COAUTHORED BOOKS

Barely Legal[††]
(with Parnell Hall)

Smooth Operator[**]
(with Parnell Hall)

TRAVEL

*A Romantic's Guide to the Country Inns of Britain
and Ireland* (1979)

MEMOIR

Blue Water, Green Skipper

[*]A Holly Barker Novel
[†]A Stone Barrington Novel
[‡]A Will Lee Novel

[$]An Ed Eagle Novel
[**]A Teddy Fay Novel
[††]A Herbie Fisher Novel

Stone Barrington gets entangled in the rarefied art business in this heart-stopping thriller by #1 *New York Times*–bestselling author Stuart Woods.

When a slam-bang of a crime brings a beautiful new client into Stone Barrington's office, little does he know his association with her will pull him into a far more serpentine mystery in the exclusive world of art. It's a business where a rare find could make a career—and a collection—and mistakes in judgment are costly. And under its genteel and high-minded veneer lurks an assortment of grifters and malfeasants eager to cash in on the game.

In the upscale world of New York City's luxury penthouses and grand Hamptons estates, it will take a man of Stone Barrington's careful discernment and well-honed instincts to get to the truth without ruffling the wrong feathers . . . because when it comes to priceless and irreplaceable works of art, the money and reputations at stake are worth killing for.

Praise for the Stone Barrington Novels

Indecent Exposure

"Another entertaining episode in what has become a bit of a soap opera about the rich and famous."

—Associated Press

Fast & Loose

"Enjoyable . . . A series of tit-for-tat exchanges leads to an exciting showdown." —*Publishers Weekly*

Below the Belt

"Compulsively readable . . . [An] easy-reading page-turner." —*Booklist*

Sex, Lies & Serious Money

"[An] irresistible, luxury-soaked soap opera."

—*Publishers Weekly*

Dishonorable Intentions

"Diverting." —*Publishers Weekly*

Family Jewels

"Mr. Woods knows how to portray the beautiful people, their manners and mores, their fluid and sparkling conversation, their easy expectations and all the glitter that surrounds and defines them. A master of dialogue, action and atmosphere, [Woods] has added one more jewel of a thriller-mystery to his ever-growing collection."

—Fort Myers *Florida Weekly*

Scandalous Behavior

"Addictive . . . Pick [*Scandalous Behavior*] up at your peril. You can get hooked." —*Lincoln Journal Star*

Foreign Affairs

"Purrs like a well-tuned dream machine . . . Mr. Woods knows how to set up scenes and link them to keep the action, emotion, and information moving. He presents the places he takes us to vividly and convincingly. . . . Enjoy this slick thriller by a thoroughly satisfying professional." —*Florida Weekly*

Hot Pursuit

"Fans will enjoy the vicarious luxury ride as usual."

—*Publishers Weekly*

Insatiable Appetites

"Multiple exciting storylines . . . Readers of the series will enjoy the return of the dangerous Dolce." —*Booklist*

Paris Match

"Plenty of fast-paced action and deluxe experiences that keep the pages turning. Woods is masterful with his use of dialogue and creates natural and vivid scenes for his readers to enjoy." —*The Sun News* (Myrtle Beach, SC)

Cut and Thrust

"This installment goes down as smoothly as a glass of Knob Creek." —*Publishers Weekly*

Carnal Curiosity

"Stone Barrington shows he's one of the smoothest operators around . . . Entertaining." —*Publishers Weekly*

Standup Guy

"Stuart Woods still owns an imagination that simply won't quit. . . . This is yet another edge-of-your-seat adventure." —*Suspense Magazine*

Doing Hard Time

"Longtime Woods fans who have seen Teddy [Fay] evolve from a villain to something of a lovable antihero will enjoy watching the former enemies work together in this exciting yarn. Is this the beginning of a beautiful partnership? Let's hope so." —*Booklist*

Unintended Consequences

"Since 1981, readers have not been able to get their fill of Stuart Woods's *New York Times*–bestselling novels of suspense." —*Orlando Sentinel*

Collateral Damage

"High-octane . . . Woods's blend of exciting action, sophisticated gadgetry, and last-minute heroics doesn't disappoint." —*Publishers Weekly*

Severe Clear

"Stuart Woods has proven time and time again that he's a master of suspense who keeps his readers frantically turning the pages." —*Bookreporter*

BOOKS BY STUART WOODS

FICTION

QUICK & DIRTY

STUART WOODS

G. P. PUTNAM'S SONS
New York

G. P. PUTNAM'S SONS
Publishers Since 1838
An imprint of Penguin Random House LLC
375 Hudson Street
New York, New York 10014

Copyright © 2017 by Stuart Woods
Excerpt from *Unbound* copyright © 2018 by Stuart Woods

The Library of Congress has catalogued the G. P. Putnam's Sons hardcover edition as follows:

Names: Woods, Stuart, author.
Title: Quick & dirty / Stuart Woods.
Other titles: Quick and dirty
Description: New York : G. P. Putnam's Sons, 2017. | Series: A Stone Barrington novel ; 43
Identifiers: LCCN 2017018244| ISBN 9780735217140 (hardcover) | ISBN 9780735217164 (ebook)
Subjects: LCSH: Barrington, Stone (Fictitious character)—Fiction. | BISAC: FICTION / Action & Adventure. | FICTION / Suspense. | FICTION / Thrillers. | GSAFD: Suspense fiction.
Classification: LCC PS3573.O642 Q53 2017 | DDC 813/.54—dc23
LC record available at https://lccn.loc.gov/2017018244
p.   cm.

First G. P. Putnam's Sons hardcover edition / October 2017
First G. P. Putnam's Sons premium edition / July 2018
G. P. Putnam's Sons premium edition ISBN: 9780735217157

Printed in the United States of America
1   3   5   7   9   10   8   6   4   2

QUICK &
DIRTY

1

STONE BARRINGTON DEPARTED the Carlyle Hotel on Madison Avenue at Seventy-sixth Street and slipped from under the Seventy-sixth Street awning into his waiting car. He had had a business lunch after departing the United Nations, where his close friend Secretary of State Holly Barker had given a well-received speech. A heavy rain was falling, and he could hardly see across the street.

"Can you see to drive, Fred?" he asked his factotum, Fred Flicker.

"Only just, sir," Fred replied. "I'll go slowly."

"As you wish." Stone found his unfinished *New York Times* crossword on the seat next to him. It was quite dark outside, and he switched on the reading light and started to work.

Traffic was slow. He saw a figure in black jogging toward Park Avenue with something in his hand, Stone couldn't tell what, and he went back to his puzzle.

They had reached Park Avenue, but just as they did

the light turned red, and since there is no right turn on red in New York City, Fred waited for it to change.

A dark blur appeared to his right in Stone's peripheral vision, but before he could turn to look at it, something struck the side window of the car with a heavy blow, and the vehicle shook slightly. As he turned he saw the figure in black seeming to bounce off his car and fall into the street. He peered out the window at the figure, who was scrambling to his feet, and noted that he carried a sledgehammer.

Then, from behind him, came another blow to the car, then one to the left rear window. Finally, the figure on Stone's side had another go, with similar results. This time a star appeared in the window glass.

Fred was turning to look at him. "What's happening?" he asked.

"Never mind the light, Fred, take a right quickly."

Fred did so, just as the light changed, and he was able to drive the length of the block before encountering another red light on Park. Stone looked over his shoulder and saw three dark figures bearing sledgehammers trotting toward the car. "Never mind the light, Fred, GO!" Stone shouted for emphasis.

Fred went and got lucky, sailing through the empty intersection. All the lights on Park turned green, and he made it to Fifty-seventh Street before they turned red again.

"What the hell?" Fred asked.

"Beats me," Stone said. "Drop me at the house, then take this over to the Strategic Services garage on Twelfth Avenue and ask them to replace my window. The other two seem to have survived intact." Stone had bought the car, already armored, from Strategic Services, the second-largest security company in the United States.

Fred pulled into the garage in Turtle Bay so Stone wouldn't get wet. "Shall I wait for the car, sir, while they repair it?"

"Yes, if they have the window in stock and can do it immediately. If not, just wait until the rain stops, then leave the car and take a cab back."

"Yes, sir." Fred pulled out of the garage and turned west as the door closed behind him.

Stone took the crossword with him into his adjacent office, where his phone was ringing. His secretary was nowhere to be seen, so he picked it up. "Stone Barrington."

"It's Dino." Dino Bacchetti had been Stone's detective partner many years before when they were both on the NYPD; by now, he had risen to the heights of commissioner of police. "Dinner tonight? Patroon at seven-thirty?"

"Sure. Funny you should ring—I need a policeman."

"Somebody take a shot at you?"

"No, but three men with sledgehammers attacked my car at Park and Seventy-sixth."

"Did you say 'sledgehammers'?"

"I did."

"Did you have anything to drink at lunch?"

"They were sledgehammers, Dino."

"Any damage?"

"One cracked window. Fred is having it replaced at the Strategic Services shop."

"That's right, you've got armored glass, haven't you? Nice to know it works."

"Yes, it is."

"Do you think they were after you?"

"I think I could be forgiven for believing that, but I've no idea why anyone would want to beat me or my car to death with sledgehammers."

"Maybe it's not you they were after, maybe it's the Bentley."

"I'm not aware of any organized hatred of Bentleys in New York, are you?"

"Give me some time, I'll see if there were any other attacks on English luxury cars today."

"Take all the time you like," Stone said.

"Oh, where were you coming from?"

"The Carlyle. I had lunch there with Bill Eggers and a client."

"Didn't you go to the UN this morning?"

"Yes, the lunch was after Holly had departed for Washington. I drove her to the heliport."

"What does Bill drive?"

"A black Lincoln from a car service, I think."

"How about the client?"

"No idea. I met him in the dining room."

"Talk to you later." Dino hung up.

Joan, his secretary, returned from somewhere with a shopping bag. "Sorry I wasn't in when you got back. I needed some office supplies. Did anyone call?"

"Just Dino."

STONE TURNED UP at Patroon on time and found Dino's black SUV parked outside with a policeman asleep at the wheel.

Dino had already ordered drinks for the two of them, and Stone slid into the booth. The drinks came, and glasses were raised.

"Well, you're not crazy," Dino said.

"I'm relieved to hear it."

"Two other Bentleys and a Rolls were attacked within six blocks and inside of an hour of your run-in."

"Anybody hurt?"

"Yours was the only one with armoring. The others ended up with a backseat full of glass, but the only passenger was in the Rolls, and he suffered some scratches from flying glass."

"Anybody I know?"

"Some guy from the Argentinian UN Consulate."

"So it's an attack on expensive English cars?" Stone asked.

"More likely an attack on just expensive."

"Any Mercedes or BMWs get the treatment?"

"Nothing reported."

"Then, on the available evidence . . ."

"Did you get a description?" Dino asked.

"A Ninja with a sledgehammer."

"That's it?"

"It was raining heavily, and all three men—I guess they were men—were dressed entirely in black."

"Leather?"

"Might have been something waterproof, given the weather. Did you check the hardware stores to see if anybody had bought three sledgehammers?"

"We didn't think of that," Dino replied.

"Well, New York's finest can't think of everything, can you?"

"Almost everything."

"I guess that's almost enough," Stone replied.

2

D INO CALLED THE FOLLOWING MORNING the moment Stone sat down at his desk. "Did you see the *Times* coverage of Holly's speech this morning?"

"I did—overwhelmingly positive, I'd say."

"Me, too. Did you see Gloria Parsons's op-ed piece?"

"I haven't gotten that far yet. What the hell is Gloria doing on the *Times* op-ed page?"

"Her boyfriend the ex-governor's influence, I expect. Also, the woman is a good writer."

"What did she have to say?"

"Read it for yourself. By the way, your guess was inspired," Dino said.

"Guess?"

"About the sledgehammers. A woman visited a hardware store on Third Avenue in the Twenties and bought three sledgehammers."

"They had to get them somewhere."

"She was about five-eight, a hundred and forty pounds,

fairly short, dark hair, age thirty to forty, wearing a trench coat over black pants."

"Did she pay by credit card?"

"That would be too easy. She paid cash."

"Did the store deliver them?"

"No, she bought a canvas carryall and took them away in that."

"So you're stuck."

"Every cop on the East Side, upper and lower, is looking for people dressed in black, carrying a sledgehammer."

"Brilliant police work."

"It will be if they spot somebody matching the description. Did you see any of these people before they started banging on your car?"

"Yes, come to think of it. As I left the Carlyle I saw somebody dressed in black—I assumed it was some sort of rainwear—and carrying something, though I couldn't tell what, it was raining so hard."

"Headed toward Park?"

"Yes, on the downtown side of the street. Does that matter?"

"I have no idea, I'm just being thorough."

"Have you had any reports of further Bentley abuse today?"

"Not yet, but I've had a hot call from the Bentley distributor, demanding action. Nothing from the Rolls people."

Stone laughed.

"Did you get your car fixed?" Dino asked.

"Yes, it took a couple of hours, but Strategic Services came up with a window and installed it. The other two windows were unmarked. The workman said they should have used a pickax."

"Why?"

"Because a pickax is pointed, and it would have had a better chance of penetrating the armored glass because it would have concentrated the force into a smaller area than a sledgehammer."

"Shall I put out an APB on people buying pickaxes?"

"Why not? Anything at all on the woman who bought the sledgehammers?"

"No, the store said she wasn't a regular customer."

"After all, how many sledgehammers does a girl need?"

"Only three, apparently. I guess they last awhile. Is there anything else your police department can do for you today?"

"Nope. Keep up the good work."

Dino hung up.

Joan came in with the *New York Post* and put it on his desk. "Your incident of yesterday made the *Post*," she said.

LUXURY CARS ATTACKED WITH SLEDGE-HAMMERS!, the headline screamed. The article was short, though, and there was no theory on why.

"I guess the *Times* ignored it," Stone said. "At least, I didn't see anything about it."

"Not shocking enough," she said, then went back to her desk.

A little farther inside the *Post* was an editorial on Holly's appearance at the UN. WOUNDED MADAM SECRETARY KNOCKS ONE OUT OF THE PARK, read the headline, and all two paragraphs were entirely favorable. "Have we got a President-in-the-making here?" it finished. Stone reflected that Dino thought the bullet was meant for him, not Holly. The ex-con gunman, shot by Fred, had not been found to have a motive to shoot either Stone or Holly, and the case had petered out.

Stone picked up the *Times* and turned to the op-ed

page. There was Gloria's piece. "Barker throws her shoulder into the ring?" read the lead. Stone read on:

"Secretary of State Holly Barker, substituting at the UN for the President, brought the General Assembly to its collective feet when she appeared with her arm in a sling, albeit a silken one from Hermès. This is surely the first time a wounded Cabinet member has risen from a hospital bed after an assassination attempt to address the world. It must be something like the reception Abraham Lincoln would have received in Congress had his wound been to the shoulder, instead of to the head.

"President Katharine Lee, who of late has been somewhat unpopular in certain quarters of the international community, thus won a victory for her policies by the simple device of not showing up, and instead dispatching her glamorous secretary of state to stand in for her.

"Secretary Barker has recently been seen with her president in half a dozen appearances where one might not expect a Cabinet member to be seen in such high company, which indicates both her high standing in her boss's opinion and maybe even a hint as to whom the President might like to see succeed her in office. There seems to be a widespread view in both houses of Congress that the President could do a lot worse than Holly Barker."

IT WENT ON like that for another six paragraphs. Stone found a pair of scissors in his desk drawer and clipped both the *Times* op-ed piece and the *Post* editorial. He buzzed Joan.

"Yes, boss?"

"Didn't somebody give me a nice leather scrapbook for Christmas a couple of years ago?"

"Yes, boss, I've been keeping it in the hope that you might do something that would engender some favorable press clippings."

"Forget about that, but bring me the scrapbook, please."

Joan hustled into his office and removed the album from its box.

Stone handed her the clippings. "You are now the official archivist for our secretary of state," he said.

"Soon to be our next President?"

"You didn't hear that from me," Stone said. She took the clippings and the album and returned to her office.

3

JOAN BUZZED STONE. "Will you speak to the secretary of state?"

"I will deign to do so," Stone replied drily. He picked up the phone. "Stone Barrington."

"Mr. Barrington, the secretary of state is on the line," a young man said.

"Good morning," Holly said.

"And to you. I trust you've seen this morning's papers."

"I have. The *Times* piece by . . . that woman was very nice."

"I thought so, too, as was the *Post*, the New York one."

"That *Post* has not winged its way to my desk as of yet, but the *Post* down here published an overnight poll showing Kate with a sixty-one percent approval rating—not at all bad for a second-term President—but me with a sixty-nine percent rating. It was very embarrassing."

"Have you heard from Kate on the subject?"

"She called me at seven o'clock this morning, laughing like hell."

"That's our Kate."

"She warned me not to try and stay out of trouble and just coast on my approval ratings. She thinks I have to deal with something controversial right away, to show I'm not an airhead. She's already looking for something to throw at me."

"Sounds like you've acquired a campaign manager."

"I'm afraid she's going to foist the new Russian president on me."

"That would certainly be good practice for you."

"I didn't like the last one, and I don't like this one, either."

"Then that's a good place to start."

"Did you hear *all* of my speech to the UN?"

"Of course."

"Then you'll remember the part where I said to the Russians that if they want the sanctions lifted, to just get out of the Crimea?"

"The whole world heard that—it's one of the reasons you're so popular this morning."

"Well, I think my next step is going to be to recommend to the President that we nominate Ukraine for membership in NATO."

"Well, *that* should be enough controversy to keep you busy for a while. Is that what Kate wants to do?"

"In the best of all possible worlds, yes, but she's unlikely to say so anytime soon."

"But you'll be on record as having proposed it."

"See how smart Kate is? Everybody will remember that I said that, and if Kate ever gets around to doing it, they'll give me the credit for moving her my way."

"Kate is very smart indeed."

"Well, I think I'll anticipate her and get started on a draft of my recommendation."

"Good idea. Call anytime."

"When you least expect it," she said, and hung up.

Joan came on immediately. "Dino called while you were talking. Want me to get him back for you?"

"Yes, please."

She buzzed, and Stone picked up. "Hello again."

"I want to read you a press release."

"Shoot."

"'The New York City Police Department has conducted a thorough investigation of the assassination attempt on the secretary of state on New Year's Eve—'"

"Wait a minute, you've concluded it was an *assassination* attempt? A few days ago you thought *I* was the intended victim."

"Shut up and listen. 'We have determined that the would-be assassin has a history of hatred of women in positions of authority and that he had several drugs in his system at the time of the shooting, including marijuana, heroin, and cocaine. We have also, after investigating his connections in prison and since his recent release, concluded that he acted alone and without the assistance of any person or organization. Although we found more than six hundred dollars in cash on his person, that is consistent with the funds withdrawn from his prison savings account upon his release. Therefore, unless new, credible evidence emerges, this investigation is now closed.' What do you think?"

"I'm pleased that my name was not mentioned as the intended victim."

"Don't ever speak those words to me again," Dino said. "This is it, as far as the department is concerned."

"I'm sure the President and the secretary of state will be glad to hear it."

"See ya." Dino hung up.

So, Stone thought, Holly is now, officially, a heroine.

AFTER LUNCH, Stone got a call from a reporter of his acquaintance at the *New York Times*.

"Hey, Stone," Edward Petter said.

"Hey, Eddie."

"I don't know if you've heard, but Dino just made a statement about the, ah, shooting business outside his building on New Year's Eve."

"Yes?"

"Let me read it to you."

"All right."

Petter read the whole statement. "You were there, Stone. Do you agree with his statement?"

"Entirely."

"There was a rumor that maybe you were the intended victim and Holly Barker just got in the way."

"I haven't heard that. I didn't know the shooter, and he didn't know me."

"Is there anybody who might want you dead, anybody who might have hired Crank Jackson?"

"No, not to my knowledge. I don't know anybody who's that mad at me."

"Did you ever represent Jackson as a defendant?"

"No, and it's been many years since I represented a criminal defendant."

"Why did your driver shoot Jackson?"

"To keep him from shooting . . . somebody else."

"You?"

"From the direction the guy was pointing his gun, Fred might have thought it was pointed at me. After all, Holly and I were walking next to each other."

"Did you and the secretary change positions while you were walking?"

"How do you mean?"

"I mean, were you walking nearer the building, then changed sides?"

"I may have done that to get her out of the wind."

"Was that the moment at which she was shot?"

"I don't remember," Stone said. "It all happened so fast."

"That's what they all say," Petter replied. "See you around." He hung up.

Stone hung up, too, hoping that was the end of it.

4

PETER RULE, the son of the President of the United States, Katharine Lee, by her first marriage to the late Simon Rule, a high CIA official, left his Fifth Avenue New York apartment to go car shopping. Peter was employed as chief of staff to his father-in-law, U.S. Senator Eliot Saltonstall of New York, but he had announced his candidacy for the other New York seat in the Senate, whose occupant had declined to run for reelection.

Peter owned several cars: three Mercedeses, one at each of his residences in New York, Washington, D.C., and East Hampton, New York, all the homes inherited from his father, who had been the only child of an old and wealthy New England family. Now he needed something he could be seen campaigning in, and no Mercedes would do. Peter had toured the state repeatedly on behalf of his boss and thus had a wide acquaintance among elected officials statewide, but he had always done so in rental cars. Now he needed something American-made that could be readily identified with him.

He carried a printout from a website containing classified ads for automobiles. His first stop was in Chelsea, where he looked at a six-year-old Ford Explorer; he didn't like it. His next stop was in the West Village, where the owner, a fifty-year-old widow, walked him to a garage on the next block to see a three-year-old Chevrolet Tahoe, which he found attractive.

"My husband and I used the car to drive to our weekend place in Snedens Landing, up the Hudson," she said. "That's why the mileage is so low. I've since sold the house, so I don't need the car."

Peter checked the odometer: 3,700 miles. Remarkable. Apart from the garage dust, the SUV looked practically new. He offered the woman her asking price, and she accepted. She produced and signed the title, and Peter produced and signed a check, and he was the owner.

He thanked the woman and drove uptown to the garage where he kept his Mercedes S550. He made a deal on the monthly rental and gave a key to the manager. "Don't wash it," he said to the man. "Not ever."

He got back to his apartment in time to have a sandwich with his wife, Celeste.

"Did you find something?"

"Something perfect," he replied, and told her about the Tahoe. "Are you ready for a week's campaigning?"

"I've already packed a bag," she replied.

"I've told the garage never to wash it—it would look brand-new. I hope to get it dirtier on this trip."

Celeste laughed. "Don't worry, rain is forecast. You can look for some mud."

"Should anybody ask you how long we've owned the car, just say it's three years old."

"Got it."

*   *   *

STONE HAD FRED drive him up to the East Sixties, to a club he belonged to that was so exclusive it didn't have a name. Its members referred to it as merely The Club, or sometimes The Place. Stone and Mike Freeman, the CEO of Strategic Services, had proposed Charles Ford—their partner in their investment firm, Triangle Partnership—for membership, and he had just been elected, so their lunch was a celebratory one.

CHARLEY WAS WAITING in the lobby of the large old house that was headquarters for The Club, and Stone introduced him to the manager and some staff, then they went up to the bar, where Mike Freeman awaited them. They found a table and ordered.

"I'm reading in the *Times*," Charley said, "that your friend Holly Barker is being talked about as a candidate to succeed Kate Lee."

"I wouldn't know anything about that," Stone said.

"Don't you read the *Times*?" Charley asked.

"Yes, but I still don't know anything about that, and I'm not going to."

"I see. I think."

"Charley," Mike said, "I think that's going to be a no-go subject, until Holly actually runs."

Charley laughed. "I was getting that picture," he said.

"There's something you need to do," Stone said.

"All right."

"I want you to go through the list of companies we own or have invested in and do some weeding."

"Everything is profitable," Charley said.

"I'm not concerned about profits," Stone replied,

"I'm concerned about what each company does and whether that might associate me with something that Holly wouldn't want to be associated with."

"You mean, like tobacco companies?"

"Exactly. Also armament companies, oil companies, and any company that might depend heavily on government contracts for its profits."

"I believe I get the picture," Charley said.

"It's well known in Washington and among the political press that Holly and I have a long-standing friendship. Since her parents are elderly retirees and since she doesn't have siblings or a husband, or even an ex-husband, that puts me in the position of someone who will be looked at for conflicts of interest."

"And you don't want to have any," Charley said. "What does she have in the way of personal assets?"

Stone thought about that. "I don't know."

"If she has any substantial holdings, she might want to think about a blind trust. I could handle that for her."

"A blind trust is a good idea, and right away, but you're not the guy—you're too close to me. You could, however, recommend the guy to handle that—or maybe better, a woman."

"Good idea. I know just the person, but perhaps I shouldn't tell you who she is—it's better if you don't know."

"I'll ask Holly to have her assistant call you for a name and number."

"Very good."

"Stone," Mike said, "have you given any thought to having some regular personal security?"

Stone looked at him askance. "Why?"

"Well, there has been talk that the New Year's Eve shooter was after you, not Holly."

"That can't be the case, Mike, and even if it were, it would only cause more such talk if I started traveling around the city with armed guards."

"It looks like Fred had that role all taken care of," Charley pointed out.

"I can't argue with that," Mike said, "and nobody can blame you if your driver is an ex–Royal Marine commando."

"I'm glad you approve," Stone said.

AS FRED PULLED OUT of the garage and turned toward Third Avenue, Stone looked across the street and saw a figure in black, walking in the same direction and carrying a sledgehammer.

5

STONE TOLD FRED TO PULL OVER, and he did. "Something wrong, Mr. Barrington?"

"A man with a sledgehammer," Stone said. "Lend me your weapon, will you?"

"I'm sorry, sir, the police have not yet returned it since the shooting."

Stone reached into the front seat and retrieved the golf umbrella that Fred kept stowed there.

"Follow me, Fred," Stone said, "but stay a few yards back." He opened the car door.

"Yes, sir. It's begun to rain again, you might open the umbrella."

"Open, it wouldn't be as useful," Stone said. He held the umbrella at the opposite end from the heavy briarwood handle and began walking rapidly down the street. The young man with the sledgehammer disappeared around the corner. Stone began to jog, and the rain began to increase in intensity. He turned the corner, the umbrella ready, but the young man in black had vanished.

Behind him, he heard the whooper of a police car, which turned the corner and continued down Second Avenue. Stone stood there in the rain, getting wet, shelter in his hand, unused. The guy must have gotten into a vehicle, he thought. As he did, another police car turned the corner, flashing its lights, whooping if anyone got in the way.

They got a report, Stone thought. Behind him a horn honked twice. He turned to find Fred waiting in the Bentley, and he got in.

"You're soaking wet, sir," Fred said. "Why didn't you use the umbrella?"

"I wanted to, but I didn't have the opportunity," Stone replied, taking a linen handkerchief from his pocket and dabbing at his face and hair.

"You'll catch your death," Fred said. "Let's get you home and dry."

"Good idea."

STONE HUNG UP HIS SUIT to dry in his dressing room, then toweled his hair, got into fresh clothes, and went downstairs to his office.

"Dino called," Joan said.

"Get him back for me, will you?"

She buzzed. "Line one."

Stone picked up the phone. "Hey."

"You sound annoyed about something," Dino said. "Did the guys with sledgehammers attack your Bentley again?"

"No, but I saw one of them as we pulled out of The Club's garage."

"Our The Club?"

"One and the same. I went after the guy on foot, but

he turned the corner at Second Avenue and dematerialized. I think that some sort of vehicle, maybe a van, was waiting for him."

"Yeah, we had two patrol cars in pursuit, after an incident at Seventy-third and Lexington. They lost him, too."

"A similar incident to before?"

"This time it was parked cars. The guy walked down Lex, looking for expensive cars. Four windshields broken—two Mercedes, a BMW, and a Bentley Mulsanne. They're expanding their repertoire to include German cars."

"Just one guy?"

"That's what the reports say. We had a call from a windshield-replacement outfit. They said their business is too good."

"And they're complaining?"

"I think they were worried that some people might think the vandals are working for them."

"Now, that would be a productive marketing technique," Stone replied.

"Their problem is, the victims' insurance companies refer them to this outfit, Windscreens Unlimited, and they don't stock those windshields. They have to order them from dealers, and they end up pissing off the car owners because it takes several days to order the windshields from the manufacturer and install them. The dealers don't like it, either, because the customers complain."

"So everybody's unhappy—the car owners, the insurance companies, the car dealers, and Windscreens Unlimited?"

"That's about the size of it."

"So who would want to make all those people unhappy?"

"Communists?" Dino offered.

"Dino, there aren't any Communists anymore, except in China."

"What about Cuba and Venezuela?"

"They're in transition after the deaths of their leaders."

"Transition to what? Capitalism?"

"Market-based economies, like the rest of the world."

"I wonder how long it takes to get a Bentley windshield in Cuba or Venezuela?" Dino asked.

Stone laughed. "Forever and a day."

"So who would want to make all those people mad?"

"My guess is some fringe political group, somebody who's very, very angry about something like global warming. Maybe they're attacking the cars they think are the biggest polluters."

"Listen, those cars have catalytic converters just like all other cars, and probably better ones."

"Such a fringe group would not overburden themselves with logic."

"That's a shame because we, the police, pride ourselves on logic. It's our most effective tool."

"I know," Stone said.

Dino explained it to him, anyway. "I'll give you an example. A woman—wife or girlfriend—is murdered. Who's our favorite suspect?"

"The husband or boyfriend," Stone said.

"The husband or boyfriend," Dino said anyway. "It's logical, right?"

"Dino, I used to be a cop, too, remember?"

"Logic is our best weapon," Dino said.

"Dino, is there anything else you want to tell me that I already know?"

"What are you talking about?"

"I don't remember," Stone said. "Is Viv in town?"

"Are you kidding? No." Dino's wife, a retired police

officer, worked as a high executive for Strategic Services and often traveled on business.

"Dinner?"

"P. J. Clarke's at seven?" Dino suggested.

"See you there."

Stone hung up and buzzed Joan. "There's a wet suit hanging in my dressing room. Will you ask Helene to press it as soon as it's only damp? I got caught in the rain."

"Wonderful," Joan said. "How does someone who rides around town in a chauffeur-driven Bentley get caught in the rain? Did Fred leave the sunroof open?"

"Don't ask," Stone said.

6

JOAN BUZZED AGAIN. "A lady to see you. She doesn't have an appointment."

"Who is she?"

"She won't give me her name."

That intrigued him. "All right, send her in." He rose to greet his visitor.

She was at least six feet tall and wearing a tightly tailored black leather pantsuit with a short jacket, diamond stud earrings with stones of at least four carats each, and coal-black hair that was a little shorter than his own. She stuck out her hand. "I'm Morgan Tillman," she said.

Stone shook the hand and found it large, soft, and strong. "Good afternoon, I'm Stone Barrington," he said. "Will you have a seat? My secretary didn't get your name."

She managed a chuckle. "I didn't give my name, on principle."

Stone didn't want to know what principle. "May I get you some refreshment? We have water, fizzy or plain, and diet soda."

"Do you have any single-malt scotch? I need a drink."

Stone refrained from looking at his watch, but he figured it was around three PM. "Certainly," he said. "I can offer you Talisker or Laphroaig. Anything more exotic than that, and I can send Joan upstairs for it."

"Laphroaig would be grand," she said. "You live over the store?" she asked.

Stone got up and went to the liquor cabinet. "Ice?"

"Just a little water."

He made the drink. "Yes, I live over the store," he said, handing her the whiskey. "And if you don't mind my asking, why do you need a drink at three o'clock in the afternoon?"

"I'm not an alcoholic," she explained, "but I've had a terrible experience, and I'm a little rattled." She raised her glass. "Will you join me?"

"I would be a poor host if I didn't," he said, retrieving a bottle of Knob Creek and pouring some over ice. He went back to his desk.

"Is your terrible experience connected to your visit here?"

"Yes, at least in part. I was having a mani-pedi uptown, and my car was parked outside within view. Someone dressed in black and carrying what appeared to be a sledgehammer smashed my windshield."

"Ah," Stone said, sipping his drink. "Do you drive a Mercedes, a BMW, or a Bentley Mulsanne?"

She took a gulp of her Laphroaig and stared at him. "That was a lucky guess," she said.

"Which one?"

"I drive a Bentley Mulsanne. How could you narrow your guess down to three automobiles?"

"I had a similar experience yesterday, except that I was in the car when he and some friends swung their sledgehammers."

"What do you drive?"

"A Bentley Flying Spur."

"And they broke three windows?"

"Only one, and that one only slightly. My car windows are armored glass."

"Are you often shot at?"

"Only occasionally."

"Then why does your car have armored glass?"

"Do you really want to know?"

"I'm dying to know," she said.

"All right, but this will take a minute."

"I have all afternoon," she replied.

"Well, some years ago, having wrecked a car, I needed one in a hurry. I went into the Mercedes showroom on Park Avenue and asked them what they had in stock for immediate delivery. I was told that they had one car ready to go, but it was armored against small-arms fire and under-vehicle explosive devices. I found that intriguing, and I asked why they had such a vehicle in stock. The salesman told me that they had special-ordered the car for a businessman of Italian-American heritage who was concerned for his personal safety. Unfortunately, the car had arrived a couple of days too late to meet his needs, and his widow had no use for it, so she had it returned and asked for a refund. He said that I would, in effect, be buying it from her, since it had already been paid for and registered, and that she would entertain offers. Almost whimsically, I made a lowball offer, and to my surprise, she accepted it. I wrote a check for the car and drove it away."

"I'm sorry, I thought you said you drive a Bentley, not a Mercedes."

"Ah, well, a couple of years after that I managed to turn the Mercedes end over end at about a hundred and thirty miles an hour. The car did not survive the accident, and it occurred to me that neither would I have, had it not been armored, so when a friend of mine who runs a security company, which includes an auto-armoring division, offered me the Bentley, I accepted with alacrity."

"That is a perfectly lucid explanation," she said, "but may I ask why you were driving a hundred and thirty miles an hour?"

"I was, as I recall, being pursued."

"At a hundred and thirty miles an hour?"

"He was gaining on me," Stone said.

She took a swig of her Laphroaig and heaved a sigh. "Your experience makes mine sound piddling by comparison."

Stone shrugged. "You are the first woman of my acquaintance who drives not only a Bentley, but a Mulsanne. May I ask what criteria you employed in making your choice?"

"Two," she said. "One, I think it's the most beautiful car currently being manufactured. Two, it's the only car I feel comfortable in while having sex in the rear seat."

"Ah," Stone said, because he couldn't think of anything else to say.

"I'm very tall, you see."

"I noticed that. Would it be rude of me to ask how tall?"

"Not in the least. I'm six feet, one inch, in my bare feet, and should it interest you, I weigh a hundred and twenty-nine pounds, naked."

"That is a very interesting set of statistics," Stone said.

"I'm glad you think so."

"I must say that even a Bentley Mulsanne sounds a tight fit for a person of your height to have sex in."

She shrugged. "You must remember that, at least in

my experience, one is rarely stretched out flat when having sex—bending is usually involved."

Stone nodded. "I take your point."

"And the rear seat is both wide and soft."

"Well," Stone said, "as interesting as I find this discussion to be, I suppose I should ask who referred you to me and how I can be of help."

"I find it interesting, too, but I should be more businesslike. I came to see you because I am outraged at how little interest the police have taken in my terrible experience. It's as though a man with a sledgehammer breaking windshields on the Upper East Side were an everyday event to them, like littering. Am I not entitled to more than that, in the circumstances? I'm told that you have some influence with the police in this city."

"And by whom were you told that?"

"By my manicurist. She seems to be a font of useful information."

Stone was momentarily flummoxed.

"Her name is Roxanne, of Roxanne's Nails. She used to work at the place where you get your hair cut."

"I see," he said, then he had a thought. "Ms. Tillman—"

"Please call me Morgan, or if you like, Mo, as my friends do."

"Morgan—Mo—I think I can offer you an opportunity to put your concerns directly to the commissioner of police—if you are available for dinner this evening."

"What time?" she asked.

"Seven."

"I am without a car. Can you collect me?"

"Of course. At what address?"

"Seven-forty Park Avenue."

Stone knew the address well; it had the reputation of being the most sought-after in the city.

"Apartment number?"

"The penthouse. Come up for a drink at six?"

"Certainly," Stone said.

"I'll need to change. How shall I dress?"

"I don't think you need to change," Stone replied. He buzzed Joan.

"Yes, sir?"

"Will you ask Fred to drive Ms. Tillman home, and I'll need him again at five forty-five."

"Thank you," she said. "You're very kind."

When she had left, Joan came into his office. "Who was that?"

"Morgan Tillman."

"Why wouldn't she give me her name?"

"I don't know. Do you recognize it?"

"Yes," Joan replied, furrowing her brow, "but I don't remember from where." She turned to go, then spun around. "Got it. The only Tillman I've ever heard of was a hedge fund guy who was murdered."

"That does sound familiar," Stone agreed, but he couldn't remember any more about it.

7

STONE STEPPED OFF the elevator into a private foyer and rang the bell. "Yes?" a voice said from a speaker.

"It's Stone Barrington."

There was a buzz and a click, and the door opened a bit. He walked into a large living room opening onto a broad terrace. Morgan Tillman was descending a staircase. She had changed her clothes, but she was wearing a leather suit that was identical to the one of earlier that day, except that it was flaming red.

"Good evening," she said, offering him her hand.

Stone shook it. "Good evening."

"I believe I owe you a drink," she said. "Knob Creek again?"

"Perfect."

She walked to a paneled bar off the living room and poured two drinks into heavy Baccarat whiskey glasses. "It's a little chilly to use the terrace," she said. "Let's sit over here." She led him to a comfortable sofa, and they sank into it. "Now," she said, "it's my turn to ask the questions."

"Shoot," he replied.

"Where were you born?"

"In Greenwich Village. I attended elementary and high school there, too, as well as NYU, for undergraduate and law degrees."

"Thank you," she said. "I like full answers. What did you do immediately after law school? Join a law firm?"

"No, the summer before my final year I took part in a program that allowed law students to ride in police patrol cars. I was impressed with the cops I met, and I joined the NYPD."

Her eyebrows went up. "Thence, your familiarity with the police."

"Thence."

"What duties did you perform with the police?"

"I was a patrol officer, then later, a homicide detective. The man we're having dinner with was my partner for many years. His name is Dino Bacchetti."

"I've seen it in the papers."

"No doubt." Stone waved a hand at his surroundings. "This is a very beautiful apartment. How long have you lived here?"

"Six years."

"All of them alone?"

"No, my husband died a little over a year ago."

Stone refrained from asking about the circumstances of his death, thinking she might tell him anyway. She did not.

"Have you ever been married?" she asked.

"Yes, I was widowed a few years ago."

"And you've been alone since then?"

"On and off," he replied.

"That's an evasive answer," she said.

"It's an accurate one. Is there anything else you want me to know about you?"

"No, I think it will be more fun for you to learn as you go."

"I'll look forward to it."

"I'll get you started. I'm British—or at least, I was born in London."

"You've acquired a perfect American accent."

"I've always had an imitative ear. Would you prefer me to speak in my native tongue?"

"Your choice."

"Oh, good," she said, suddenly perfectly British. "It's easier for me to relax. Have you spent any time in Britain?"

"I have. In fact, I have a house there, in south Hampshire, on the Beaulieu River."

"Does the house have a name?"

"It's called Windward Hall."

"Oh, that's Sir Charles Bourne's house. I dined there years ago. He and my father were friends and fellow members of the Royal Yacht Squadron."

"I'm a member as well. Sir Charles died, as you probably know."

"I saw his obituary in the *Times*. When did you buy the estate?"

"Shortly before his death. He was renovating the house at the time of his death, and he lived the last year of his life in a cottage on the estate, while the work was in progress."

"And how did you come to learn about Windward Hall?"

"A friend of mine, one of his neighbors, insisted on my seeing the house, and I was immediately smitten. How did you happen to move to New York?"

"I met my husband, as he was to become, in London. We had a whirlwind romance, and I returned to New York with him. We were married shortly after that, and shortly after our marriage he had the opportunity to buy this apartment. He knew the previous owner, so it never went on the market, and he saved himself a few million dollars, since he wasn't bidding against anybody." She took a thoughtful sip of her drink. "How did you come to own your house?"

"I inherited it from a great-aunt—my grandmother's sister."

"It seems to be in beautiful condition."

"It was a bit run-down when she died. I had saved enough money to redo the electrical system and the plumbing, and after that I did much of the work myself."

"And how did you come by those skills?"

"My father was a cabinetmaker and furniture designer. I grew up in his shop."

"Would you like another drink?" she asked.

Stone consulted his watch. "Why don't we have it at the restaurant? It's time we left."

She got her coat, and they went downstairs and got into the car. Soon they drew up in front of Clarke's.

"My God," she said, "I haven't been here for years."

"You'll find it little changed," Stone said.

They found Dino in the bar and introductions were made. Morgan towered over him. They chatted for a few minutes, then Morgan excused herself to find the ladies' room.

"You know about her?" Dino asked Stone when she had left them.

"Not very much. She's British and married a hedge fund guy—that's about it."

"You know he was murdered?"

"Yes," Stone said. "I think I read something about it. I was in England at the time, and it got only a mention in the *International Herald Tribune*. How'd it happen?"

"The story was he came home and found a cat burglar in the apartment. There was a tussle on the terrace, and Tillman went over the railing."

"A long fall," Stone said.

"The burglar got away with a small van Gogh, said to be worth something in the neighborhood of forty million dollars."

"Did it ever turn up?"

"Not yet."

"Was an arrest made?"

"Not yet. There may not have even been a cat burglar. Morgan Tillman was our chief suspect."

"And what did you think, personally?"

"I liked her for it," Dino said. "I still do."

8

THEY HAD THEIR SECOND DRINK at the table, and everybody ordered steaks. Stone picked a nice wine from the list.

"Dino," he said, "Morgan has a bone to pick with you."

"Oh?" Dino responded.

"I do, I'm afraid," Morgan said. "You see, while I was having a pedicure this afternoon I saw a man with a sledgehammer break the windshield of my car."

"There's a lot of that going around, I'm afraid. What kind of car do you drive?"

"A Bentley Mulsanne," she replied.

"Don't ask her why," Stone said.

Morgan laughed. "He's right. Now, I telephoned the police, and *eventually* a uniformed officer in a patrol car turned up."

"It was a busy afternoon," Dino said.

"I told him how it happened, how I had to run outside barefoot through broken glass. He didn't seem to think the incident was worth investigating. He just took a report."

"Taking a report is investigating," Dino said. "The perpetrator had gone, so his job was to report the incident, then interview any witnesses, who was you. He also filed his report and should have given you a copy."

"He did."

"You can use that to get your insurance company to pay for the replacement of your windshield."

"That's not as easy as it sounds," Morgan replied. "The car is at the dealership, where they have had to order a replacement from England. You see, there were a limited number in stock, and these incidents have used them up."

"I'm afraid there's nothing we can do to hurry that process."

"Don't these incidents constitute something of a crime wave?" Morgan asked. "And shouldn't you pursue the, ah, perpetrators as criminals?"

"It is a crime wave of a very small nature," Dino said. "However, we are most assuredly pursuing the perpetrators. We very nearly caught yours this afternoon, as did Stone, who was armed, but the man disappeared, probably into a waiting vehicle."

"You pursued him?" Morgan asked Stone.

"Yes. I was armed with an umbrella."

"My hero," she said, patting him on the thigh.

It was the first time she had touched Stone, except to shake his hand, and it gave him a little electric thrill.

"My office will be in touch the minute this has been resolved," Dino assured her. "Perhaps you'll be able to attend the trial."

"I'd prefer to attend the hanging," Morgan said.

"Heh, heh," Dino replied.

Mercifully for Dino, their steaks arrived, and for a few minutes there was more chewing than talking.

"I understand your wife is some sort of security guard," Morgan said when she could.

Dino choked on his steak.

Stone jumped in quickly. "Vivian Bacchetti is executive vice president and chief of operations for Strategic Services, the second-largest security company on the planet."

"Forgive me," Morgan said to Dino.

Dino managed to swallow his steak. "That's quite all right. Is there anything else your police department can do for you today, Mrs. Tillman?" he asked.

"Thank you, no, that will be all, until you capture the perpetrator, at which time I would very much like to have ten minutes alone with him. I'll bring my own sledgehammer."

"I'll try to remember that, Mrs. Tillman."

"Then please remember that it's Morgan or Mo," she said. "We mustn't stand on formality."

Stone ordered another bottle of wine, because he thought Dino might need it.

AFTER DINNER FRED drove them uptown. "Would you like to come up for a nightcap?" Morgan asked.

"Certainly," Stone replied. As they got out of the car, Stone said to Fred, "If I'm not back in half an hour, go home, I'll get a cab."

She was silent on the elevator ride, but she was looking very carefully at him. The elevator door opened and she shed her coat, went to the bar, and picked up two brandy glasses. "What would you like?" she asked.

"Brandy," Stone replied.

She poured two and led him to the sofa. Before sitting down, she removed her red jacket, revealing a black blouse cut low in the back.

Stone observed that only one large button secured it.

She sat down close by his side and facing him. "In recounting my history," she said, taking a gulp of her brandy, "did I mention that I have not had sex since my husband died?"

"No," Stone replied. "How can I help?"

She reached behind her and undid the button securing her top, lifted it over her head and tossed it away, revealing uncaged breasts that Stone could only think were perfect. "Anything you like," she replied, leaning over and kissing him.

Then she stood up, took him by the hand, and led him upstairs to a bedroom, which was baronial in proportions.

While Stone shed his clothes, she carefully turned down the bed and plumped the pillows. Finally, she lay on her back, and there was nothing between them but air.

"Come here," she said, holding out a hand.

"Yes, ma'am," Stone replied, climbing aboard.

TWICE DURING THE NIGHT she woke him from a sound sleep for an encore performance. Stone wasn't sure he was up to the second one, but she persuaded him that he was.

THE NEXT TIME he woke it was because of a ringing telephone, which she answered. "Yes, Lila?" She covered the phone and poked Stone in the ribs. "What would you like for breakfast?"

"Two eggs, scrambled soft in the English style, bacon, English muffin, orange juice, and strong black coffee."

She repeated his order into the phone, then pulled back the sheet and inspected Stone's body closely. "Once more unto the breach, dear friend, once more!"

"God for Morgan, England, and Saint George!" Stone responded. They had just enough time before breakfast arrived.

Riding home in a cab, Stone thought Morgan had come along just in time to save him from a life of celibacy.

9

STONE LEANED AGAINST the limestone shower wall and let the water cascade over him. He was feeling something oddly like guilt, a rare emotion for him.

Holly Barker, with whom he had been entwined for years, but nearly always separated from by work or distance, had, at their last meeting, renewed her granting of his sexual freedom, as long as it was committed outside the city limits of Washington, D.C. While he had played by her rules, he gave himself a moment to regret the night before. After that moment, his regret evaporated. He had needed that night as much as Morgan had.

He dressed and went down to his office.

Joan came in with some messages and dropped them on his desk. "Uncharacteristically late, aren't we?" she asked.

"I overslept," he replied.

"I'm sorry, overwhat?"

"Please go away," he said, and she did.

Dino's message was on top of the pile, and he dealt with that first.

"Bacchetti."

"Good morning, it's Stone."

"Well," Dino said, "that was quite a dinner last evening."

"I'm glad you enjoyed it."

"I mean, if you didn't mind the occasional whiff of sulfur."

"What's that supposed to mean, Dino?"

"I mean that Morgan Tillman has a first-rate chance of being the actual Antichrist."

"Are you coming over all Catholic on me?"

"I have my ecclesiastical moments—especially in the presence of evil."

"All right, all right, lay out your evidence."

"Gladly. Her story is, she came home from shopping and as she entered the living room she saw her husband struggling with another man, dressed in black, on the terrace outside. She dropped her shopping bags and ran to help him, but as she did, he was pushed backward and tumbled over the parapet."

"Wait a minute, what does the building code say on the minimum height of parapets?"

"How the fuck should I know? Am I a bricklayer? In any case the parapet was undergoing repairs, and several running feet of bricks had been removed in aid of the work. It was low enough that he could have tripped over it and fallen. Shall I continue?"

"Please do."

"The man ran along the parapet, and she noticed that he had some sort of canvas bag slung over his back. She looked down and saw her husband sprawled in the alley in a spreading pool of blood. She looked back at the 'burglar,' and he was rappelling—she used that word—down a rope that was hooked to the parapet. At that point she ran into the house and called nine-one-one. While she was waiting for them to answer, she noted a bare spot on the wall a few yards from her, where her husband's prized van Gogh had been affixed. When the operator answered—we checked, it was on the fifth ring, they were busy that day—she said that her husband had been fighting with someone on their terrace, and that he had been pushed over the parapet and was lying in the alley, fifteen stories below, and to send an ambulance and the police."

"Did you listen to the tape?" Stone asked.

"I did, and it substantially matched her story. We had a patrol car there in under four minutes and a pair of detectives three minutes after that."

"Pretty good response."

"Thank you. While she was being questioned, Mrs. Tillman took the uniforms to the parapet and looked down to see paramedics attending to her husband. The detectives arrived and she showed them the parapet, then took them further along to where the perp had hooked his rope to the bricks, leaving scrape marks. She suggested the burglar must have had some technique for unhooking his rope. The detectives spent nearly an hour with her, going over her story again and again—you know how that goes—and questioning her about her background and her marriage. They noted that she was unusually calm and lucid during the questioning and answered them without hesitation."

"Unusually calm as compared to what?"

"You get a wide range of emotions on such occasions, ranging from hysteria and weeping all the way down to calm and reasonable, or as one detective described it, 'cold and calculating.'"

"How did the other detective describe it?"

"'Calm and reasonable.' She also pointed out the bare spot on a wall of pictures and said it had contained a small painting of some golden fields, by Vincent van Gogh, when she had last seen the wall, and she suggested that the picture must have been in the bag slung onto the burglar's back."

"And I'm sure your people did all their work thoroughly, with respect to the burglar."

"Your confidence is not misplaced," Dino replied.

"Now tell me how she might have killed her husband herself."

"All right, she came home from shopping and immediately fell into an argument with her husband that may have become physical on either or both of their parts. The argument moved to the terrace, where there may have been a struggle such as that she described with the burglar, and her husband went over the parapet."

"What reason do you have to think that his going over wasn't an accident?"

"It's possible, but all those involved felt that she engineered it."

"And they felt that on what basis?"

"The couple had a history of domestic disputes. Some of the building's staff had heard them at it, and she had called the police on one occasion. The officer's record states that they were both calm when he arrived, and she told him she had overreacted to something he had said to her, and he had since apologized and everything was now fine."

"And that's it?"

"Did I mention that she is six feet one inch tall and

very fit, and that her husband was seven inches shorter and a doughboy?"

"You can't blame a girl for going to the gym."

"No, but you can blame her for planning his death and executing her plan."

"What about the van Gogh?"

"The apartment was thoroughly searched and it was not found."

"When she came home from shopping, did any of the staff see her?"

"The two men on the desk both saw her go upstairs."

"And how long after that was the call to nine-one-one?"

"Six minutes, as far as we can tell."

"Was the elevator on the ground floor when she arrived?"

"Yes, it's passenger-operated and trained to return to the ground floor after delivering a passenger. We feel that six minutes is a little too much time to have elapsed, if her story were true."

"Had there been any reports in the city of a cat burglar operating?"

"Three in the two months prior."

"So her account is plausible?"

"Then how the fuck did the guy get up to the penthouse? Do you really believe he could climb, hand over hand, on a rope, fifteen stories? And how the hell would he have gotten the rope hooked on the parapet?"

"Two ways spring to mind. One, he fired a rocket that took the rope to the top. That's how the soldiers on D-Day got up the cliffs at Normandy."

"Implausible. What's your second theory?"

"He somehow got into the building and made his way to the penthouse and hooked on the rope before continuing. The husband interrupted him just after he had detached the painting from the wall. Rappelling down was a one-way trip."

"That building is arguably as secure as any on the East Side."

"I've been in that building a couple of dozen times. I had a client there for a while, and I've never noticed anything in the way of security, except the two men at the desk."

"There's a camera in the elevator, so a burglar didn't get in that way."

"How many people used the elevator in the hour before she called nine-one-one?"

"Thirteen, four of them men, who were noted by the deskmen."

"How many of the men were workers or repairmen?"

"All of them."

"Did they keep a record of them at the desk?"

"No, but they recognized two of them, and they called up to ask the occupants if they were expecting visitors."

"Did they call Mr. Tillman for that purpose?"

"No, he had told his wife that he didn't feel well and was going to take a nap."

"How was his body dressed when the EMTs got there?"

"Pajamas."

"Dino, if Morgan were tried in court on the basis of that evidence, the jury wouldn't be out for an hour before they acquitted her, and half that time they would have spent filling out the required forms."

"That doesn't mean she's not guilty."

"Sorry, pal, you've got nothing but suppositions."

"Yeah, that's what the DA said, and Tillman was a friend and campaign contributor of his."

"And you still smell sulfur?"

"Yeah. What was she like in the sack?"

"That's a rude question. Like somebody who hadn't had sex since her husband died. Did you find a boyfriend in her life, before or since her husband's death?"

"No."

"I didn't think so. See ya." Stone hung up, fuming.

10

AROUND ELEVEN AM JOAN buzzed him. "Arthur Steele on one."

Arthur Steele was chairman and CEO of the Steele Group, a conglomerate of insurance companies, which was one of Stone's major clients. He also served on their board. He pressed the button. "Good morning, Arthur."

"Good morning, Stone. Could we meet for lunch at The Club? There's something important."

"Of course."

"Twelve-thirty. I have a private dining room."

"See you there."

STONE ASKED FOR MR. STEELE on his arrival and was sent to a floor above the main dining room, where a staff member directed him to a small dining room.

Steele was seated already, and his briefcase was on the table. He stood and greeted Stone cordially, and they sat down. "I've taken the liberty of ordering for us," he said. "Would you like a drink?"

"I'll have a glass of wine with lunch," Stone replied.

"I have a lot of talking to do," Steele said, "so we may as well get at it."

"Please do, Arthur."

"It has been reported to me that you spent last night, from around ten PM until nine this morning, in the apartment of Morgan Tillman, presumably in her bed."

Stone was surprised. "Arthur, have you had someone following me?"

"No, I've had someone following Morgan Tillman. Last night, it was pretty much the same thing."

"I have nothing to say about that, Arthur. Go on."

"Are you aware that Mrs. Tillman was, perhaps still is, the principal suspect in the death of her husband?"

"I was made thoroughly aware of that by our police commissioner earlier today. He laid out his case."

"And what did you think of it?"

"I thought that, in the unlikely event that she were tried, she would be acquitted in short order."

"I'm afraid that's what I thought, too," Steele said.

"I suppose your interest in this business has something to do with insurance?"

"It certainly does. We insured the van Gogh in the value of sixty million dollars."

"I'd heard it might be worth forty million."

"People always over-insure," Steele said. "It's one of the ways we make our money."

"Did you pay the claim?"

"Mark Tillman's policy states that if the painting is stolen, we have a grace period of eighteen months before payment is due, to give us and the authorities time for a thorough investigation. Our time is up soon, and I'm afraid that unless the picture is recovered, we'll have to pay."

"I trust you laid off some of your liability on a reinsurer?"

"Lloyd's took fifty percent of it. They're very interested in the investigation, as you might imagine, and I'm speaking to you with their concurrence."

"Arthur, what, exactly, are you speaking to me about?"

"Is Morgan Tillman your client?"

"We have no formal arrangement, nor even an informal one. She sought advice on dealing with the police when the windshield of her Bentley was smashed. I expect you'll be receiving a number of claims for similar events."

"Yes, I've heard about that rash of breakages."

"I introduced her to Dino so that she could vent. She did so, and that was the extent of my involvement in her affairs."

"So she is not your client?"

"I don't intend to bill her, so no, I guess not."

"All right, from here on we are operating under the strictest degree of confidentiality. Agreed?"

"Arthur, you are already my client, so agreed."

"We—I, at least—feel that the stolen van Gogh may be a fake."

"Arthur, surely you took steps to authenticate the painting before you insured it for sixty million dollars."

There was a knock at the door and a waiter entered, pushing a cart. He served them a cold soup.

"Just leave the cart," Steele said to him. "We'll deal with the main course." The man departed, closing the door behind him.

"We did take steps," Steele replied, pouring them both a glass of Meursault. "Mark Tillman insisted that it be inspected at his apartment. For security reasons, he did not want it to leave the premises."

"I don't blame him," Stone said.

"We had three experts—one from the Van Gogh Museum in Amsterdam representing Lloyd's, one from the Metropolitan Museum, which expected to acquire the painting as a gift from Tillman's estate upon his death, and an eminent authority on van Gogh, representing us."

"And did they render their opinions?"

"They all agreed that it was genuine."

"Then why do you believe that it might not be?"

"This is rather a long story, so drink your soup and listen."

Stone picked up his soup spoon and Arthur began.

"Are you aware of the circumstances of Vincent van Gogh's death?"

"I believe he committed suicide," Stone said.

"That was the official verdict," Steele said. "On Sunday, July twenty-ninth, 1890. He told the police later that he had shot himself in the abdomen. There has also emerged a theory that he might have been accidentally shot by one of three boys who were playing with a pistol near where he sat. The theory holds that he didn't want to implicate the boys, and he wanted to die, anyway."

"Now that you mention it, I think I read something about that."

"You probably also know that Vincent's brother, Theo, who was an art dealer in Paris, represented him in the sale of his work?"

"I do, and I believe he was singularly unsuccessful in that pursuit."

"Quite right. No van Gogh painting was sold during Vincent's lifetime. Theo, who believed strongly in his brother's work, supported Vincent and dealt with all his affairs. He received a telegram on Monday morning, from the keeper of the inn where Vincent lived, telling him of the painter's wounding. The telegraph office had been closed on Sunday. He took a train immediately for Auvers-sur-Oise, where Vincent had been living. When he arrived, he found several completed paintings in Vincent's room, and he had them packed later and took them back to Paris with him on the train after the burial. But before Vincent died he told Theo that he had completed another painting."

"And what had happened to that?"

"Vincent had taken his painting gear and his easel with him when he left the inn on Sunday morning. He painted the picture, a landscape of a local field with many flowers, then left his gear leaning against a haystack while he had lunch. The shooting, one way or another, took place soon afterward, and Vincent was able to make his way back to the inn, but he was unable to carry his gear. Later, when the police went looking for it, it was gone—including the picture he had painted."

"Was it ever found?"

"No. It was posited that one of the boys had taken it, but all of them denied everything. There was an investigation, instigated by Theo, but it was cursory. No one ever tried to sell it, and the police had little interest in a work by a madman who was an unsuccessful artist of no reputation."

"Then how did this painting come to be in Tillman's hands?"

"The story continues. The young boy died many years later, and his son sold the contents of his father's small house to a junk dealer in Arles. The painting is said to have been among his belongings. The junk dealer, failing to sell the picture, gave it to a woman who owned a framing shop, but oddly, she seemed to have no appreciation of it. She was apparently interested in framing, but not art. It reposed in the workroom in her shop for years. Upon her death it was discovered by an art dealer who had come to retrieve a picture she was framing for him, and, recognizing that a painting he saw there was a van Gogh, he bought the entire stock of the store, so that the picture's existence would not be noticed. He then sold the picture to a Paris dealer, who then contacted Mark Tillman, to whom he had earlier sold a Monet. He needed money badly and could not wait for an auction, and Tillman paid him fifty thousand dollars for it. It was cheap, because it could not be authenticated by the usual means—no one had ever seen it and it had never been photographed."

"Arthur, you still haven't told me why you think the picture is a fake."

"I believe that the whole story was contrived to support the authenticity of the painting. Have you ever heard of a man named Angelo Farina?"

"I believe I heard from my mother about him." Stone's mother, Matilda Stone, had been a well-known painter.

"I believe the picture was painted by Farina."

11

STONE WAS INTRIGUED. "Why do you think that?"

"Farina, in his youth, was a very expert and successful forger of art. He worked as an art restorer, repairing hundreds of old paintings, and he learned how they were made and with what materials. He is alleged to have sold hundreds of forgeries, many of which are said to be hanging in museums all over America and Europe, undetected. When law enforcement finally took an interest in him, he stopped doing forgeries and earned his living by selling his own paintings or copies of those of others', identified as such, and by his art restoration business.

"It has been fifteen years or so since he says he stopped forging, and the statute of limitations has expired for any fakes he may have executed. Also, he left no paper trail—no receipts, bills of sale, no provenance, nothing—so it would have been difficult to convict him, anyway."

"You still haven't told me why you think Angelo Farina painted the supposed van Gogh."

"Angelo lived about two hundred yards from Mark Tillman's house in the Hamptons."

"So they were friends?"

"They were. Mark would go over to Angelo's studio and watch him paint. I believe that Mark, over time, concocted the story of the painting and asked Angelo to paint it for him. If that is so, then he probably faked the theft of his painting for the insurance."

"Could Angelo paint in the style of van Gogh?"

"Angelo could paint in any style. He needed only a picture to copy. In this case he would probably have looked at several photographs of van Goghs in museums, then copied his style and brushstrokes. And that is what makes it so difficult to deny that the picture is a fraud—it is not a copy of anything, so no direct comparisons can be made."

"But there are differences between old and new paints and canvases. Surely that would have been checked."

"Of course, but Angelo is highly expert at using old materials and paints." Steele opened his briefcase and handed Stone a book, entitled *Art for Art's Sake*. "He explains his techniques in his autobiography. I think you'll find it interesting. For instance, he will buy a cheap painting from the period in question, remove the oil paint from the canvas, apply a gesso, or primer coat, of his own invention, which is made of ingredients that cannot be dated. Then he uses his own paints or old ones, the formulas of which have not changed for centuries. He has special techniques for aging the finished painting—like baking it in the sun for days to produce the cracks associated with age, and even adding what appear to be fly specks, which are common on old paintings. He uses pieces of old wood from period furniture for the backings, and he has a large collection of period frames. The results are masterful." Arthur went back into his briefcase and came out with an 8x10-inch color transparency. "This was taken by our expert during the examination, in sunlight."

Stone's breath was slightly taken away. "This is glorious," he said.

"All of Angelo's work, that we've actually seen, has been glorious," Arthur said. "The FBI has quite a collection of his, ah, works, but of course they can't prove that he painted any of them."

"This is all very intriguing," Stone said.

"One more thing, and this happened when I was present as the experts were examining Mark's picture. The man from the Van Gogh Museum wanted to clean a small area of the painting to see what might be underneath more than a century of dust and dirt. He had brought acetone, the best cleaner, with him, but Mark would not allow him to use it, saying that it might damage the painting. Instead, he offered the man a bottle of mineral spirits, which would clean the picture fairly well without damaging it. You see, the varnish on paintings hardens very slowly, over a period of decades, to the point where it will not be harmed by acetone, and even Angelo has not been able to replicate this characteristic, so he can't allow acetone to be used."

"Very clever of him."

"And very necessary. I've heard of a case where a man bought an old and expensive picture at auction, and when he got it home and tried to clean it with acetone, it melted. It seems obvious, after the fact, that it was a contemporary forgery."

"This is all very interesting, Arthur," Stone said, "but I still don't know what you want from me."

"Simple. I want you to find the picture and bring it to me so that I can have it cleaned with acetone. Then I will know, one way or another, if it is a genuine van Gogh, and I can pay or deny payment, as is appropriate."

"Simple? The NYPD and the FBI have already failed to find it, but you expect that I can?"

"But you have something they don't, Stone."

"And what is that?"

"Access to Morgan Tillman—perhaps even her trust. That is why I am prepared to offer you a finder's fee, for the recovery of the painting, of twenty percent."

"Twenty percent of what?"

"Forty million dollars."

"But you have insured it for sixty million, Arthur."

"Oh, all right," Steele said grumpily, "twenty percent of sixty million dollars." Steele opened his briefcase and extracted one of two identical envelopes. "And here is a letter to that effect—a contract, if you like."

Stone opened the unsealed envelope and read the letter inside. "You have neglected to sign it, Arthur."

Steele took the letter from him, signed it with a flourish, and handed it back. "There you are."

"I expect the other envelope contains a letter mentioning forty million," Stone said.

"That's neither here nor there," Steele replied, offering his hand. "Do we have a deal?"

Stone shook it. "How long do I have?"

"Two weeks from today, at noon," Steele said. "It must be in my hands by then to have time for it to be reexamined."

Stone put the letter back into its envelope and tucked it into the inside pocket of his jacket. "I'll be in touch," he said. Then he stopped for a moment. "You realize, Arthur," he said, "that if you're wrong about this, the picture is the very last one painted by van Gogh."

Steele made a little groaning noise.

12

STONE WENT BACK to his office and said to Joan, "Send two dozen yellow roses to Morgan Tillman, at 740 Park Avenue."

"Gotcha, boss." Joan leered.

"Immediate delivery, please."

"But of course."

Stone called Dino.

"Bacchetti."

"Hey. Were you at the Tillman house when it was searched?"

"Most of the time," Dino replied.

"Did you order the search?"

"Yes."

"What were you searching for?"

"Signs of a burglar—prints, DNA, whatever we could get."

"Did you tell your people to search for the stolen painting?"

"I don't think so. We thought it was stolen, so it wouldn't still be there."

"Did you have your art squad on the premises?"

"They came in after I was gone."

"What were they doing there?"

"The art squad always goes in after the theft of a picture or sculpture or valuable book—things like that."

"And what do they do during their visit?"

"They affirm that the stolen object is absent from its usual place. They look for evidence of a modus operandi of the thief and compare it to what they know about others. Did he jimmy a window? Knock down a door? Or just pick the lock and walk in through the front door?"

"Who runs the squad?"

"Arturo Masi—called Art, appropriately enough. An Italian, of course."

"Of course."

"He's an expert on everything."

"Except things he hasn't seen," Stone said.

"Huh?"

"He didn't see the van Gogh—it was gone."

"Oh, yeah."

"I'd like to talk to him."

"On the phone or in person?"

"In person, in my office, if possible."

"He'll give you a call," Dino said.

"Thanks. See ya." Stone hung up.

SEVEN MINUTES LATER, Joan buzzed. "Art Masi on one."

Stone picked up the phone. "Mr. Masi?"

"Art. The commissioner would like me to come and see you. When's good?"

"Anytime today."

"How about in five minutes? I'm in your neighbor-hood."

Stone gave him the exact address and told him to come ahead.

ART MASI WAS TALL, solidly built, and handsome, with thick salt-and-pepper hair brushed straight back, leaving a prominent widow's peak and olive—or maybe just tanned—skin. He was sharply dressed in a handmade Italian suit. Stone wondered how he could afford it on a policeman's salary.

Masi took the offered chair, and he seemed to have read Stone's mind. "In addition to being a cop and commanding the art squad, I do freelance consulting work. The department feels it's important that I know what's going on in the art world. What can I do for you?"

"I'd like to hire you as a consultant," Stone said, "at your usual rate."

"A thousand dollars a day," Masi replied coolly, "or any part of."

"Done," Stone replied. "I expect you recall being in the apartment of one Mark Tillman, who, at the time, was very recently deceased."

"I do. He had a small but very fine collection, many of them very expensive pieces."

"How long were you and your squad in his apartment?"

"The better part of two hours."

"And what were you looking for?"

"Evidence of a crime against art."

"Define 'a crime against art.'"

"Theft, vandalism, forgery, possession of stolen goods."

"Define 'forgery.'"

"The copying of a work of art for the purpose of deceiving, or for gain during a sale or exchange."

"Exchange?"

"You swap me your fake Modigliani for my real Picasso, sell the Picasso, and pocket the difference in value."

"Of course. Do forgeries have an intrinsic value?"

"If you buy a picture because you like it, having been informed by the seller that it's a copy, its intrinsic value is whatever you paid for it."

"So it's not a crime to sell a forgery as long as the forger identifies it as such."

"No, then it's just a copy or a reproduction. If a forger is in the business of selling reproductions, he will change something about his work to make it identifiable to an expert as a copy. I know of a perfect copy of Modigliani's *Reclining Nude*, which sold at auction a couple of years ago for two hundred and sixty-four million. In the copy, the nude's eyes are closed, and the picture is four inches longer than the original."

"Who painted the copy?"

"Angelo Farina."

"And you say it's perfect?"

"If her eyes had been open and the copy exactly the same size as the original, the forgery could have been substituted for the original, before, during, or after the sale, and no expert would have been the wiser."

"Farina is that good?"

"He's that good. He has told me that more than a thousand of his forgeries are hanging in museums and private collections all over the world. Many of them have been auctioned or sold in fine galleries—some of them several times, and in so doing, authenticated by experts on each occasion."

"So experts can be wrong?"

"They're wrong at least half the time. Say you're an expert, and somebody brings you a Rembrandt for authentication. It's a new find, not in any catalog or sales record, never exhibited. You're immediately suspicious, because Rembrandt's oeuvre has been very well documented for centuries. In the absence of any forensic evidence that it's a forgery, you're going to say that, in your opinion, it's a real Rembrandt and an important discovery."

"Why?"

"Because you'll make everybody happy—the owner will be happy, the gallery that's going to auction it will be happy, and the buyer will be happy. When the buyer dies, his heirs or the museum he bequeathed it to will be happy. And you'll always be known as the expert who recognized a real Rembrandt. Who wants to piss in everybody's punch? You won't get much new work that way, and if nine other experts say it's real, you'll be the schmuck who couldn't tell the difference."

13

STONE TOOK THE TRANSPARENCY of Tillman's van Gogh from his briefcase and handed it to Art Masi. "There's a light box right behind you."

Masi turned and, without leaving his chair, placed the transparency on the light box and switched it on. He gazed at it for perhaps half a minute. "Do you have a loupe or a magnifying glass?" he asked.

Stone opened a desk drawer, retrieved both items, and placed them on his desk. "Take your pick," he said.

Masi picked up the magnifying glass, wiped it with a tissue from the box on Stone's desk, and slowly looked at the transparency from top to bottom, side to side. He placed the magnifying glass on Stone's desk, then repeated the process with the loupe. "What are its dimensions?" he asked.

"About fourteen by sixteen," Stone replied.

"Has it ever been thoroughly cleaned?"

"Only with mineral spirits, not with acetone."

Masi handed the transparency back to Stone, holding

it delicately by its corners. "This is the most gorgeous piece of art I have ever seen," he said. "And I've seen *everything*."

"Is it a forgery?" Stone asked.

"A forgery of *what*?" Masi asked. "That term would imply that an original exists. I've heard the story of this, and it's entirely plausible. It could have happened exactly the way Tillman said it did."

"If it's not a forgery, then is it an original work by Vincent van Gogh?"

"On the basis of a photographic examination, I could not say that it is not an original. I understand that three world-class experts, one from the Van Gogh Museum in Amsterdam, have pronounced it as the real thing. Is that the case?"

"Yes."

"And they were allowed to perform whatever tests they wanted to?"

"Yes, except Tillman would not allow it to be cleaned with acetone, only with mineral spirits."

"That's a red flag, but a very small one. If I owned the painting, I wouldn't allow it to be cleaned with acetone, either. I mean, even if it had been painted on July twenty-ninth, 1890, there would still be the possibility of damaging it. What we're talking about here is the last thing van Gogh ever painted, and on the day he was mortally wounded."

"Did you search the Tillman apartment for the painting?" Stone asked.

"No. I was told that it had been stolen."

"Did it not occur to you that the report might be false, and that it might have been hidden in the apartment?"

"Yes, but I reasoned that if Mrs. Tillman had hidden it, she would not have permitted a search of the apartment without a warrant, and the process of obtaining that would have given her time to remove the painting from the apartment and hide it God-knows-where. After all, it's not very big, it would fit in a small suitcase or a large briefcase, or even a large envelope, if it were out of the frame. I assume it was framed."

"I assume so, too. I don't know, but I can find out. Art, do you have any vacation time coming from the NYPD?"

"About five weeks, I think."

"If you can take two weeks off and find the painting in that time, I'll pay you a million dollars."

Masi blinked. "I assume the insurance company has offered you considerably more than that."

"You may assume anything you like. There are conditions. You may not break any laws during your search, and that includes harming anyone."

"I'm going to need it in writing," Masi said.

Stone took a sheet of his personal notepaper, picked up a fountain pen, and wrote, after the date: *I, Stone Barrington, agree to pay Arturo Masi the sum of one million dollars if he can recover, undamaged, a lost painting, ostensibly by Vincent van Gogh, formerly the property of Mark Tillman, deceased, by noon two weeks from today, as long as Mr. Masi does not violate any law in his search or harm any person. The painting is to be authenticated by comparing it to an 8x10-inch transparency of the work, which is in my possession.* He buzzed Joan.

"Yes, sir?"

"Joan, will you please come in here and bring your notary's stamp?"

"Right away." She came in, he signed the document, and she notarized it. Stone handed it to Masi, along with an envelope.

Masi read it carefully, then he folded the document and tucked it into an inside pocket of his jacket. "The clock is ticking," Masi said. "I'd better get going."

"Don't bother trying to gain access to the Tillman apartment," Stone said. "I'll take care of that myself."

"As you wish," Masi said, handing Stone a card. "That has all my contact information." The two men shook hands, and he left.

Joan buzzed.

"Yes?"

"A Mrs. Tillman on one for you."

Stone picked up the phone. "Hello there."

"I trust you're having a good day," she said.

"It's easy to have a good day after a good night."

"I must agree. Have you any plans for the weekend?"

"Not yet."

"Would you like to come out to my place in the Hamptons today?"

"I'd love to. May I drive you? You're still short of a car, aren't you?"

"Yes, but that won't be necessary. My husband thoughtfully left me a helicopter. May we meet at the East Side heliport at four o'clock?"

"Certainly."

"Bring a coat, it's cold out there this time of year."

"I'll do that. I won't bring a swimsuit, either," he said.

"You wouldn't need one, even if it were a hot day."

"I'm glad to hear that."

"I'm having some people over for dinner tomorrow evening, but it will be casual. You won't need a suit or a dinner jacket."

"I'll see you at four."

"I'll look forward to it." They both hung up.

Stone picked up Art Masi's card from his desk and called his cell number.

"Yes, Mr. Barrington?"

"Change of plans," Stone said. "Mrs. Tillman will be out of her apartment for the weekend. That should give you time to obtain a search warrant."

"The whole weekend?"

Stone gave him his own cell number. "Leaving today, not returning before Sunday. Ring me before you go in. If I say you got a wrong number, she won't disturb you. If I say I'll have to call you back, it won't be safe."

"Got it."

Stone hung up and went upstairs to pack.

14

T HE HELICOPTER ROSE from the pad and climbed to one thousand feet, just short of the overcast clouds, then headed for the shoreline. Once over the sea, the pilot descended to five hundred feet and followed the coast.

"I always ask him to fly low," Morgan said. "I love the view this way."

"Well," Stone said, "there's nothing to bump into."

Three-quarters of an hour later the chopper slowed, flew over a large, shingle-style house, and made an approach into a tennis court, from which the net had been removed. Stone and Morgan alit, then two men ran onto the court and removed their luggage from the machine, then it lifted off.

"They'll hangar it at the East Hampton airport," Morgan said as she led Stone into the house.

The place was spacious without being overwhelming, and was beautifully decorated. "Mark Hampton did the decor," she said, "years ago when my husband first bought the house. It's nearly a hundred years old."

They settled into a small sitting room off the big living room. "Would you like a drink?" she asked.

"A cup of tea would be nice," Stone replied.

"Do you have a preference?"

"Earl Grey, if you have it." It began to rain outside.

She ordered tea from a staffer. "I love it when the weather is like this," she said, getting up and lighting a fire that had already been laid.

The tea and an assortment of cookies arrived, and Morgan poured, then settled onto the sofa next to Stone. "I'm so glad you could come," she said.

"So am I, and I like this weather, too."

"It makes the house cozier."

They finished their tea, and she stood up. "Let's go upstairs and unpack."

Stone thought he knew what that meant, and he was right. They unpacked, undressed, she lit another fire, and they got into bed. Half an hour later they were spent and asleep.

When they woke up, darkness had fallen. They got dressed and went down to dinner, which was served on a small table in a handsome library.

"Give me your brief bio," Stone said after the wine had been poured.

"Typical," she said. "Born at my parents' country house in Wiltshire, sent to Lady Eden's School in London—all the fashion at the time—then a girls' school near the country house, and a finishing school in Switzerland, where I was taught French and to cook and to set a table. There was no thought of university for me, but I insisted, and I got a first at Oxford. Then I went out and got my own job in a training program at an advertising agency. I spent a few years at that, along with a lot of partying with girls of a similar background and a lot of Hooray Henrys, then I met Mark, and the next thing I knew, I was married and living in New York."

"Are your parents still living?"

"My father is. Mother died when I was sixteen."

"Do you see him much?"

"Not really—once or twice a year. He likes his books and his horses in the country and his club in London. He does the Cowes Week regatta every other year, when they run the Fastnet Race. He'd rather I'd been a boy, and he never seems to know what to say to me. All in all, I'd say he prefers his own company to that of anyone else."

"Would I like him?"

"When he decides to be charming, you would. He would find you exotic, because you're an American—but acceptable, because you have a house in England and belong to the Squadron."

"Do you love him?"

"Madly."

"That speaks well of you."

"Thank you."

They moved to a leather Chesterfield sofa for brandy and gazing into the fire. Somehow he discovered that she wasn't wearing underwear, and they entertained each other for a while, then went upstairs and entertained each other some more.

THE FOLLOWING MORNING was brilliantly sunny and windy; they managed a short walk on the beach, before nearly freezing and running back to the house. They had a lobster stew for lunch and the warming of their bones.

THE DINNER GUESTS began arriving a little after six. The first were a middle-aged couple named Joe and Martha Henry, then three more arrived: a man of about sixty, beautifully dressed and sporting an open-necked shirt with an ascot, something Stone could pull off, and a younger couple—an athletic-looking man of around thirty and his date.

"Stone," Morgan said, indicating the older man, "this is Angelo Farina. And this is his son, Pio, and Pio's friend Ann Kusch. All three of them are artists."

Drinks were served, and people warmed themselves before the fire. When they were well thawed and well oiled everyone became gregarious, and Stone enjoyed their company.

AT DINNER, Stone was seated between Morgan and Ann Kusch, who seemed curious about him. "Where have I heard your name?" she asked.

"You tell me," he replied.

"What do you do?"

"I'm an attorney, with Woodman & Weld."

"My father, Antony Kusch, was a partner there until he retired a few years ago."

"I remember him," Stone said, "though I didn't know him well. I work out of a home office, so I don't see much of the partners."

"Why do you work out of a home office?"

"When I first joined the firm I had already established my office, and I didn't bother to move. It's worked out well, though. I'm very comfortable there."

"Now I know where I've heard your name—you were mentioned in a magazine piece about Holly Barker."

"You know the secretary of state?" Morgan asked before Stone could blush and stammer a reply.

"We're old friends," Stone said.

Then someone changed the subject, for which Stone was grateful.

*　　　*　　　*

AFTER DINNER, over brandy, Stone and Angelo Farina fell into conversation. "You're a painter, are you not?"

"I am," Farina said.

"My mother was a painter—Matilda Stone."

"Oh, yes, I know her work. She had a remarkable gift for bringing New York City to life in her paintings, particularly Greenwich Village."

"Thank you," Stone said. "I'd like to see your work sometime."

"I live just down the road. Why don't you come around for coffee tomorrow morning? I'll show you my studio."

"I'd like that," Stone said, then Ann Kusch came around again, and Stone turned his attention back to her.

THAT NIGHT IN BED, when they had exhausted themselves, Morgan said, "You and Angelo got on very well. He doesn't like many people."

"He invited me around to his studio for coffee tomorrow morning."

"Oh, good, then I'll be rid of you while I'm talking with my decorator about curtains for the guest rooms."

"Have you seen a lot of Angelo's work?"

"Oh, yes, he and Mark were good friends. He used to be an art forger, you know."

"Ah, that's where I've heard the name."

"He does his own work now, but he'll whip you up a Monet, if you like, or an old master. He's really quite brilliant."

15

THE FOLLOWING MORNING, after a good breakfast, Stone pulled on his sheepskin coat and gloves against the wind, and put on a soft trilby, then he walked past the tennis court/helipad and followed a stone path for five minutes until he came to an inviting stone-and-shingle cottage. Angelo Farina answered the door wearing a well-smeared painter's smock.

"Good morning, Stone, come in and get warm." He hung Stone's coat and hat in a hall closet and led the way through a well-used living room and into a large studio that had been attached to the rear of the house. There were dozens of paintings and drawings and a few sculptures, as well as many empty frames of all sizes and shapes. On a large easel rested a newly begun painting of a haystack. "This one will be 'after Monet,'" he said. "I was a very serious forger in my youth, but now I have to be careful to distinguish between my work and that of the original and make it just a tiny bit different, to protect myself from damnation." He poured Stone a mug of coffee. "How would you like it?"

"Just black," Stone replied, accepting the mug. "May I look around?"

"Of course, that's why you're here, isn't it?"

Stone took a sip of the coffee. "That and the coffee, which is excellent." He started at his left and walked slowly around the big room. "It's like being in a museum," he said. "So many old friends—Rubens, Leonardo, Matisse, and I love the Picasso Blue Period things."

"Who is your favorite painter?" Farina asked as he brushed at his canvas.

"After my mother, I particularly like Amedeo Modigliani, and of course van Gogh—everybody loves van Gogh."

"Of course," Farina said. "Let me show you something." He went to a cupboard and removed a canvas covered with a cloth and set it on an easel. "Perhaps you know this one." He pulled away the cloth, revealing Modigliani's *Reclining Nude*. "It sold at auction a couple of years ago for nearly half a billion dollars."

Stone stared at the woman; her skin was creamy, her pose, welcoming. He wanted to crawl into bed with her. Her eyes, he noted, were closed. "It's breathtaking," he said, "but weren't her eyes open?"

"They were, but it would be too easy to let someone have it who might try to resell it as the original. It's a defensive move."

"May I buy it?"

"Please accept it as my gift," Farina said. "I'll choose a suitable period frame from my collection and send it to your home."

"You are very kind," Stone said, and he meant it.

"It will be my pleasure."

Stone looked around some more. "Could you paint me a van Gogh?" he asked.

"I've never done a van Gogh," Farina said, "but it would

be an interesting exercise. What would you like? Some irises? A portrait, perhaps a self-portrait? Pre- or post-ear?"

Stone laughed. "A van Gogh to order," he said. "I like it." He looked some more. "Perhaps a landscape, a bit of sunny Provence?"

"Let me look through my books and find something to, ah, inspire me. I expect I could have something done for you in a couple of weeks, perhaps sooner. Quick and dirty, as they say."

"And this time, it must come with a bill," Stone said. "You've been too generous already."

"As you wish."

Stone accepted a second mug of coffee, then sat down and watched Farina paint, as he had so often as a boy watched his mother. The man was astonishingly quick. Consulting a large art book on a separate easel, he held the brush and it flew around the canvas, and as Stone watched, a Monet haystack emerged. By the time Stone rose it appeared finished. "I promised Morgan I'd be back for lunch," he said, "so I should go."

"I'm so glad you could come over," Farina said. "May I have your address for the Modigliani?"

They exchanged cards. "I'll look forward to hanging it," Stone said. "I'll go home and start clearing a perfect place for it."

Farina got him his coat and hat and walked him to the door. "Drop in anytime," he said. "I enjoy performing for an audience."

They shook hands, and Stone walked back to Morgan's house, where interesting aromas were emanating from the kitchen.

"Sea bass for lunch," Morgan said, kissing him. "It slept last night in the ocean."

Stone hung up his things.

"Would you like a drink before lunch?"

"I'll wait and have a glass of wine with the fish."

They sat down on a sofa. "Did you enjoy seeing Angelo's work?"

"I certainly did. I watched him paint a Monet haystack, and he gave me a Modigliani."

"Then Angelo must like you very much indeed. I've only rarely known him to give anything away."

"What sort of a painter is his son?"

"He does mostly abstracts. He and his girlfriend, Ann, share a studio. She's a sculptor." She looked out the window. "Something disturbing happened this morning," she said.

"What happened?"

"I got a call from the front-desk man at my building. The police turned up with a warrant to search my apartment."

Stone sat up. "Do you have any idea what they're looking for?"

"I expect it's Mark's van Gogh, the one that was stolen."

"Ah, I see. They think it might still be somewhere in the apartment."

"What should I do, Stone?"

"Are you concerned about what they might find?"

"No. In fact, I'd be very pleased if the picture turned up."

"Then leave them to it. They won't wreck the place, and you'll have all that out of the way."

"I guess you're right," she said. "The helicopter is coming for us at four. Will you have your bags ready?"

"Of course."

They were called to lunch, and the sea bass was delicious, as was the Cakebread Chardonnay served with it.

"I've really enjoyed our weekend," Stone said. "It's nice to get out of the city."

"Do you have a country place?"

"Yes, but it's in Maine."

"How long does it take to drive up there?"

"Oh, I don't drive. I fly myself to Rockland, then take a small plane to the island."

"Which island?"

"Islesboro."

"I've heard it's lovely."

"Then when the snow is gone, we'll go up there together."

"I'd love that."

When Stone got home it was nearly six o'clock, and there was a package waiting for him in the front hallway. He set it on the hall table and opened it. The *Reclining Nude* greeted him with a little smile.

"Hello, beautiful," he said. "How did you get here so fast?" He took it into the living room, got out the ladder, and cleared away two other paintings, then hung the nude and adjusted the ceiling spotlight to its best advantage. He put away everything, then stepped back and viewed her.

"You are gorgeous!" he said to her.

16

STONE HAD JUST SAT DOWN at his desk on Monday morning when Joan buzzed. "Art Masi on one," she said.

Stone pressed the button. "Good morning, Art. Did you get your work done?"

"We went over the place twice with a fine-toothed comb. All we found was a frame of about the right size, which the thief must have discarded. It's in the hall coat closet."

"That makes sense. Morgan said he had a canvas bag slung on his back."

"Something else we found. There's a back door to a service stairway with a broken mechanism. It couldn't be locked from either the inside or outside."

"So that's how a thief could have gotten in and out, except Morgan says she saw him go over the parapet and rappel down."

"He'd need a hundred and fifty feet of rope. I suppose he could carry that up the stairs. It would probably weigh fifty pounds or more."

"Less, if it was something like nylon, and it wouldn't be more than a quarter of an inch in diameter."

"You have a point, Stone."

"I spent the weekend at her house in the Hamptons, and although I had a good look around, I never spotted anything like a good hiding place."

"The deskman at the building let us have a look around the basement, which is divided into storage areas, all of them padlocked. We checked the furnace room, too, and couldn't find anything."

"Maybe you should get a search warrant for the East Hampton house."

"I'll do that."

"Do you have any grounds for a warrant for Angelo Farina's house?"

"I'm not sure a judge would go for it, but it's worth a try," Art said.

"There are so many pictures there that it will take you a day just to get through his studio."

"I'll get on it." Art said goodbye and hung up.

Stone called Dino.

"Bacchetti."

"Good morning, Commissioner."

"Where were you this weekend?"

"At Morgan Tillman's house in East Hampton, and while I was gone, your art squad got a warrant and searched her apartment for the van Gogh. Twice. He also searched the basement and the furnace room."

"And what did he find?"

"Zip."

"Well, she's had plenty of time to hide it by now."

"He did find a frame, which a burglar could have discarded."

"I'll tell Art to search her East Hampton house."

"He's already on it, and Angelo Farina's house and studio, too, but I'm beginning to get the feeling that we aren't going to find it there, either."

"Well, shit."

"Yeah. Oh, one thing Art did find was a broken lock on a back door leading to a service stairway, a perfect entry for a burglar—the door couldn't be locked from either side."

"My nose still tells me," Dino said.

"Maybe you'd better stop listening to your nose."

"You like Mrs. Tillman, don't you." It was an accusation.

"Yes, I do. You'd like her, too, if you spent a little time in her company. Why don't we all have dinner this week, and you can find out what Viv's nose tells her?"

"Her nose will agree with mine."

"We'll see. Tomorrow at seven-thirty at Patroon?"

"All right."

"Tell Viv to bring her nose." Stone hung up and called Morgan.

"Good morning. Did you sleep well?"

"I certainly did. When I got home, Angelo's gift was waiting for me. It looks wonderful in my living room."

"Write him a note, he'll love that. Angelo's a stickler for the courtesies."

"I have already done so," Stone lied, taking a sheet of paper from his desk drawer. "How about dinner with Mr. and Mrs. Bacchetti tomorrow evening?"

"Love to."

"I'll pick you up a little after seven."

"Wonderful. See you then."

Stone composed a genuinely grateful thank-you note to Angelo Farina. *It looks wonderful in my house. Give me a call the next time you're coming to town, and come for a drink. I'll show you some of my mother's work, too.* He signed it and gave it to Joan to mail.

MORGAN AND VIV GOT ON as if they were old school friends, somewhat to Dino's annoyance. When the women went to the ladies', Stone said, "Well?"

"All right, Viv likes her," Dino admitted.

"Could she like a murderer and art thief?"

"She could, if she didn't know."

"Surely she knows your theory."

"Well, yeah."

"And?"

"And I don't think she buys it. You been talking to Viv?"

"Haven't seen her since the last time."

The two women came back from the restroom, and Morgan stopped at another table to visit with some people for a moment.

"That girl wouldn't kill a fly," Viv said to Dino, "let alone a husband. And why would she need to steal that painting? She would have inherited it anyway."

"Touché," Stone said.

"Oh, shut up," Dino riposted. "You two are ganging up on me."

Morgan joined them. "Old friends of Mark's," she said, indicating the other table with a nod.

"Why don't you all come back for a nightcap?" Stone said. "I've got something to show you."

THEY WENT BACK to Stone's in Dino's police car; Morgan asked to sit in the front. "May I turn on the siren?" she asked.

"Absolutely not," Dino said. "I'd have to cite you under the noise ordinance."

"Oh, come on, Dino," Viv said.

"All right, just once."

The driver pointed out the switch and she hit it, scattering a group of pedestrians crossing the street.

"That was fun," Morgan said happily.

STONE SWITCHED ON the living room lights. "My new companion," he said.

"This can't be true," Viv said, clapping her hands together. "You're not that rich, Stone."

"You are correct. It's by a forger, but a very fine one."

Viv inspected it closely. "I don't remember her eyes being closed."

"That's what makes it a copy instead of a forgery," Stone explained.

The Bacchettis had their drinks and left Stone and Morgan sitting in his study.

"I love your house," Morgan said.

"Would you like a tour of the master suite?" Stone asked.

"Yes, please," she replied.

17

LATER IN THE WEEK Stone got a call from Arthur Steele.

"Good morning, Arthur."

"Good morning, Stone. Have you found the painting?"

"Not yet, Arthur, but I can tell you that the art squad of the NYPD obtained a search warrant for Mrs. Tillman's apartment and went over it twice."

"And found nothing?"

"They found a frame that the burglar probably discarded."

"Nothing else?"

"They found a back door to a service stairway that has a broken lock, which gives the burglar a way in."

"And supports Mrs. Tillman's story," Arthur said glumly.

"Cheer up, Arthur, they're going to search her East Hampton house, too, and they're trying for a warrant for Angelo Farina's house and studio, too."

"They won't find anything at Farina's place," Steele

said. "He's far too smart to have it there. Do you have any other ideas?"

"Not yet, but you have motivated me very well, Arthur."

"It occurs to me that I have not agreed to pay your fee if the NYPD finds the picture."

"The head of the art squad is in my employ as a consultant, Arthur, and it's too soon in the game for you to start trying to get out of our agreement."

"I won't do that," Steele replied.

"Arthur, why don't you take a few days off and put this whole thing out of your mind? You'll feel better."

"No, I won't. Keep in touch." Steele hung up.

Stone had been feeling guilty about working for Arthur Steele and, possibly, against the interests of a woman he liked. He picked up the phone and invited Morgan to lunch.

THEY SAT IN THE DINING ROOM at The Club, perusing the menu.

"What is this place?" Morgan asked. "I thought I knew every restaurant on the Upper East Side."

"It's a club," Stone said, "but it doesn't have a name."

"Wait a minute," she said, "do the members just call it The Club?"

"Yes."

"Mark tried for years to get into this place, but he didn't know the right people. How is it you know the right people?"

"A friend proposed me—Dino, too. In fact, Dino was a member before I was, and he had never mentioned it to me."

"I'm impressed," she said.

"Thank you."

"With Dino."

They ordered, then Stone took a deep breath. "Tell me," he said, "which would you rather have—the van Gogh or sixty million dollars?"

"The van Gogh," she said, without hesitation. "It was my favorite thing in my marriage."

"That's good."

"Why?"

"Because your insurance company is trying very hard to find the painting, and if they find it they won't have to pay you. You must understand that the Steele Group are my clients. I shouldn't have told you this, and you can't tell anybody I did."

"Is that what all these search warrants are about?" she asked. "They're searching the East Hampton house, as well."

"Yes."

"Well, I hope they find it, because I certainly couldn't."

"You've been looking for it?"

"Yes, indeed. I've been over the apartment and the house from stem to stern. I'm obsessing about it, I think."

"I'm glad to hear that. I would not like to have thought that you were concealing the painting from the authorities."

"If I were, that would lend credence to the suspicions of the police, wouldn't it? And that would make me complicit in Mark's murder."

"I don't think it's possible that you had anything to do with his death."

"You'd be surprised at how many people think it is, including some I thought were my friends."

"You seem to be handling that very well."

"What other choice do I have? I can't prove that I didn't kill my husband."

"As long as nobody can prove you did, you'll be all right."

"Not as long as anyone still suspects me. I'll have to live with it the rest of my life."

Stone didn't have an answer to that. Their lunch came and they relaxed and enjoyed it, and he felt much better now that he had told her about Arthur's hunt for the picture. Of course, he hadn't told her that he would profit if it was found. He'd save that for another time.

THE FOLLOWING DAY Art Masi came to see Stone. He took a seat. "I'm at my wit's end," he said. "We found nothing in the East Hampton house, and I couldn't persuade the judge that I had grounds to search Angelo Farina's place. What do you want me to do next?"

"Well," Stone said, "you could work on the assumption that Morgan Tillman has always told the truth about her husband's death and try to solve the crime."

"I'm an art specialist," Art replied, "not a homicide detective."

"It's in your interest to become one," Stone said.

"Believe me, I understand that."

"Art, what do you know about Pio Farina?"

"Angelo's son? Not much. He's an abstract painter, and he has a girlfriend who's a sculptor—Ann Kusch."

"Is he any good?"

"Yes, he is."

"Does he make a living at it?"

"I think he does all right. He and the girl live in East Hampton village, but not on the beach. They have a show opening tomorrow night at the Wilder Gallery, on Madison Avenue, in the Seventies." Art thought for a minute. "Are you thinking he could be the burglar?"

"He's young and fit enough to be a cat burglar. I have nothing more than that to go on."

"That's not evidence."

"There's a computer over there," Stone said, pointing. "Why don't you run a check on him?"

Masi went to the computer and logged into the NYPD website, then entered his password to be admitted to a deeper level. He sat and stared at the screen.

Stone could see a photograph of a much younger Pio Farina over Masi's shoulder. "What's his sheet say?"

"He was arrested on suspicion of three burglaries in the Hamptons when he was nineteen."

"Was he convicted?"

"He wasn't charged—lack of evidence. After that, there were no more burglaries."

"Well," Stone said, "that's a start."

18

THE FOLLOWING MORNING, Stone got an invitation to a gallery opening featuring the works of Pio Farina and Ann Kusch. He called Morgan.

"Good morning," she said.

"Good morning. I got an invitation to an opening for Pio Farina and Ann Kusch."

"So did I."

"Would you like to go? We can have dinner afterward."

"Love to. What would you like to do after dinner?"

Stone laughed.

"So would I," she said. "The opening starts at six. Pick me up at six-thirty."

"Certainly."

BY THE TIME they arrived the gallery was full of people drinking cheap wine, talking to each other, and ignoring the art.

"Would you like a drink?" Stone asked Morgan.

"Of that stuff? No thanks."

"Then let's look at the work. Maybe we'll start a trend."

Pio's abstracts covered the walls, and Ann's sculptures were scattered about the gallery on pedestals. Stone was only mildly interested in abstract painting, and not on this occasion. The sculptures, however, interested him.

They were small bronzes, and of tools: here, an ax, embedded in a tree trunk; there, a hammer, driving a nail; and over there, a sledgehammer, smashing a rock. "What do you think of the sledgehammer?" he asked Morgan.

"I've had enough of sledgehammers," she said. "I finally got my car back, and I'm afraid to take it out of the garage."

Stone wasn't attracted to the sledgehammer, either. He flagged down a gallery worker and bought the ax.

"A good choice," the young woman said. "It will be available at the end of the show, next week."

"Please send it," Stone said, handing her a credit card and his business card.

"Certainly," she replied.

They went over to where Pio and Ann stood and greeted them.

"Are you enjoying the work?" Ann asked.

"I am. I just bought your ax."

"A good choice."

"That's also what the gallery worker told me, so it must be true."

They moved on so that others could meet the artists, then Stone looked up and saw Art Masi walk into the gallery.

"Do you know that man?" he asked Morgan.

"He was in my apartment right after Mark's death," she replied.

"He was probably there more recently than that," Stone said.

"Executing a search warrant?"

He nodded. "Let's go to dinner."

ART MASI HAD A LOOK AROUND, and when the crowd began to thin out he walked over to Pio Farina and showed him a badge. "May I speak with you in the manager's office?" Art said.

"Of course," Pio replied, and the two of them walked to the rear of the gallery and sat down at the manager's small conference table.

"What can I do for you?" Pio asked. "I can promise you that none of the art here is stolen."

"I'm more concerned about another piece of art," Art said. He mentioned the date of Mark Tillman's death. "Where were you on that day?"

Pio took an iPhone from his pocket and consulted the calendar app. "Let's see, that was a Saturday. I was at home in East Hampton, watching a football game. It's right here, on my schedule." He held up the phone.

"Who was playing, and who won?"

"The University of Georgia and Alabama. Alabama won. I forget the score, but it was close."

"Anyone watch it with you?"

"No, Ann was visiting her mother in Connecticut. I watched it alone."

"Have you ever visited the apartment of Mark and Morgan Tillman?" Art asked.

"Yes, a couple of times. Once for a drink, once for dinner."

"On what dates?"

Pio consulted his calendar again. "Drinks on July

fourth, two years ago. Dinner two nights before Mark died."

"Did you take any notice of the art in the apartment?"

"Oh, yes. Mark had a very good collection, mostly impressionists and post-impressionists."

"Do you recall seeing a van Gogh among them?"

"Of course. It would have been impossible to miss. A fabulous work, if a little small for van Gogh."

"Small enough to put in a backpack?"

"I expect so."

"Do you own a backpack, Mr. Farina?"

"I do."

"Can you describe it?"

"Beautiful leather, nut brown, from Ralph Lauren."

"Mr. Farina," Art said, "have you ever done any mountain climbing or rock climbing?"

"Once, at a big sporting goods store, I climbed a wall installed there."

"On any other occasions?"

"No, I didn't enjoy the experience. I'm afraid of heights, even the twenty or so feet of the store's wall."

"Can anyone attest to that?"

"My girlfriend, Ann, can. She was there. Ann is more adventurous than I—she's fearless."

"Would that be Ms. Kusch, whose work is being shown?"

"Yes, she was standing next to me when we met."

"I'd like to speak to her," Art said.

"Alone?"

"Yes, please. Would you ask her to join me here?"

"Of course. I'll be right back."

A moment later, Ann Kusch appeared in the doorway. "You wanted to speak to me?" she said.

Art stood. "Yes, please. My name is Masi, I'm with the art squad of the NYPD. Please have a seat."

She sat down.

"Ms. Kusch, where were you on the day that Mark Tillman was killed?" Again he cited the date.

"Let me see, I believe I was visiting my mother, in Washington, Connecticut."

"Can she confirm that?"

"Sadly, no, she died four months ago."

"Was anyone else present at your meeting with her?"

"We had lunch at the Mayflower Inn, in Washington. Perhaps the maître d'."

"Did you see any other people who knew you?"

"I'm afraid I don't remember," Ann said. "You see, my mother had asked me to come to see her because she wanted to tell me that she was ill and had only a few months to live. That sort of conversation tends to concentrate the mind and shut out everything else."

"I quite understand," Art said. "Thank you for speaking to me." He stood as she left. "Oh, Ms. Kusch," he said.

"Yes?" she asked, turning.

"May I ask, how tall are you?"

"Five feet ten inches, in my stocking feet," she replied.

"And forgive me, but your weight?"

"A hundred and forty pounds," she replied.

"One more question. Have you ever done any mountain or rock climbing?"

"Both," she replied. "I enjoy risky sports."

"Thank you. Good day."

19

JOAN BUZZED STONE. "Art Masi on one."

Stone pressed the button. "Good morning, Art. Did you enjoy the opening?"

"I like Kusch's sculptures," he said. "Pio's stuff was good, too. You left as I arrived."

"Yes, we were going to dinner. How long did you stay?"

"Long enough to interview both Pio and Ann."

"With what result?"

"They've both visited the Tillman apartment on a couple of occasions." He told Stone of their claimed whereabouts on the day of Tillman's death.

"Do their stories hold up?"

"There was a Georgia–Alabama game on that day, and Alabama won by three. That doesn't mean he stayed home and watched it, though."

"Where was Ann?"

"She says her mother invited her to Washington, Connecticut, to tell her that she had only a few months to live."

"I know the town, I used to have a house there."

"Do you know the Mayflower Inn?"

"Of course."

"Ann says they had lunch there, but I spoke to the maître d' this morning. He knew both mother and daughter, but he has no record of a lunch reservation for them on that date. It's a busy place, reservations are usually necessary, especially on a weekend, and that was a Saturday. And her mother died four months ago, so she can't help with her daughter's alibi.

"Washington is about an hour-and-three-quarters drive from where Tillman lived. Even if she was telling the truth about the lunch, she still could have easily made it to the Upper East Side by late afternoon."

"What brought Ann Kusch to your attention?" Stone asked.

"She's five-ten, a hundred and forty pounds, and athletic. She admitted to having done both mountain and rock climbing. She also has rather small breasts, so dressed in something loose, with her hair and face covered, a woman her size could have passed as a man."

"That's an interesting theory, Art. What are you going to do with it?"

"I'm going to investigate them both until their pips squeak."

"Then I'd better let you get on with it," Stone said, and hung up.

STONE CALLED DINO and related his conversation with Art Masi. "Looks like the burglar could have been a woman," Stone said.

"What burglar?" Dino asked. "There was no burglar,

just Tillman and his wife—who was, by the way, bigger and probably stronger than he was."

"Then what is Morgan's motive?"

"Money—she inherited a ton of it."

"Then she also inherited the van Gogh, right?"

"Yeah."

"So what was her motive for stealing it from herself?"

"It was worth sixty million bucks," Dino pointed out.

"But you've just told me she inherited a ton of money from her husband. How much?"

"A little over half a billion dollars."

"I'm surprised it wasn't more. Those hedge fund guys are mostly billionaires, aren't they?"

"Yeah, until they aren't," Dino replied. "And Tillman had been through a rough patch. His fund lost a lot of money that year. If he had died the year before, he'd have left her something like three billion."

"Dino, you still haven't told me why Morgan would steal the painting from herself. You've told me she inherited half a billion dollars. If she had needed money she could have sold it at auction."

"Maybe she needed money in a hurry?"

"Why? Was the estate slow to complete probate?"

"No, Tillman had arranged his estate planning so as to avoid probate. She was very rich from her first day as a widow."

"So she had no motive for stealing a painting from herself. And it was a painting that some people think is a forgery."

"Maybe that's why she didn't want to auction it," Dino said. "An auction would have brought more scrutiny to bear, whereas the insurance company had already accepted that the painting was a real van Gogh, so if the painting disappeared, they wouldn't have a leg to stand on, they'd have to pay the claim."

"Okay, I'll give you that," Stone said. "It's the first thing you've said that makes any sense."

"Gee, thanks," Dino said.

"Of course, they had an eighteen-month delay in paying off on the policy."

"I'll bet money that neither of the Tillmans knew that. Who reads an insurance policy?"

"You have a point there, too. I still haven't read my household policy."

"And that eighteen months must be about to expire?"

"Very soon," Stone said.

"That's interesting," Dino said. "It puts pressure on everybody, and when people are under pressure, they make mistakes."

"I agree, but let me ask you another question," Stone said.

"Do your worst."

"With regard to motive, why would either Pio Farina or Ann Kusch want to steal the van Gogh? If it's a fake by Angelo, they might very well have known it. Why risk a murder for a forged painting when they could just ask Angelo to paint another one?"

"I'm surprised that Art Masi hasn't mentioned this," Dino said, "but big-time art thieves usually have a buyer waiting. That picture could be hanging on some rich man's wall in Hong Kong or someplace, and the guy wouldn't be in a position to question the authenticity of the painting. He can't call the Hong Kong cops and say, 'Hey, I paid a guy to steal this painting and murder the owner, and the picture's a fake!'"

"I guess the guy wouldn't get a very sympathetic hearing."

"I think," Dino said, "that what's going to happen is, the eighteen months will expire, the insurance company will pay the loss, and we'll never hear from the painting again, unless the guy in Hong Kong dies and somebody notices that it's a fake."

"More likely," Stone said, "his estate will auction it off, and then the picture is a free-floating objet d'art that will end up on some other rich guy's wall, or in a museum, which is *not* going to question its authenticity. I've been reading Angelo Farina's book, and that's how his work ended up in so many museums—he sold his paintings to schmucks who got tired of them and sold them at auction or donated them and took the tax break."

"You know what I think?" Dino asked.

"What do you think?"

"I think that neither you nor I will ever solve this one."

"You could be right," Stone replied.

20

PIO FARINA AND ANN KUSCH drove back to East Hampton village in separate cars, so they had no time to talk on the way. Once in the house, Pio made them a drink and brought hers to her in her study.

"Okay," he said, "what did the cop ask you?"

"Probably the same things he asked you," she said. "Don't you remember the questions?"

"Like where were you when Mark Tillman died?"

"There you go. I stuck to the plan. It's not like he can call my mother and ask if I was there. Did you stick to the plan?"

"Georgia–Alabama game. I expect he checked."

"Isn't Masi the art squad guy?"

"Yes, he is," Pio answered. "Dad's known him for years."

"Then why is he investigating Mark's death?"

"Because of the picture, I guess."

"That was investigated by the regular cops at the time, wasn't it?"

"Yes, they talked to me, but not to you."

QUICK & DIRTY 101

"Gee, I feel left out," she said.

"I expect we've heard the last of it," Pio replied. "Drink your drink and forget about it."

They sat quietly for a while, then the doorbell rang, and a moment later Angelo Farina walked into the room.

"Hi, Dad," Pio said. "Would you like a drink?"

"Scotch, please," Angelo replied.

Pio brought it to him.

"How'd your show go?" Angelo asked.

"I sold eight," Pio replied. "All of Ann's sculptures went, one of them to Stone Barrington."

"I'm delighted to hear it," Angelo replied. "I talked to Abe at the gallery, and he said the police were there."

"Just one—Art Masi, from the art squad."

"Is he still looking for the picture?"

"That didn't come up. He seemed more interested in Mark's death," Pio said.

"He talked to me, too," Ann said, "and on the same subject."

"Did he give the impression that he had something new to go on?" Angelo asked.

"Not to me," Pio replied. "They were just routine questions."

"There was something he asked me that I'll bet he didn't ask you," Ann said.

"What was that?"

"He asked me my height and weight."

"Ah," Angelo said, "Art is thinking."

"Now that I think of it," Pio said, "he asked me if I had any rock climbing experience. I told him I was afraid of heights."

"He asked me that, too," Ann said. "He asked about mountain or rock climbing."

"And what did you tell him?" Angelo asked.

"I told him yes. He would have found out anyway, and I thought it best not to lie to him."

"You're absolutely right," Angelo said. "If a policeman catches you in a lie, he'll never believe you again, and I think our credibility is important. Pio, you shouldn't have told him you're afraid of heights—that could come back and bite you on the backside."

"How is he going to disprove that?"

"Suppose he looks up your prep school yearbooks? He'll find out you were on the rock climbing team."

"I hadn't thought of that."

"If you tell the truth, you don't have to worry about things like that. Now, if he finds out about the team, he'll work all the harder to find out about you."

"He didn't ask me about the burglaries."

"I've no doubt he already knew," Angelo said. "That would have required only a few keystrokes. If it ever comes up, admit it immediately—tell him the truth, that you were young and stupid."

"Please don't start on that again, Dad," Pio said.

"I told you at the time that it would come back to haunt you."

"I know, I know. Please just drop it."

"I will, if you'll stop lying to the police."

"So," Ann said, "am I a suspect now, because I'm big for a girl?"

"Don't forget flat-chested," Pio said sourly.

"That again? Do you want me to have a boob job?"

"Children, children," Angelo said, "let's not start opening old wounds. Everyone just needs to be calm. This will be over soon, and life will go on as usual."

"I'm going to make an appointment with Dr. Bassey, in the village," Ann said. "Boobs are his specialty."

Pio started to say something about who the boob was,

but he thought better of it. "I like you as you are, but as always, you can do whatever you like."

"I will," she replied. "Don't you worry."

Angelo tossed off his scotch. "I'm going to leave you two to this conversation," he said, then left.

"Why did you lie to the police?" Ann asked when Angelo had gone.

"Just a reflex. I've never trusted cops."

"Well, now they're not going to trust you."

21

ART MASI SAT AT HIS COMPUTER and Googled Pio Farina; he found a website. Art went there and clicked on Bio. Pio had attended a coed, arts-oriented prep school in New Hampshire for four years. He found the school's website and did a search for Pio; in a moment he had found the school yearbook for his senior year.

There was a photograph of the young Pio with lots of hair, and underneath, a list of school activities: *Sketch Club, 123&4; Drama Club, 3&4; Climbing Club, 123&4, captain, 3&4*. Art didn't need to read any further. Pio had lied to him about his fear of heights. Art loved it when suspects lied to him, and in this case, badly.

The two could have said they had both stayed home and watched the football game; instead, they had contrived to put Ann in Connecticut, and Pio thus had no one to back up his alibi. And since Ann had lied about her lunch at the Mayflower with her dying mother, neither did she. They had blown each other out of the water. How stupid could they be?

Art looked up Pio's number in East Hampton and called. Pio answered. "Hello?"

"Mr. Farina, this is Art Masi from the NYPD."

"Oh, yes, we met at our opening."

"I'd like for you and Ms. Kusch to be in my office tomorrow at noon, to answer some more questions."

"What?"

"I believe I spoke clearly."

"In New York?"

"That is correct."

"You want us to drive all the way to New York to talk to you? If you like, I'll put Ann on the extension and you can talk to both of us now."

"I'm sorry, this meeting will have to be face-to-face."

"It's a four-hour drive!"

"That's why I scheduled our meeting for noon. Would one o'clock be more convenient? That's the only other available time."

"I'm sorry, Mr. Masi, but we're not going to make a trip into the city just to answer some questions that we can just as easily answer on the phone."

"I can arrange for you to be driven to the city in a police car, if you like. Handcuffed."

"What are you charging us with?" Pio demanded.

"We'll discuss that at our meeting. One o'clock. The address is One Police Plaza. Ask for me at the front desk. Good day."

Art hung up.

"JESUS CHRIST!" Pio said.

Ann came in from the next room. "What's wrong?"

"That art cop, Masi, just called. He says he wants us in his office at one o'clock tomorrow to answer some questions."

"He doesn't really expect us to drive all the way into the city just to see him, does he?"

Pio looked up at her. "He offered us a ride in a police car, handcuffed."

"Oh, shit."

ART CALLED Stone Barrington.

"Hello, Art."

"Stone, I've called Pio Farina and Ann Kusch in tomorrow at one for questioning."

"Don't they live in East Hampton?"

"They do."

"Do you think they'll show up?"

"As an alternative, I offered them a ride in a police car."

Stone laughed. "That should do it."

"I'm going to question them separately, and I'd like you to observe, if you have the time."

"Sure, one o'clock. Are you downtown?"

"Yes, just ask for me at the desk. Make it twelve-thirty."

"I'll bet they bring a lawyer," Stone said.

"I don't think so, they still think I don't have anything on them."

"Do you?"

"They both lied to me when I questioned them at the gallery, and I can prove it."

"So you're going for a confession?"

"I may not be a homicide detective, but I'm a pretty good interrogator."

"I'll see you at twelve-thirty," Stone said.

*   *   *

"**WE'D BETTER CALL A LAWYER**," Pio said.

"Bringing a lawyer is as good as a confession," Ann said. "Don't you ever watch TV?"

"We watch all those cop shows together. If somebody lawyers up, they have to let them go."

"Look," Ann said, "we've got one more shot at getting Masi off our backs, before we get lawyers involved."

"We don't even know a lawyer," Pio said.

"Sure we do," Ann replied. "His name is Stone Barrington."

22

STONE ARRIVED AT One Police Plaza at 12:30 and was immediately sent up to the art squad offices. Art Masi greeted him.

"How is this going to work?" Stone asked.

"We've got two interrogation rooms," Art replied, "and my colleague—" He was interrupted by a knock at the door, and a handsome woman in her forties entered. "Stone, this is Adrian Halstead, my colleague. Adrian, this is Stone Barrington, who has an interest in this interrogation."

They shook hands. "Just what is your interest in this case, Mr. Barrington?"

"Call me Stone, please. I represent the insurance company that covered the van Gogh."

"Adrian has been fully briefed on this case, and she will conduct the interrogation of Pio Farina, while I interrogate Ann Kusch. We have two interrogation rooms set up, each with two-way mirrors, and there is a small room between the two, so you can witness both interrogations simultaneously."

"I hope I can keep up," Stone replied.

The phone on Masi's desk rang, and he answered it. "Thank you, please send them up to my office." He hung up. "Stone, let's get you in position."

Stone followed him down a hallway and into a small room with blinds on either side. Masi raised both, revealing standard interrogation rooms. "There are speakers for each room above," he said, pointing upward. "There are volume knobs on the table."

Stone sat down at the table; he had never seen a setup quite like this. Masi left him there and closed the door behind him.

Stone took the moment to check his e-mail; there was one from Dino. "Dinner with girls, Rotisserie Georgette, 7:30?"

"Done," Stone said. He forwarded the message to Morgan, who responded quickly.

"I'll meet you there. Looking forward."

Then the doors to the adjoining rooms opened simultaneously, and the interviewers and their subjects entered and took seats. Masi and Halstead spoke together: "I'm required to read you your rights. You have the right to remain silent. You have the right to an attorney. If you cannot afford an attorney, one will be appointed to represent you at no cost to you. If you choose to speak to me, your answers may be used as evidence against you in a court of law. Do you wish an attorney?"

"No," Pio said.

"Not at this time," Ann replied.

Masi and Halstead produced documents for their signatures. "This document says that you have been read your rights and have declined to have an attorney present during your questioning. If you agree, please sign and date."

Both of them signed.

"Now, Mr. Farina," Halstead said, "on a previous occasion you spoke to my colleague Lieutenant Masi, did you not?"

"I did."

MASI BEGAN: "Ms. Kusch, do you recall speaking to me two days ago at an art gallery?"

"Yes," she replied.

"Do you recall being asked about your whereabouts on the date of the death of Mark Tillman?"

"I do."

"And what was your response?"

"I told you that I had had lunch in Washington, Connecticut, with my mother."

"At the Mayflower Inn?"

"Yes."

"The headwaiter there, who was acquainted with both you and your late mother, denies that you were present in his dining room on that date. He recalls because the restaurant was very crowded that day, and he was turning people away. His reservation book does not contain either of your names."

"I suppose we must have had lunch in the bar that day," she said. "They don't require reservations there."

"They do on weekends," Masi said. "Why did you lie to me?"

HALSTEAD STARED INTO PIO'S EYES. "Do you recall telling Lieutenant Masi that you have no experience mountain or rock climbing?"

Pio blinked. "I'm not sure I recall being asked that," he said.

"It was only two days ago, Mr. Farina."

"I still don't remember."

"Do you recall telling my colleague that you are afraid of heights?"

"I may have said something like that, jokingly."

"In fact, Mr. Farina, at your prep school in New Hampshire you were a member of the climbing club for four years and captain for two, were you not?"

"Um . . ."

"So it says in your school yearbook."

"Then that must be the case."

"Tell me, what do members of the climbing club climb? Stairs? Trees?"

"Mountains and rocks," Pio replied.

"MS. KUSCH," Masi said, "did you spend that particular day with your boyfriend, Pio Farina?"

"I may have, I'm not sure."

"Do you recall watching a football game together on TV? Georgia versus Alabama?"

"Oh, yes, I believe I did watch that game with him."

"Who won?"

"Ah, I'm not sure. Georgia, I think."

"Alabama won by three points."

"If you say so. I'm not very interested in football. In fact, I was probably reading a book while the game was on."

"What book?"

"I don't remember. I'm usually reading a book, and it was more than a year ago."

"MR. FARINA, where were you on the date of the death of Mark Tillman?"

"I was at home, watching a football game."

"Were you alone?"

"Yes."

THE DOOR OPENED and Halstead walked in, handed Masi a note, and left.

Masi unfolded the note. "Ah, Mr. Farina has said that you were not present when he watched the Georgia–Alabama game, that you were out of town."

"Well, he's wrong."

"Just as you were wrong about being in Connecticut?"

"I believe we had lunch at my mother's house, since the restaurant was fully booked."

"What did you have for lunch?"

"Tuna fish sandwiches."

"I WAS WRONG," Pio said. "I remember now that Ann was there."

"Watching the football game?"

"Yes."

"Is Ann very interested in football?"

"Yes, very. She enjoys it."

Art Masi entered the room, handed Halstead a note, and left.

Halstead read the note. "Ann Kusch says that she doesn't like football and read a book during the game. I'm sorry, didn't she say she was in Connecticut?"

"She was somewhere," Pio replied. "I just assumed it was Connecticut."

"So you were alone?"

"Yes."

"Entirely? Did anyone else visit you?" Halstead asked.

"No."

"So no one can corroborate your contention that you watched a football game on that date?"

"My father may have dropped in for a drink. He does that sometimes, unannounced."

Halstead wrote something on a pad. "Your father's phone number?"

"Why do you want it?"

"To ask him his whereabouts on that day."

"He doesn't have a very good memory, he's getting on in years."

Halstead consulted her notes. "I see that your father is sixty years old and in excellent health," she said.

"I think I'd like to speak to an attorney," Pio said.

"MS. KUSCH," Masi said, "it seems that since your mother is now deceased, there is no one who can confirm your whereabouts on the day Mark Tillman died."

"I'd like a lawyer," she said.

"Of course you would," Masi replied, closing his notebook.

23

STONE WAITED WHILE Farina and Kusch vacated their interrogation rooms, then Art Masi came for him. "Did you hear everything?"

"Yes. I'm glad I'm not representing them."

"If you were, they'd have done better," Art said.

"If I were, I would have been there, and they would have declined to answer questions."

Art laughed. "Typical lawyer."

"I suppose so," Stone said, looking at his watch. "I'd better get back to my office. I have an appointment." They shook hands, and Stone departed.

STONE HAD BEEN BACK in his office for, perhaps, half an hour when Joan buzzed him. "An Ann Kusch on one. She says you know her."

"I do," Stone said, picking up the phone. "Ann?"

"Yes, Stone, thank you for remembering me."

"How could I forget? I own your ax."

"That's right, you do."

"How can I help you?"

"Pio and I are outside in the car. May we come and see you?"

"Of course, come right in." He hung up and buzzed Joan. "Two people are arriving. Please show them in."

A moment later, the two walked into Stone's office. He directed them to the sofa, where he thought they might feel more comfortable. They declined refreshments.

"Now, how can I help?"

Ann did the talking: "The police seem to have somehow gotten the idea that we had something to do with the death of Mark Tillman and/or the theft of his van Gogh."

Stone held up a hand. "Before we continue, I'm obliged to declare an interest in that case. I represent the Steele Group, who insured the van Gogh and whose desire is to recover the painting. Does that trouble you in any way?"

"I don't see why it should," Ann replied. Pio shook his head.

"As long as you know. Please continue."

"Anyway, a Lieutenant Masi of the art squad questioned us at the gallery during our opening."

"Were you troubled by that?"

"No, his questions were straightforward, and we answered them. Then we got a phone call from him demanding that we come to his office for further questioning."

"Demanding?"

"He said that if we didn't come voluntarily, he'd send a police car for us, and we'd be handcuffed."

"It sounds like the lieutenant got a little too enthusiastic about his work. What did he ask you?"

"He seemed most concerned about where we were on the day that Mark Tillman died."

"And what did you tell him?"

"I'm afraid that we got a little confused about where we were and what we were doing—after all, it's been more than a year."

"Did you give him truthful answers?"

"We tried to, but he and another detective did their best to trip us up and make us contradict each other."

"And where were the two of you on that day?"

"I went to Washington, Connecticut, to see my mother," Ann said. "We had lunch at her house, but at the first questioning, I thought we had gone to the Mayflower Inn, which turned out to be my mistake."

"And, Pio, where were you?"

"Watching the Georgia–Alabama football game at home."

"Alone?"

"Ann came back late in the afternoon, while the game was still on."

"Ann, what route did you take going home?"

"I drove down to Bridgeport and took the ferry to Long Island. It saves a lot of time to avoid the city."

"So can anyone prove that you didn't visit your mother, or in Pio's case, stay home and watch the game?"

"No," they both said.

"Was there anything else of note they asked you?"

"They wanted to know if I had done any mountain or rock climbing," Ann said, "and I told them I had. Masi also asked me my height and weight."

"Which is?"

"Five-ten, a hundred and forty."

"Masi asked me the same thing," Pio said, "but I told him, jokingly, that I was afraid of heights."

"Are you afraid of heights?" Stone asked.

"Not in the least," Pio said. "I was captain of my climbing team at prep school."

"Did you later tell them that?"

"Before I could, they looked up my school yearbook and found out for themselves."

"Are we in any trouble?" Ann asked.

"Did either of you have anything to do with Mark Tillman's death or the theft of the painting?"

Neither of them answered.

"Is there something you'd like to tell me about that day?" Stone asked.

They looked at each other and Pio nodded, then Ann spoke up. "Mark knew that we would be in the city that day, and he invited us for a drink."

"What time of day?"

"At two-thirty," she replied.

"And what ensued?"

"Not much. We had a drink, chatted, then excused ourselves, saying that we had to drive back to East Hampton. Then, on the way out, Mark asked us if we'd drop off a package at a FedEx store on Second Avenue. It was on our way, so I said sure."

"And did you?"

"Yes. There's a drop box outside the store."

"How big a package was it?"

"It was a standard-size FedEx box, about yea big," she said, showing how big with her hands.

Stone buzzed Joan. "Will you please bring me a small and a large FedEx box?"

A moment later she entered with the boxes.

Stone sealed one end of each and held them up. "Which one?"

"The larger one," Ann said.

"Did you have any idea what was inside?"

"No. It didn't weigh a lot, though."

"Did you notice to whom it was addressed?"

"I never gave it a thought," Ann said. "We dropped it in the box and drove home."

"And what time did you get home?"

"I'm not sure, but the game was still on, and we watched the last quarter."

"There are two ways to address a FedEx box," Stone said. "One is with the multi-copy form that you fill out by hand. The other is one that you print out on a computer. Which way was the package labeled?"

"I honestly don't remember," Ann said.

"Do you remember how you both were dressed that day?"

"Well, Pio wears mostly black, no matter what the occasion. I think I was wearing a black denim suit—pants, not skirt."

"Blouse?"

"I wear either white or black with that outfit," Ann said. "I don't remember which that day."

"Where did you have your drinks?"

"On the terrace," Ann said. "It was an unseasonably warm day."

"When you left, did Mark see you to the door?"

"Now that you mention it, no," Ann replied. "He said he was going to enjoy the last of the afternoon and finish his drink."

"Where was the FedEx package?"

"It was on a table in the front hall. Mark called out and asked us to take it."

"And he stayed on the terrace?"

"Yes, he never got up. He seemed drowsy and had his feet up on an ottoman."

"Might he have dozed off out there?"

"I wouldn't be surprised," she said. "He was on his second drink, and the sun was warm."

"On your way out of the building, did you encounter anyone?"

"There was a man on the front desk, but he barely took notice of us."

"Did you cross paths with Morgan?"

"No."

"Where were you parked?"

"Outside the building on Seventy-eighth Street."

"Did you see anyone you knew on the way to the car?"

"No."

"All right," Stone said, "here's where we are. You've lied to the police about your whereabouts when Mark Tillman was murdered. You may well have been the last people to see him alive, except for Morgan. You removed a package from the apartment that may have contained the van Gogh that Morgan says disappeared."

"We did so at Mark's request, and we had no idea what it contained, and we didn't care."

"Did you know that Mark owned a van Gogh?"

"Yes, he had shown it to us when we had dinner there a few weeks before. Angelo was there, too, and he saw it."

"Has either of you ever expropriated a work of art belonging to someone else?"

"Certainly not," Ann said. "Why would we do that?"

"For money?"

"We earn a decent living from our work," Pio said. "We don't need to steal."

"Tell me, Pio," Stone said, "suppose you suddenly came into, say, twenty million dollars, tax free. What would you do with it?"

"I'd buy a house," Pio said.

"Where?"

"Either in East Hampton or in Paris."

"Ann? How would you spend it?"

"The same way," she replied.

"All right," Stone said, "I'm going to have a conversation with Art Masi and tell him what you've told me today. Have I your permission to do that?"

"We're going to look awfully bad to him," Pio said.

"You already look bad, because he knows you lied to him," Stone pointed out. "You're just going to have to live with that and hope, now that you've told the truth, that will be enough for him. You can both expect to be questioned again, and next time longer and much more thoroughly. My best advice is to be contrite about lying to them, and don't do it again."

"Couldn't we just refuse to answer any further questions?" Ann asked.

"You could, but the police would see that as a virtual confession of both murder and grand theft, not to mention colluding in insurance fraud. They would investigate you for weeks or months, maybe years. At least half the people you know would believe that you're guilty, and that would last the rest of your life. It would be mentioned prominently in your obituaries. So unless that's how you want to live your lives, you'd better be very, very cooperative with the police from now on. When they question you again, don't ask for a lawyer, and tell the truth. When you're done, come back to see me."

"Oh, all right," Ann said, and Pio nodded; then they left. Stone was disgusted with them.

24

STONE WAS THINKING about leaving his desk early when Joan buzzed him and said Art Masi wanted to see him.

"All right, send him in," Stone replied.

Masi came in and sat down.

"Art, after your interview with Farina and Kusch, what are your feelings about the case?"

"Well, they're lying, and I don't know why, except that they're hiding something incriminating."

"Which crime do you think they may have committed?"

"Either one, or possibly both."

"They came to see me after your interview. I'm now representing them."

"But, Stone, the last thing you said to me was that you were glad you weren't representing them."

"I'm still not crazy about the idea, Art, but after speaking with them at some length, I don't believe they committed either crime."

"Well, that's a pretty fast turnaround," Masi said.

"No, I've never said I believed they were involved, and now I feel more strongly than ever that they're not."

"Explain to me why, please."

"Let me tell you what they told me this afternoon."

"I'm all ears."

"They admit having been present in Tillman's apartment on the afternoon of his death."

"Well, that's hardly exculpatory, is it?"

"They say that Tillman knew they were going to be in town, and he invited them for a drink at two-thirty. They showed up, had their drink, then made to leave. Tillman asked them to drop off a box at the FedEx store on Second Avenue. It was on their way to the tunnel. They agreed. The box was on the hall table, and they took it and deposited it in the receptacle outside the FedEx store."

"Who was it addressed to?"

"They didn't bother looking to see—they had no interest." Stone picked up the large FedEx box beside his desk. "This was the kind of box. They identified it. Does that give you any ideas?"

"You think the van Gogh was in the box?"

Stone tossed him the box. "Wouldn't it fit easily into that?"

"I suppose so," Masi said. "But why would Tillman FedEx it to somebody?"

"Maybe he had an accomplice."

"An accomplice in what?"

"In the theft of a valuable piece of art. You've searched his apartment twice and his beach house once, and you haven't found it."

"Who would he choose as an accomplice?"

"Well, on the available evidence, now that these kids have told the truth, he sent it to *somebody*. Is there a likely suspect among the people involved in the case?"

"Perhaps his wife?"

"He lived with her. He could have just handed her the package."

"A friend?"

"What friend? He didn't seem to have many. From what we've heard, he worked all the time."

"A business partner?"

"His hedge fund had lost a lot of money. That's not the sort of event to seal a friendship among partners."

"He left his wife half a billion dollars," Art said. "What would he need with another sixty million?"

"His estate was almost entirely in trusts, so that his executor could avoid probate. He wouldn't have had access to those funds, and if he were a little short of money, sixty million might have been very welcome."

"So he stole the painting from himself?"

"No, he stole it from his insurance company, then he sent it to somebody for safekeeping. Fortunately, Federal Express keeps records."

"Then I'd better get over to that FedEx store and find out what packages were collected in their deposit box that Saturday afternoon," Art said, rising.

"Good idea," Stone said, and Masi turned to go. "Art?"

Masi turned. "I think I may know who he sent it to, but I don't want to prejudice you." Stone took a sheet of paper, wrote something on it, sealed it into an envelope, and handed it to Masi. "That's my best guess. See if I'm right after you've traced the package."

Art tucked the envelope into an inside pocket of his jacket. "I'll call you when I know something," he said.

Masi drove uptown and found the FedEx store, with its outside deposit box. He went inside, where a young woman was behind the desk. "May I speak to the manager, please?" She looked far too young to be the manager.

"Who shall I say wants him?" she asked.

Masi produced his badge. "Lieutenant Masi of the NYPD. Tell him not to worry, he's not in any trouble."

She disappeared into the rear of the store and came back with a young man who appeared to be even younger than his staffer. "I'm Rich Mann," he said.

"Congratulations," Masi said. "About eighteen months ago"—he gave him the date—"a Saturday afternoon, someone deposited a large FedEx box in your outside receptacle. I'd like to know to whom it was addressed."

"You got a tracking number?"

"No."

"An address?"

"No, but it was sent by a Mr. Mark Tillman of 740 Park Avenue."

The boy went to a computer and began typing. "Mr. Tillman has two accounts with us—one at his office, one at his home, at 740 Park."

"Good."

"Nothing was shipped from either address on that date."

That brought Masi up short. "Suppose he used a blank waybill that he picked up at this shop, or one like it, and suppose he used another name as the sender."

"And what name would that be?"

"I don't know," Masi replied.

"That's not very helpful," the boy said.

"Somewhere in your computer, don't you have a record of what was sent from this shop on that date?"

"Yes, but that could be hundreds of packages."

"Is there a separate list of what was put into the deposit box?"

"No, those packages would be sent with all the others. There were, let's see"—he tapped some more keys—"two hundred and eight packages dispatched from this store on that date."

"And none of them sent by Mark Tillman?"

"No, sir."

"Thank you," Masi said, and turned to go.

"Just a sec," the boy said. He was staring at his screen.

"What?" Masi asked.

"We got one package that was sent *to* Mr. Mark Tillman, at 740 Park."

"You mean that on the waybill Tillman was listed as the addressee?"

"That's right. It was sent for third-day delivery, and it was delivered to 740 Park on the following Wednesday at ten fifty-four AM and signed for by a doorman."

"Can you print me a copy of your screen, please?"

"Sure," the boy said. He pressed a key, and a moment later a printer spat out a sheet.

"Thank you very much for your help," Masi said, and walked out of the shop, tucking the page into an inside pocket, where he ran into an obstruction. He removed an envelope from his pocket, the one Stone Barrington had given him. He opened it and found a single sheet of paper with a name written on it:

MARK TILLMAN

25

STONE WAS ON HIS WAY uptown in a cab to meet Dino, Viv, and Morgan for dinner when his cell phone rang. "Hello?"

"It's Art Masi."

"Hello, Art. How did you do with Federal Express?"

"I did okay. How did you know?"

"Know?"

"Who the package was addressed to."

"I guessed. Obviously, I was right."

"You were. Why would Tillman send the painting to himself?"

"He sent it to the only person he trusted," Stone said. "He didn't have a lot of friends, and apparently none he would entrust with his art treasure. Did you find out when it was delivered?"

"He sent it for third-day delivery. The following Wednesday a doorman in his building signed for it. The homicide guys missed that."

"It's understandable. Why would they be interested in

a package that arrived three days after his death? Would you have thought to look for that?"

"No," Art replied.

"Neither would I," Stone said. The cab pulled up in front of Rotisserie Georgette. "I've gotta run. Let me know if you come up with something else." He hung up and got out of the cab.

Dino was there, alone. "Hey."

Stone sat down and immediately a waiter set down a High Rock on the rocks. They didn't serve Knob Creek. "Where are the girls?"

"Where are they ever?" Dino asked. "Viv wasn't home when I left to walk down here. She probably went to the apartment to fix her makeup or something. Morgan is your problem."

"Right," Stone said, tasting his New York State bourbon. It was lighter than his usual, but flavorful. "I had an interesting day," he said.

"I wish I could say that," Dino replied. "Regale me with the events."

"Well, I learned that Pio Farina and Ann Kusch were at Mark Tillman's house on the afternoon he died."

Dino sat up straight. "Why didn't you tell me that before?" he demanded.

"Because I learned about it only today." He explained how Art Masi had called them in for questioning. "After that they came to my office and asked me to represent them."

"Do you think they offed Tillman?"

"No."

"Why not?"

"Because the evidence doesn't support a charge. They got there at two-thirty, had a drink, then left."

"Did you check that with the doormen?"

"No, did your people?"

Dino glowered at him. "Don't be a smartass."

"I haven't been back to the building, or I would have asked, but I would have thought that your people, as a matter of routine, would have inquired if he had any visitors that day."

Dino whipped out his cell phone and pressed a button; a brief conversation ensued, then he hung up. "They inquired and were told by the doormen that Tillman had no visitors, until his wife went up."

"Something else," Stone said. "When they left, Tillman asked them to drop off a package for him at a FedEx office on Second Avenue."

"How big a package?"

"Not big, but big enough to hold the van Gogh."

"I'd like to know who he sent it to," Dino said. "I'll have somebody check with FedEx."

"Don't bother, Art Masi has already done so. Tillman sent it to himself."

Dino stared at Stone blankly. "What the fuck?"

"That's pretty much what I thought, until I realized he had sent it to the only person he trusted. He sent it three-day. It arrived on the Wednesday morning after his death."

"Does Morgan know about this?"

"She would have been the only one home on that Wednesday," Stone said.

"Have you mentioned it to her?"

"No, but Masi has searched the apartment twice, and it wasn't there. He searched the East Hampton house, too, and found nothing."

"He's an art guy," Dino said, "not a homicide detective."

"He knows how to look for a painting," Stone pointed out.

"Here come the girls," Dino said. "Keep your mouth shut about this."

"We bumped into each other on the way in," Viv said, "and we did a little window-shopping."

Everybody kissed everybody else.

AFTER DINNER, Stone took Morgan home and stayed the night. After sex, she always slept like a stone, and she did so that night.

In the middle of the night, Stone crept out of bed and walked downstairs. He switched on the lights in the living room and had a look around. Now, where would somebody put a package that had been delivered? He looked under the furniture, then checked the coat closet in the entry hall. There, he found an empty frame, about the size to have held the van Gogh, but no package.

He walked back into the living room and looked at the wall of pictures; they were thickly hung. Without counting, he estimated fifteen or twenty. The space where the van Gogh had hung had not been filled; it was between a Matisse still life and a Utrillo Paris street scene.

He checked the wall with the pictures for a secret panel, then the same with the bookcases. Nothing. He went into the kitchen and opened the cabinet doors, one by one, then he checked the freezer.

"What are you doing naked in my kitchen?" Morgan's voice said.

Stone jumped, then turned to find her behind him, also naked.

"I woke up and couldn't go back to sleep, and I felt a little peckish."

"How about some cheese?" she asked.

"Perfect." She lifted a bell jar and put the stand on the

table, exhibiting a Saint-André, a Humboldt Fog, and a Pont-l'Évêque. "Choose something," she said, sitting down with a box of crackers and a cheese knife in her hand.

Stone chose the Pont-l'Évêque and sat down. "This chair is cold," he said.

"It will warm up in a minute." She found an open bottle of red and poured them both a glass. "This will help."

"You're right, the chair is getting warmer," he said.

They finished their cheese. Stone wondered if she had seen him searching her apartment. "What time does your maid come in?" he asked.

"Why do you want to know?"

"Because I don't want to be seen naked in your kitchen, eating cheese," he said.

"Don't worry, she doesn't get in until around six-thirty, and she leaves at one. Let's go back to bed," she said. "There's something I'd like to do to you."

There was, and she did.

ON THE WAY out of the building, Stone stopped at the front desk.

"Good morning, Mr. Barrington," one of the men said.

"Good morning. Mrs. Tillman asked me to check and see if a FedEx package had arrived for her or Mr. Tillman—"

"Not this morning, sir. Not yesterday, either."

"I was about to say that this would have been about eighteen months ago." He mentioned the date. "They were expecting something, but it never arrived."

The man produced a ledger from under the countertop and looked up the date. "No, sir, nothing arrived on that date, or the days before and after."

"FedEx says it was signed for by a doorman."

The man shook his head firmly. "No, sir, we log in every package that arrives."

"Thank you." Stone went home, annoyed.

26

AFTER BREAKFAST STONE went back to his house and
entered through the street door.

"Good afternoon," Joan said.

"It's ten past nine."

"Your mail and messages," she said, handing them to
him.

"Do I detect a whiff of disapproval?" Stone asked.

"I don't disapprove of anything you do," she replied.
"Even when it's stupid."

"Oh, thank you." He went to his office. The message
on top was from Arthur Steele. Stone called his direct
line.

"Good morning, Stone. Have you found my picture?"

"Not yet, Arthur, and I'm going to need another ten
days."

"That's a negotiating tactic," Steele replied. "You want
another week."

"No, Arthur, I need another ten days. I know your
deadline won't expire before then. You were just building

in an edge. I also know that your eighteen months runs not from the day of the theft, but from the day a claim was filed."

Steele ignored that. "Are you making progress?"

"Yes, in the sense that I'm eliminating possibilities."

"Oh, all right, you can have another ten days," Steele said, "but that's about it."

Stone knew the "about" meant he had longer than that. "Thank you, Arthur. I'll be in touch." He hung up before Steele could ask any further questions.

Joan buzzed. "Art Masi to see you."

"Send him in."

Masi came in looking desolate and flopped into a chair. "I'm done," he said. "I can't meet your deadline."

"It's all right, Art," Stone said, "I got us another week."

"How did you do that?"

"Never mind, I got it. We're making progress, Art, don't be discouraged."

"Why shouldn't I be discouraged? Every idea I've had has been a dead end."

"You're eliminating possibilities, Art."

"Name a possibility I've eliminated."

"Mark Tillman didn't commit suicide. That was a possibility."

"How do we know that?"

"Because he wouldn't send himself a package containing a sixty-million-dollar work of art if he didn't expect to be there to receive it."

"He would have expected his wife to receive it."

"Then he would have addressed it to her."

"It wasn't even insured."

"Not with FedEx, maybe, but his household insurance covered it as a listed piece of art, and because it's listed, he wouldn't even have to pay a deductible."

"That is correct."

"Oh, by the way, I checked with the doorman this morning, and he says they never received a FedEx package for Tillman on or about that date."

"But FedEx says a doorman signed for it."

"They don't know the doormen—anybody could have signed for it."

"How about the maid?" Art asked.

"Nope, she's there mornings only, gone by one o'clock. The doormen never delivered it to the apartment."

"You think the doormen are art thieves?"

"Maybe. They know more about what goes on in the building than anybody else, including who owns important art."

"Okay, I'll investigate the doormen."

Stone handed him a card. "This contains the names and numbers of everyone who's employed by the building. I took it from a tray on the front desk."

"While I'm at it, I'll see if I can find out why they didn't see Pio Farina and Ann Kusch enter the building the afternoon of Tillman's murder."

"Don't bother. Pio and Ann rang Tillman's bell at the service entrance, and he buzzed them in. They left the same way."

"How do you know all this stuff?"

"Because I've spent more time in the building than you have," Stone replied. "I've come to know how it works. I'll give you an example. Suppose you wanted to buy an apartment in the building. Who would you call?"

"I'd find out which Realtor sold the last unit that went and call her."

"No, a waste of time, and very expensive. You'd be smarter to let a doorman know that there's ten thousand dollars in cash available if you can find the right apartment there."

"How would the doormen know?"

"Because they know everything that goes on in the building. They know who's having an affair and whether it's with someone in the building. They know which couple is about to divorce. They know which tenant is chronically late with his maintenance payments, meaning he's had a downturn in his business and can't afford the place anymore. They know who's dying, creating a vacancy. They don't have to wait for the obituary to run in the *Times*. Did you know that when the news got out that Marilyn Monroe had died, there was a long line of people waiting to bribe the doorman for a shot at the place?"

"I didn't know that," Art said.

"The doormen hold the keys to the kingdom, especially in a building as desirable as that one. You find a doorman who has a low credit score, or who owes his bookie too much money, and that will be the guy who's helpful when it comes to making a package disappear."

"I see your point," Masi said.

"Mark Tillman, before he sent the package to himself, would have crossed a doorman's palm handsomely and said, 'I'm expecting a FedEx on Wednesday. Don't deliver it, just put it in my storage unit,'" Stone said. "By the way, did you search Tillman's storage unit? Every apartment has one, and the doormen have a key."

"We had a look around the storage area, but we didn't have a key to the Tillman unit," Masi said. He excused himself and left.

Stone picked up the phone and called Pio Farina's house in East Hampton. Ann Kusch answered. "Yes?"

"Ann, it's Stone Barrington."

"Good morning, Stone."

"I have a question for you. When you and Pio went to Mark Tillman's apartment on the day he died, how did you enter the building?"

"Through the service entrance. Mark said there was some work being done on the elevator, and that it might not be working. He told us to go to the service entrance, call him from downstairs, and he would buzz us in."

"And how did you depart the building?"

"The same way."

"Thank you, Ann, that's all I need to know."

He hung up. He had been right when he had told Art that.

27

THERE WAS STILL SOMETHING itching in Stone's brain, something he needed to know that he didn't know. He called Art Masi's cell number.

"Lieutenant Masi."

"Art, something I forgot to ask you. When you visited the FedEx store, did you see the signature of the door-man who signed for the package?"

"No, I just got a printout of the packages they had delivered on that day."

"Go back to the store and see if they have a facsimile of the waybill that the doorman signed. If they do, I want to know what his name is. Even if it's illegible, I want to know that."

"All right, I'll call you back."

Stone hung up. What he wanted to know was why the doorman didn't log in the package, as was their standard practice.

*　　*　　*

HALF AN HOUR LATER, Art called back. "The guy who signed for the package was Gino Poluci," he said. "It's a plain signature, doesn't look like he signed it in a hurry."

"Thank you, Art." Stone hung up, slipped on his jacket, and got a cab uptown. He walked into the building and saw the doorman he had spoken to earlier at the desk.

"Good morning again, Mr. Barrington," the man said. His name tag read "Ralph Weede."

"Good morning, Ralph," Stone said. "Is Gino Poluci on today?"

"No, sir, he's off, he'll be back at work tomorrow."

"Ralph, I need your help with something."

"Of course, Mr. Barrington, what can I do for you?"

"You recall that I asked about a package that was delivered here after Mark Tillman died?"

"Yes, sir, we had no record of it."

"Ralph, I'm an attorney, and I represent the Steele Insurance Group, who have the household insurance on the Tillman apartment."

Ralph's eyes narrowed a tiny bit. "Yes, sir?"

"There was something in that package that I need to look at. The company is offering a ten-thousand-dollar reward to anyone who can produce it. Does that interest you?"

"Well, sure, Mr. Barrington," Ralph said cautiously. "Since you're a lawyer, can you tell me if there's any legal liability attached to having some knowledge of that package?"

"No liability whatsoever, Ralph, I just want to see the package, and I'll produce the ten thousand in cash within the hour."

"Tell you what, let me have a look in Mr. Tillman's

storage unit," Ralph said. "I'll get the key." He walked to an open door behind him, disappeared inside for a minute or so, and came back with the key. "I'll be back in ten minutes," he said to somebody in that room. He walked back to where Stone stood. "I'll go have a look."

"I'll have a look with you," Stone said.

Ralph hesitated. "Nobody's allowed down there but the tenants and the doormen," he said. "I don't want to get in any trouble."

"Ralph, the only way you can get into trouble is by not telling me the truth," Stone said.

"This way, sir." He led the way to a door that opened onto a stairway and walked down the stairs. The storage units were neatly divided into rows, and he walked down one, then stopped. "Here we are," he said. "Fifteen A." He opened the padlock securing the door, swung it open, and switched on an overhead light. Fluorescent lamps blinked on.

Stone followed him inside. The room was about twelve by fifteen feet and contained several pieces of furniture stacked on top of each other. There were some lamps, no shades, a rolled-up carpet, and a few pictures in bubble wrap. "Just a minute," he said to Ralph. He went through the pictures: two portraits, what appeared to be a Hudson River School landscape, and an abstract painting. No van Gogh.

"Let's continue," he said to Ralph. There was a clothing rack filled with zipped-up covers, then, at the end of the aisle, two steel filing cabinets and a large steel cabinet. He tried to open them. Locked. "Do you have the keys, Ralph?"

"No, sir, we just keep keys to access the unit. We don't have keys for anything inside."

Stone reached for his own keys, which included one for his office files. He tried it in the locks and had no luck.

"No package," Ralph said. "Are you satisfied, Mr. Barrington?"

"No, Ralph, I'm not. I'm going to have to come back with a locksmith."

"Why don't you just ask Mrs. Tillman for the keys?" Ralph asked.

"I don't want to trouble her, Ralph, and I don't want you to, either. Do you understand?"

"Yes, sir, I'll be discreet."

Stone took two hundreds from his pocket and handed them to the man. "For your trouble today," he said. "I'll come back with a locksmith, and we'll see if we can get you the ten thousand."

"Yes, sir," Ralph replied. "I'm on all day, then off for two days."

They went back upstairs. "If I don't get back today," Stone said, "I'll speak to Gino Poluci when he comes in tomorrow and see what I can find out. You can make your own financial arrangements with him." They parted company. Back on the street, Stone called Bob Cantor, his go-to guy for any sort of technical work, mechanical or electronic.

"How you doing, Stone?"

"Pretty good. I need to get into a couple of locked pieces of office furniture. Can you meet me at Park and Seventy-eighth?"

"Sorry, Stone, I'm in the middle of a major alarm installation, and I've got to be finished by tonight. As it is, I'll probably be here until midnight. How about tomorrow?"

"Okay," Stone said.

"What kind of office furniture?"

"Standard steel stuff, like you'd see in a hundred of-fices."

"That shouldn't be a problem," Bob said. "I just don't have the time today."

"I understand, Bob."

"Stone," Bob said, "just about any locksmith can open those cabinets."

"I'd rather wait for you, Bob."

"Okay, you know best."

"Okay." Stone hung up; he was just going to have to be patient until then.

28

STONE MET BOB CANTOR at 740 Park at ten the following morning. A doorman wearing a name tag with the name "Gino Poluci" greeted him at the reception desk. "Good morning, Mr. Barrington," Gino said. "Ralph called me last night and said you'd like to get into the storage area for 15A?"

"That's correct, Gino," Stone replied. "This is my associate, Bob Cantor."

"Oh, yes, we've met before, haven't we? You've done some security system work here." The two men shook hands.

Gino got the key and led them down to the storage unit. Stone found it apparently undisturbed from the day before. "Back here, Bob," he said, leading him to the three pieces of office furniture.

Cantor knelt and produced a key ring containing a couple of dozen similar keys, and he began working his way through them, inserting them into a filing cabinet lock. "If we get one that works, chances are it'll be keyed to all three pieces," he said. "If not, then I'll have to do some picking." Nothing he had worked.

Stone watched as Bob took a small zippered case from his shirt pocket and chose two of a number of lock picks.

"I made these myself," Cantor said, "cut and ground from hacksaw blades." He started on a filing cabinet, and after a minute or two, he opened the drawer.

"Go ahead and finish all three," Stone said, standing back and giving him more room.

Cantor had all three done very quickly.

Stone knelt and began going through the file drawers, first looking for the painting itself, then glancing at the names of files. This drawer was mostly old tax returns. He went through the second drawer in the cabinet, then did the same with the second filing cabinet. All that remained was the larger storage cabinet. He swung the door back to reveal a stack of reams of printer paper. On top rested a FedEx box. Stone picked it up gingerly, by the corners: it was addressed to Mark Tillman. It was empty. "Okay," he said, "let's go back upstairs."

"Find what you're looking for, Mr. Barrington?"

"I found the FedEx box, but not the contents."

They went back up the stairs. As they arrived at the desk a man in a FedEx uniform placed an envelope on the desk and gave Gino an electronic box on which to sign. Stone watched as the doorman scrawled his name: only the G and the P were legible; the rest was a scrawl.

Stone thanked Poluci and he and Bob Cantor left. Outside, Stone stopped and handed the FedEx box to Cantor, his hand inside it. "Bob, I know this is a long shot, because a lot of people may have handled it, but I'd like for you to go over this box very, very carefully, see if you can find any legible prints, and if you do, run them against every database you've got."

"Okay, I'll go back to the office and start on it now," Cantor said. "I'll try to have something for you late this afternoon."

The two men shook hands, and Stone sent Cantor on his way. He decided to walk back to Turtle Bay; it was thirty blocks or so, but the exercise wouldn't kill him. He began thinking his way through the steps of assembling and sending a FedEx package. You had to put stuff inside, then you had to fill out a waybill or print one from your computer. You'd seal it, then it would begin its journey through the system. Finally, it would be received at the front desk of the building and delivered to the recipient. Except this one wasn't delivered, because the recipient was dead. It apparently didn't get to Morgan or her housekeeper, either. It was emptied and the box placed in a locked storage cabinet in a locked apartment storage unit.

The last thing to happen would be for the FedEx box to be discarded, but that hadn't happened. Someone had opened two locks in order to place it in a steel cabinet, to save it as if it were important. Why? It couldn't be reused, and it didn't make any sense to save it.

By the time he got home his feet were hurting, and so was his head.

STONE SAID TO JOAN as he passed her desk, "Hold my calls, will you, please?" He took off his jacket, stretched out on the leather sofa in his office, and dozed.

SOMEBODY TOOK HOLD of Stone's shoulder and shook him gently. "Bob Cantor's on the phone," Joan said. "He said you'd want to hear from him."

Stone sat up and reached for the phone on the coffee table. "Bob?"

"Hey. I got your package done."

"What did you find?"

"I got four legible prints off it—two of them were Fed-Ex employees, who would have handled it in the course of business. One was a Margaretta Fernandez, who, according to her Social Security records, is employed as a house-maid for one Mark Tillman. The other is Pio Farina. This one had a juvie record of being a suspect in several bur-glaries, but no charges were brought. That's it."

"Thank you, Bob, that's very helpful. Send me your bill."

"Okay. Call when you need me."

Stone hung up the phone. Pio's print made perfect sense: he would have handled it on the way to the FedEx store to send it. The maid? She might have received it from one of the doormen. Not Gino, because someone else had signed his name; probably not Ralph, because he had had a chance to pick up $10,000 and didn't. Cer-tainly it was someone who had a key, not just to the stor-age units, but to the steel file cabinets, as well. Morgan? She fit the bill. So did the maid, who might have known where the key would be kept in the household.

Stone picked up the phone and called Morgan.

"Hello, there," she said. "It's been forever."

"It was the day before yesterday."

"In my book, it's forever. What can we do about that?"

"Let's have dinner tonight," Stone said.

"I am agreeable to that. Why don't I cook something for us?"

"I was not aware that you possessed that skill set."

"My dear, I am a certificated graduate of Cordon Bleu—London, not Paris. I was sent to the forty-day bride's course, created for young women of good family who are unacquainted with the concept of boiling water."

"And how did you do?"

"Top of my class," she said.

"Then I'll risk it. What time?"

"Say, seven o'clock?"

"You're on."

"Please wear tearaway clothing," she said. "Cooking makes me amorous."

"I'll see what I can do."

29

STONE TURNED UP on time and, in addition to a kiss from Morgan, was welcomed by an inviting aroma from the kitchen. She sat him down on a living room sofa and brought them both a drink from the bar. "Now," she said, tapping his glass with hers, "tell me about your day."

"Did you learn that at Cordon Bleu?" Stone asked.

She laughed. "As a matter of fact, I did. We had a few side lectures to the cooking course, one of them attuned to one's conduct with the gentleman who is the recipient of the evening meal one has just prepared."

"Aha. I thought it must be something like that."

"But I really would like to know about your day," she said, kissing him on an ear. "I can't imagine what it is you do when you're not with me."

Stone decided it was time to be frank with her. "Well, I spent a good part of my day rummaging around in a storage room, looking for something."

"One, what were you looking for? Two, and in whose storage room?" she asked.

"One, a Federal Express box," he replied. "Two, yours."

Her brow wrinkled. "My what?"

"Your storage room."

She sat back and looked at him as if he were a naughty child. "Are you perfectly serious?"

"Perfectly."

"Tell me what this is about, and I may not punish you."

He set down his drink, took her by the shoulders, and pushed her into the sofa cushions. "All right. It's not a simple story, and I'd like you to wait until I've finished before you ask any questions."

"That level of restraint is not in my character," she replied, "but I'll do the best I can."

"Here we go. I have learned that early on the afternoon of Mark's death, he was visited by Pio Farina and Ann Kusch, at his invitation. He gave them a drink, they chatted for a while, and as they left, he asked them to drop off a package at the Federal Express store on Second Avenue, which was on their way to the tunnel. They did so, depositing it in the box outside the store."

Morgan raised her hand, like a schoolgirl.

"Not yet," Stone said.

She pouted, then lowered her hand.

"Subsequent investigation by the police revealed that Mark had addressed the box to himself, for third-day delivery."

"Not yet," Stone said.

She rolled her eyes.

"The box arrived downstairs on the Wednesday following Mark's death."

"The day of his cremation," she said.

"I'm not finished. Someone signed for the package,

using Gino Poluci's name, but it wasn't Gino. Subsequent to that—I'm not sure when—the package was opened, the contents removed, and the empty box was placed in a locked steel cabinet inside the storage unit of Apartment 15A, where I found it today."

She raised a hand again.

"What?"

"I have a list of questions before you continue."

Stone sighed. "All right, go ahead."

She held up a finger. "One, why would Mark send a package to himself?"

"Because he knew this apartment would be searched, and he didn't want the contents of the package found."

She held up two fingers. "What was in the package?"

"I can't be certain, but I believe it was the missing van Gogh."

Her jaw dropped.

"Do you have any further questions?"

"Yes, but I forgot what they were. Continue, please."

"I had the box checked for fingerprints," Stone said, "and four were found and identified. Two belonged to FedEx employees, one belonged to Pio Farina, and . . . one belonged to Margaretta Fernandez."

Morgan stared at him. "Why . . ."

"Be specific."

"Why was Margaretta's fingerprint on the package?"

"Because at some point she handled it. Perhaps a doorman delivered it to her while you were out."

"And did you say you found the empty box in my storage unit?"

"I did, inside a steel cabinet, which was locked and to which the doorman did not have a key."

"Back up a step," she said. "How did you get into my storage unit?"

"Simple—I bribed a doorman."

"Which one?"

"I'm not going to tell you."

"All right then, how did you get into the steel cabinet without a key?"

"I engaged a person with a deep knowledge of locks, and he picked it."

"One more question," she said. "Where is the painting now?"

"I don't know, but I'd like to ask Margaretta that question. Would she have access to the key to the steel cabinet?"

"All my keys are in a drawer in the hall table," she said.

"And does Margaretta know that?"

"Yes."

"Anyway," Stone said, "that's how I spent my day, and now I'm hungry."

"Come with me, you have to help."

Stone followed her into the kitchen. She poured the contents of a saucepan into a double boiler, already simmering, and handed him a rubber spatula. "That is béarnaise sauce. Please stir it until it thickens."

Stone took the spatula and started stirring.

Morgan turned on three eyes on the gas range and dropped two boned chicken breasts into a small skillet with some butter and olive oil. She sautéed them quickly on both sides, then put them on two plates and added haricots verts and new potatoes from the other two pans, then held out the plates. "Now pour the béarnaise onto the two plates."

He did so.

"Now turn off the stove and follow me." She led him around a corner to a small dining nook, where two places had been elaborately set and a bottle of wine decanted.

Stone set down the plates and pulled her chair out for her, then he sat down.

He picked up the wine bottle. "Haut-Brion '59. Wherever did you get that?"

"From the gigantic wine cupboard in the kitchen, which you failed to notice. There's a lot like that in there."

They raised their glasses and drank, then began to eat.

"Wonderful," Stone said.

"I'll have more questions when we're finished," she said.

30

MORGAN DID NOT consider them finished until they had left the dinner table, gone upstairs to the bedroom, and made love twice.

"Now," Stone panted, "do you have any further questions?"

"Not at the moment," she said. "I am unable to organize my thoughts just yet."

"Organize this," Stone said. "I'm going to need to ask Margaretta some questions when she arrives tomorrow."

"I think I understand the necessity of that," Morgan said, "but not until we have finished breakfast. I don't want to throw her off her stride."

"She does make very good scrambled eggs," Stone said, and they were soon asleep.

THE FOLLOWING MORNING, when they were awake, Stone said, "I have another question for you, and it's a very important one."

"Go ahead, I think I can handle it now."

He took the remote controls, sat up both their beds, and turned to look her in the eye. "I once asked, if you had to choose between the van Gogh or sixty million, which you would pick. Does your answer still stand?"

"It does," she said.

"You're absolutely certain of that?"

"Absolutely."

"You're going to have to sign a document to that effect," he said.

"Gladly. Do you have it on you?"

"No, I'm naked at the moment, but I will produce it in due course, when we have the picture back."

"How are we going to get it back?"

"We're going to start by my questioning Margaretta."

There was a knock at the door and Margaretta entered, wheeling their breakfast on a cart. Greetings were exchanged, breakfast was served, and she left them.

AFTER BREAKFAST, Stone shaved, showered, and dressed, and Morgan slipped a cashmere dressing gown on over her nightie. "All right," she said, "let's go see Margaretta."

They went downstairs; Morgan retrieved Margaretta from the kitchen and invited her to sit down on the sofa opposite them. "Margaretta," Morgan said, "Mr. Barrington needs to ask you some questions, and it's important that you give him honest answers."

Margaretta looked alarmed. "Did I do something wrong, Mrs. Tillman?"

"I hope you didn't," Morgan replied, but Margaretta did not look less alarmed.

"Margaretta," Stone began, "on the Wednesday after

the Saturday Mr. Tillman died, was a package from Federal Express delivered to this apartment?"

Tears appeared in Margaretta's eyes and began to roll down her cheeks. Morgan got up and gave her a box of tissues, then sat down.

"Yes," Margaretta said.

"Who delivered the package?"

"One of the doormen."

"Which one?"

"Ralph."

"Did Ralph sign for the package when Federal Express delivered it?"

"Yes, but not his name."

"Whose name?"

"Gino."

"Do you know why Ralph signed Gino's name?"

"Ralph didn't want anybody to know he signed it."

"When you received the package, had it been opened, or was it still sealed?"

"It was open," Margaretta said. "Ralph opened it."

"Do you know why he opened it?"

"I think maybe he thought it was something valuable, and since Mr. Tillman had died . . ." She didn't finish the sentence.

"What was inside the package?"

"A picture," she said, then pointed at the wall. "The one that used to be over there."

"What did you do with the picture?"

"Ralph said I should take it home," she said.

"Why did he say that?"

"He said it would look pretty in my living room, and Mr. Tillman wouldn't need it anymore. So I took it home, and I bought a frame at the store, and I hung it on my wall."

"Did Ralph say anything to you about the value of the picture?"

"No. He just said I deserved to have a pretty picture."

"What did you do with the Federal Express box?"

"I took it downstairs to the storage room and locked it in a gray cabinet."

"Why did you keep the box?"

"Because if anybody asked about the picture, I wanted to put it back in the box, like it was delivered."

"Margaretta," Morgan said, "where was I when the box was delivered?"

"At your hairdresser's, ma'am."

"Ah, yes, it was Wednesday, wasn't it?"

"Ma'am," Margaretta said, sniffling, "am I in any trouble?"

"Stone," Morgan asked, "is Margaretta in any trouble?"

"No," Stone said.

"Oh, thank God," Margaretta said.

"Not if we get the picture back."

Margaretta began to cry again.

"What's wrong, Margaretta?" Morgan asked.

She kept crying, and Morgan went and sat next to her on the sofa and consoled her. Finally, she got herself under control.

"Now, Margaretta," Stone said, as gently as possible, "is the picture still on your wall? All we have to do is go and get it, then you won't be in any trouble."

Margaretta began to cry again.

Stone looked at Morgan and shrugged helplessly.

"Margaretta, please answer Mr. Barrington," Morgan said.

Margaretta continued to sob.

Stone was beginning to get a very bad feeling. "When you're ready, Margaretta," he said.

Morgan went to the bar, poured a glass of sherry, and returned to the sofa. "Here, Margaretta, drink this, it will make you feel better."

Margaretta sipped the drink, then took a bigger sip.

"When you're ready," Stone said again.

Finally, she made the effort. "No, Mr. Barrington, it is not still on my wall."

"Where is it, Margaretta?"

"The picture was stolen."

"What?"

"Two days ago," she said.

"Do you know who stole it?"

Margaretta nodded. "Yes, I think."

"Who?"

"Manolo."

"Who is Manolo, Margaretta?"

Morgan held up a hand to stop him. "Manolo is her son," she said, "and Manolo has a drug problem."

"He steals things to get money for drugs," Margaretta said.

"Do you think he thought the picture was valuable?"

"I think he thought he could sell it for enough to buy drugs. He needs drugs every day."

31

MARGARETTA WAS CRYING nonstop now, so Stone put his questions to her through Morgan, as it seemed to work better.

"Margaretta, does Manolo live with you?"

Margaretta nodded, then shook her head. "Sometimes," she said.

"Would he be there now?"

She shook her head. "He has been gone for two days."

"Margaretta, what is Manolo's cell phone number?"

Every junkie had a cell phone.

Morgan handed her a pad of paper and a pen. "Just write down the number, Margaretta."

"Will you hurt him?" she asked, handing the pad back to Morgan.

"No, of course not," Stone replied. "If he returns the picture at once, he will get a thousand-dollar reward."

Margaretta began to recover herself. "Please," she said, taking her phone from her apron pocket, "let me call him so he won't be frightened."

"All right," Stone said, "but please speak English."

Margaretta blew her nose, then pressed a button.

"Yeah?"

"Manolo, it's Mama. I have good news."

"Mama, I'm busy right now."

"Could you use a thousand dollars?"

A brief silence. "What are you talking about?"

"If you bring home the picture, you will get a thousand dollars."

Stone rubbed his thumb against his fingers.

"Cash," she said.

"A thousand dollars?"

"Yes, truly, but you have to bring the picture home now."

"Mama, I already sold the picture. I got a hundred dollars for it."

Stone said a silent "Who?"—exaggerating his lip movement.

"Who did you sell it to, Manolo?"

"I can't tell you, Mama. He would hurt me. I gotta go now." He hung up.

"What can I do?" Margaretta asked. "You heard."

"Margaretta," Stone said, "please leave it to me. We'll find Manolo and learn who bought the picture, and your son will not be hurt, I promise. And he may still get the thousand dollars."

Margaretta looked at Morgan for confirmation.

Morgan nodded vigorously. "Now you can go back to work, Margaretta. Everything will be all right."

"Oh, Margaretta?" Stone said.

She turned. "Yes, sir?"

"Do you have a photograph of Manolo?"

She fished in her other apron pocket and came up with a wallet. She found it and handed it to Stone.

"Thank you, Margaretta," he said. "I'll see that it's returned to you." She went to the kitchen, and he looked at the picture: it was a school photo, taken when the kid must have been sixteen or so. He was angelically beautiful.

"Now what?" Morgan asked.

Stone motioned for them to go out onto the terrace, pointing at his ear. When they had closed the doors behind them, he said, "I'll take care of this."

"What are you going to do?"

"Find Manolo, for a start."

"How are you going to find a junkie in Spanish Harlem?" she demanded.

"Please, Morgan, go inside."

Reluctantly, she went inside and closed the doors behind her.

Stone called Dino and got sent directly to voice mail. Stone left an urgent message, then went inside, where Morgan stood, hands on hips.

"What did you do?"

"I left someone a message."

"Dino?"

"Yes."

"What can he do?"

"Morgan, Dino is the commissioner of police. Now I'm going to go home and try to get some work done. I'll call you when we have some results." He kissed her, retrieved his jacket, and left.

ALL THE WAY home in the cab, Stone thought about what had to be done. This was not good. Morgan's question was appropriate: How was he going to find a junkie in Spanish Harlem? All he had was a cell number, and he hoped it was enough.

* * *

BACK IN HIS OFFICE, Stone checked and Dino had not yet returned his call. He called Dino's secretary, and it went straight to voice mail. In desperation, he called Viv.

"Hello, Stone."

"Good morning, Viv. I'm having trouble reaching Dino. Do you know where he is?"

"Yes, he's at a policeman's funeral, a patrolman who was shot last week."

Stone remembered the news report. "When am I likely to be able to reach him?"

"Oh, God, it could take half the day or longer. There's a parade, then a very long funeral service, then the wake—the boy was Irish—and you know how that can go. Did you leave him a message?"

"Yes."

"Well, stop calling him, he'll get back to you as soon as he can."

"Right," Stone said. "I'll wait for his call. Bye." He hung up and called Art Masi.

"This is Lieutenant Masi. I'm attending a police funeral. Leave a message, and I'll call you back later in the day."

Stone sighed and called Bob Cantor.

"Hey, Stone."

"Listen, Bob, I've got to locate a guy, and all I have is a cell phone number."

"Give it to me. Let me fire up my cell search engine," Cantor said. "I'll call you back."

Stone waited impatiently; ten minutes later, Joan buzzed him. "Bob Cantor on one."

He grabbed the phone. "Yes, Bob."

"I've got your guy," Cantor said. "He's in Spanish Harlem."

"I figured. Can you put him at an address?"

"He's moving, in a car or a cab. No, wait, he's stopped. He's on the street. Hang on, I'll superimpose my street map. I've got him going into a building near the corner of Fifth Avenue. He's still moving, he must be climbing stairs."

"Give me the address, Bob."

Cantor recited it. "Hang on, he's moving funny."

"What do you mean, funny?"

"It's like he's dancing."

"Dancing?"

"Short, choppy movements. Hang on."

"What's going on, Bob?"

"He seems to be on the sidewalk again. Oh, shit, I think he went off the building."

"How can you tell that?"

"It's like he was scuffling with somebody, and he lost the fight. He was on an upper floor, maybe the roof. Now he's on the sidewalk."

"I'd better get up there," Stone said.

"He's not moving," Cantor said. "You'd be better off calling nine-one-one."

32

S TONE CALLED 911 and reported the incident, then he ran outside, got into a cab, and headed uptown.

IT WAS A GOOD twenty minutes before Stone arrived at the scene. A patrol car and an ambulance had one side of 125th Street blocked, and a small crowd lingered, hoping for a look at the body, which was a lump under a sheet. A supervising sergeant had arrived and was standing next to the lump, taking notes from a conversation with one of his officers.

Stone waited for them to finish, then approached the officer and showed him his retirement badge. "Sarge, do you mind if I have a look at the body? It's about another case."

The sergeant looked at him narrowly. "Are you Barrington?"

"Yep."

"Yeah, I remember you from the One Niner. What case?"

"Art theft. The kid stole a valuable picture, then sold it, and I have to find out who to."

"Awright," the cop said, turning his back on the corpse. "Be quick about it."

Stone pulled back the sheet and saw that the angelic good looks of the sixteen-year-old had fled him. He was scrawny and unshaven and his hands and fingernails were filthy; his head rested in a pool of drying blood. Stone pushed up his sleeves and found fresh track marks. He checked his pockets and found a wad of bills, something over fifty dollars, and a business card from a bar, with a phone number written on the back of it. He palmed the card and returned the cash to the pockets. "Thanks, Sarge," he said. "Did he go out a window or off the roof?"

"The roof. We got a couple of witnesses to that."

"Anybody see who threw him off?"

"Of course not. You get what you needed?"

"Not much to get," Stone replied.

"That's life, pal."

Stone departed the scene and walked down 125th Street. He had a look at the card: Sam Spain's Bar, maybe a block down the street. His cell phone buzzed.

"Yes?"

"It's Dino. I'm at a wake. What do you need?"

"I needed to locate a junkie, but I got there too late."

"A particular junkie?"

"The son of Morgan's maid. He stole something, and I was trying to get it back, but he's already sold it."

"Any idea where?"

"Not really, but there was a business card from a bar in his pocket. I thought I'd check it out."

"What bar?"

"Sam Spain's on 125th Street."

"Don't you go in there alone," Dino said. "I mean it.

On any given day there are half a dozen people in there with a reason to knife you."

"You want to join me?"

"I'm tied up here for another hour, then I've got to spend the rest of the day catching up on what I didn't get done during the funeral. Meet me at Clarke's at seven, and we'll figure it out."

"Okay."

"But, Stone, *don't go into that bar alone!*"

"Got it. See you at seven." He hung up.

By now, Stone was across the street from Sam Spain's. It looked very ordinary: big neon sign, a Schaefer Beer sign in the window, also neon, also saying OPEN. Schaefer Beer, an old-time New York brewery dating back to the nineteenth century, had gone out of business, what, twenty, thirty years ago? A man approached the place on the bar's side of the street, a familiar face. But who? Stone couldn't remember.

His phone rang again.

"Yes?"

"It's Art Masi. Something up? Talk fast, I'm at a wake."

"I've got a lead on the picture. Margaretta Fernandez, Filipino lady, Mrs. Tillman's maid, received the FedEx box, took the picture home with her, and hung it on her living room wall, from where her son, a junkie, stole it and sold it."

"Have you caught up with him?"

"No, but somebody did about half an hour ago, tossed him off a roof on 125th Street."

"Swell."

"The cop let me go through his pockets, and I found a card from Sam Spain's Bar, just down 125th. I'm standing across the street from it now."

"I wouldn't go into that bar alone if I were you," Art said.

"You're an art cop," Stone replied. "What do you know from dangerous bars?"

"Sam Spain is a fence. I know from fences. If you go in there you'll come out with a knife between your ribs."

"I've heard that."

"I'm tied up for another couple of hours," Masi said. "When can we meet?"

"P. J. Clarke's at seven. The commissioner will be there, too."

"Okay, I'll hang on while you find a cab."

"Art, I'm fine."

"Are you carrying?"

"No."

"I'll hang on while you find a cab."

"Oh, all right." It took only a couple of minutes to flag down a cab. "Okay, Art, I'm in a cab."

"See you at seven," Masi said, and hung up.

Stone gave the driver the address.

"You had me worried for a minute," the driver said. "You looked like you were thinking about going across the street into Sam Spain's."

"I was thinking about it."

"You don't want to go in that place without an armed escort, pal," the driver said.

"Gee, everybody's looking out for my welfare today," Stone said.

"You look like you could use some looking out for. You go into Sam's dressed like that, and it's like wearing a sign on your back that says, 'Please knife me and take my wallet.'" He turned down Fifth Avenue.

"Dressed like what?"

"Ain't that a cashmere jacket?"

"Oh, yeah, I guess so. I get your point. How did Sam Spain's get such a lousy reputation?"

"They worked at it. I went to high school with Sam's daughter, who would fuck anything that moved, but if Sam found out about it, the fucker got dead in a hurry, and nobody would go near the fuckee. I felt sorry for her."

"Is Sam mobbed up?"

"Not in the way of the traditional Italian mob," the driver said. "Sam's a Filipino and an expert with blades."

"I appreciate both your concern and the information," Stone said as the cab drew up at his corner.

"You really were gonna go in there, weren't you?" the driver said, accepting a fat tip.

"I was thinking about it," Stone said. He slammed the door, and suddenly he remembered who the familiar face was; he hadn't made him without his uniform. He was Ralph Weede, the doorman from 740 Park, Margaretta's boyfriend.

33

STONE GOT TO P. J. CLARKE'S and found Art Masi waiting for him.

"Bring me up to date," Masi said.

"Wait until Dino gets here, I don't want to have to do it twice." They ordered drinks.

Dino got there half a drink later. "Let's sit down, I'll order at the table."

They got a table. "Okay, now what the hell is going on?" Dino asked. "You first," he said to Stone.

"Okay. On the day he was killed, Mark Tillman invited Pio Farina and his girlfriend, Ann Kusch, over for a drink in the early afternoon. They say he was still alive when they left, and he asked them to drop off a package at FedEx, on Second Avenue. Art tracked it down. Tillman had sent it to himself, and it was delivered on the following Wednesday."

"The van Gogh?" Dino asked.

"As it turns out, yes. A doorman named Ralph Weede signed for the package but used his colleague's name, then he opened it, had a look at the contents, and delivered it to the apartment, where Margaretta Fernandez, Morgan's maid, took charge of it. She took it home, hung it on the wall, and a couple of days ago her junkie son, Manolo, stole it and sold it to somebody for a hundred bucks."

"Good buy," Dino said.

"I got Bob Cantor to track the kid's cell phone. He went into a building on 125th Street, near Fifth Avenue, went up to the roof, encountered someone there who tossed him six stories onto the sidewalk. This is about a block down the street from Sam Spain's Bar, and Manolo had their card, with a phone number written on the back, in his pocket. Come to think of it, a cell phone number, area code 917. A few minutes later I saw Ralph Weede, the doorman, walk down 125th and into the bar. I didn't recognize him at first because he wasn't in his uniform."

They ordered steaks.

"So that's where we are?" Dino asked. "Masi, you got anything to add?"

"Sam Spain has a lot of pictures on the walls of the bar," Masi said. "Posters, stuff he got off the Internet, nothing real, but he fancies himself a collector. Manolo might have picked him for a buyer."

"Tell you what," Dino said, "after dinner we'll go uptown and take a look at the art collection of Sam Spain."

"Just the three of us?" Stone asked.

"Who else?" Dino replied.

"You and Art both made it sound like we'd need a platoon of uniforms to tackle the place."

"You and I have walked into worse places and come out alive," Dino reminded him.

"We were younger then, and stupid," Stone reminded him.

"Well," Dino said, "sometimes we're still stupid."

FORTIFIED WITH a couple of drinks each and a shared bottle of Cabernet, the three of them piled into Dino's SUV.

"What's your plan?" Stone asked.

"I thought we'd walk in there, slap Sam Spain around a little, then relieve him of the picture," Dino replied.

Masi made a little groaning noise. "Let's not do anything that might damage the picture."

"Yeah," Stone said, "Arthur Steele wouldn't like that."

IT WAS FAIRLY LATE, but it was the shank of the evening in Sam Spain's, and everybody looked and sounded drunk. Stone let Dino take the lead, followed by Masi, and then he did what he used to do in places like this: he watched the crowd at the bar for signs of discontent. Then something happened: somebody opened an office door at the rear of the place, and for a millisecond before the door closed, Stone caught sight of a picture on the wall above the desk that was the color of sunshine.

The man who'd left the office ducked behind the bar and replaced a large, older man on the stool in front of an old cash register. The older man, who had big shoulders and a flat gut, spotted Dino and pretended to smile. He pointed his chin at Stone and said, "Hey, Dino, who's the civilian?"

"He doesn't look it, Sam," Dino said, "but he's the meanest sonofabitch you ever met, and he's heeled."

Sam Spain snorted. "Yeah? If you say so."

Dino said, "You don't mind if we have a look around the place, do you, Sam?"

"Especially in the office," Stone said.

"You mean tear it apart and run off my customers?" Spain asked. "You're going to need a warrant for that, and I'll still sue your ass and the department's when you're done."

"Sam," Dino said, "you know a junkie named Manolo, don't you?"

"I know three or four guys who match that description," Spain replied.

"Last name Fernandez," Stone said. "This afternoon he ended up in a puddle of his own blood on the sidewalk, just down the street, after a dive off a rooftop."

"Oh, yeah, I know that kid. He's always offering me stuff he's stolen. I never want any of it."

"Sure you do, Sam," Dino said. "You buy stuff from everybody. Anything to turn a buck."

"I got no objection to turning a buck, but I do it by selling booze," Spain said, waving a hand at the array of bottles behind the bar. "Have one on the house."

"I'm too young to go blind," Dino said. "Why don't you unlock the office door?"

"Is that door locked?" Spain asked with a smirk.

Dino turned around, walked to the door, and delivered a kick just above the doorknob. There was a splintering sound as the jamb gave way, and the door flew open. He walked in, looked around, then opened another door that led to the alley beside the bar.

Stone ran outside and checked the alley from the other end; nothing but garbage cans. He came back inside, looked at Dino, and shook his head. "It was there a minute ago," he said, "now it's not."

* * *

BACK IN DINO'S CAR, he turned toward Stone, who was in the rear seat with Masi. "Did you actually see it?"

"For just a second, when the guy came out. It was hanging over the desk in a cheap frame."

"Have you ever even seen the picture?" Dino asked.

"I have an eight-by-ten transparency of it," Stone replied. "It makes an impression that stays with you."

"Masi, did you see it?" Dino asked.

"No," Art replied, "I was looking for blades."

"Dino," Stone said, "check your computer and see if you can find a record and an address for Ralph Weede, with an *e* at the end."

Dino pulled the car's computer around on its supporting arm and did some typing. "He has a conviction for assault and battery twelve years ago," Dino said. "Suspended sentence. I wonder how he got the job at 740 with a record for violence?"

"I wonder, too," Stone said.

"Oh, and we just passed the building where he lives, sixth floor."

"That's the building where Manolo Fernandez took a swan dive off the roof," Stone pointed out.

Dino did some more typing. "We'll get him in for questioning," he said.

"I can put him at Sam Spain's half an hour after the murder."

"I'll mention that to Homicide," Dino said.

34

I T WAS TOO LATE to call Morgan when he got home; he'd call her in the morning.

Bright and early, Morgan called him. "Are you enjoying your scrambled eggs?" she asked.

"Speaking of scrambled eggs," Stone said, "Margaretta is unlikely to come to work this morning."

"Funny you should mention that—she's half an hour late. What do you know that I don't know?"

"Yesterday somebody threw her son, Manolo, off a roof in Harlem, six stories to the sidewalk."

Morgan made a moaning noise. "Poor Margaretta, she's been expecting something like this for a couple of years. I'm sorry it finally happened to her."

"There's more. Manolo went off the roof of the building where one of your doormen, Ralph Weede, lives."

"What makes you think Ralph is mixed up in this?"

"He's mixed up with Margaretta," Stone said. "He's the guy who's been shtuping her for a while, and he's the genius who suggested a van Gogh would look nice in her living room."

"Ralph wouldn't know it was a van Gogh."

"Those doormen know *everything* that goes on in your building. You think they would miss the theft of a sixty-million-dollar painting? Ralph wanted the picture stashed somewhere quiet, where nobody would look for it, until he could figure out how to unload it. He didn't count on a strung-out junkie lifting it and selling it to a bar owner named Sam Spain, who fancies himself something of an art collector."

"Does *he* know it's a van Gogh?"

"If he didn't then, he does now. I saw Ralph Weede go into his bar yesterday, and I'm sure their chat included a brief lecture on art history."

"How would a bar owner in Harlem dispose of a sixty-million-dollar painting?"

"Do you know what a fence is?"

"Like a garden fence?"

"No. A fence is sort of a freelance broker who buys and sells stolen goods—in your Limey parlance, things that fell off the back of a truck."

"Lorry."

"Sorry, lorry. You get the picture, so to speak."

"Yes, but surely he's a small-timer who's never dealt with something like this."

"Just as fences know their neighborhood thieves, like Manolo, they know other fences, who know still other fences, including some who may be way out of their neighborhood league. There are so-called 'reputable' art galleries on the Upper East Side where you could walk in with that van Gogh in a shopping bag and walk out with a million bucks in cash."

"Which galleries?"

"That's the trick, knowing which ones, and Sam Spain knows people who know people who know people who have a good eye for art, a greedy heart, and a lot of untaxed cash. In a week, that van Gogh could be hanging in a very private collection in Hong Kong or Macau, and a man in New York named Arthur Steele would be crying his eyes out."

"Who's Arthur Steele?"

"He's the guy who insured your painting."

"You're right," she said, "I'm beginning to get the picture."

"No, you're beginning to *lose* the picture, unless I can find a way to short-circuit the sales process before the painting leaves Sam Spain's hands."

"And how are you going to do that?"

"I'm going to pay Mr. Spain a visit," Stone said.

"Stone, wouldn't that be dangerous?"

"Possibly, but I will arrive bearing gifts that may turn Mr. Spain's head."

"I don't want you to lose yours in the process."

"Neither do I. If you haven't heard from me in, say"—he consulted his wristwatch—"two hours, call Dino and tell him I've got my tit caught in a wringer in Harlem." Without another word, Stone hung up.

AN HOUR LATER Stone arrived at Sam Spain's Bar, just as Sam himself was turning the CLOSED sign to OPEN. He walked in and set his briefcase on the bar; Sam was already behind the bar at an adding machine, counting last night's take.

"Good morning, Sam," Stone said.

"Sez who?" Sam grumbled.

"My name is Barrington," Stone said.

"Ah, you're the ex-cop, now a civilian."

"Today I'm in the business of buying art."

Sam swept a hand toward the junk on his walls. "Take your pick—five hundred bucks."

"I want to pay more than that."

"Okay, a thousand bucks."

"Even more, Sam. I want to buy the picture you bought from Manolo Fernandez, and I'm willing to give you a handsome profit on the transaction."

"Now, listen—"

"No, you listen. I'll make this easy for you. If you hang on to that picture or try to move it, the earth is going to fall on you. You'll be hounded by the NYPD, the FBI, and the state police forces of a dozen countries. There will be so many cops in here, from so many places, there won't be room for the people who buy your booze, let alone fence their goods, and you'll end up doing some very serious time. That's not a good prospect for somebody your age, Sam. Think about it."

"Okay, I'm thinking. How much should I be thinking about?"

"I'm authorized by the insurance company to offer you one million dollars in cash for the return of the picture—today."

Sam looked surprised. "Is there a million bucks in that briefcase, or are you packing something else?"

"There's a substantial down payment in the briefcase," Stone said. "I can have the rest of the cash here in a couple of hours."

"How substantial?"

"Thirty-five thousand dollars."

"Show me half a million, then we'll talk about the other half."

"I don't walk around with that kind of money," Stone

said, "and I'm not going to. The rest of the money will be delivered to your back door by a security company."

"Listen," Sam said, "I know what that picture is worth. If your insurance company wants it back, they're going to have to cough up half its value, and we both know how much that is."

"Sam, there's something you don't know about that painting."

"Yeah, what's that?"

"It's a fake. It wasn't painted in France in 1890, it was painted by a guy out on Long Island last year. If you try to sell it, the prospective buyer is going to have it subjected to every possible test, and it's going to fail one or more of them. Then the picture will be worth about three thousand dollars."

"I don't believe you," Sam said.

Stone heard the sound of the front door opening and closing, but Sam didn't even glance at it. Stone started to turn, and then something hit him on the side of the head, hard.

He didn't even feel the floor rising to greet him.

35

ART MASI WALKED into Stone's outer office.

"Good morning, Lieutenant Masi," Joan said.

"Good morning, Joan. Is he in?"

"I'm afraid not," she said. "He left about forty minutes ago, and he didn't say when he'd be back."

Art stared at her. "Was he carrying anything?" he asked.

"Just a briefcase."

"Joan, not to pry, but does he keep much in the way of cash around the office?"

She looked at him. "He has a safe," she said.

"Oh, shit," Art muttered.

STONE WOKE UP, slowly and painfully, in the office at the back of Sam Spain's Bar. He was alone in the room, but he wasn't going anywhere. His hands and feet were duct-taped to a heavy wooden armchair; there was a ball of something cottony in his mouth and a strip of tape around his head to keep it there.

He took a few deep breaths through his nose to clear his head and, he hoped, help the pain in his head go away. That didn't work. He looked at a clock on the wall and did some arithmetic: he'd been out for twenty minutes or so. He felt nauseated, but he couldn't afford to vomit—he could easily strangle to death.

The office door opened and a man walked in: short, dark, mustached, carrying something in his hand. Stone closed his eyes and prepared to be hit again. Instead, something cold was pressed over and around his left ear.

"It's just some ice," the man said. "It'll make you feel better."

It did. The nausea backed off, and so did the pain, a good bit.

"It was an old-fashioned cosh," the man said. "A couple of pounds of lead shot in a leather bag. My wife sewed it."

Stone tried to thank him, but all he could produce was a grunt through his nose.

"I'll take off the gag if you promise not to yell. Then I'd have to cosh you again."

Stone nodded.

The man snatched off the tape.

Stone took a deep breath and blew the wad out of his mouth. "Ow," he said, if a little late.

"That's better, isn't it?"

"Much better, thanks. How about my hands and feet?"

"Not just yet," the man said. "Sam's gonna come in here and talk to you in a minute, and my advice is to be nice. If you cooperate, you might get out of here under your own steam. If not, well, there's a little river under this place that runs pretty fast all the way to the East River. It would be something like getting flushed down a really big toilet. You getting the picture?"

"That's the question I came here to ask," Stone said.

The door opened and Sam Spain walked in. "And I'm ready to answer it," he said. "I want five million."

"I'll have to ask," Stone said.

"Ask who?"

"The CEO of the insurance company."

"So call him."

"Hard to do," Stone said, "in the circumstances."

"Free up his left hand," Sam said to his man.

The man did so.

Stone flexed his fingers to get rid of the numbness. "Give me a minute," he said.

"Take your time," Sam said.

"JOAN," ART MASI SAID, "can you get Dino Bacchetti on the phone for me? If he's tied up, tell whoever answers it's an emergency."

"Sure," Joan said, and made the call.

"OKAY, I THINK the hand's working now," Stone said.

Sam picked up Stone's iPhone from his desk, where it rested near his little Colt Government .380, and placed it in Stone's hand.

"It has to read my right thumb," Stone said, "or it won't turn on."

Sam nodded to his man, who cut loose Stone's other hand.

Stone pressed his thumb against the phone and it opened. He went to his contacts and selected Arthur Steele's private line.

Arthur answered immediately. "Yes?"

"It's Stone. A man who says he has the picture wants five million for it."

"Have you seen it?"

"Hang on." Stone looked up at Sam Spain. "I have to see the picture," he said. He watched very carefully as Spain walked to a large safe and tapped in a code.

Spain reached into the safe and extracted a laundry bag. He opened it, produced a picture, sans frame, and held it in front of Stone.

"It's upside down," Stone said.

Sam turned it 180 degrees. "Well?"

"In my briefcase there's an envelope containing a photograph of the painting. I'll have to compare the two."

"Go get his briefcase," Sam said to his man.

"Hang on, Arthur," Stone said.

"COMMISSIONER, THIS IS ART MASI."

"Be quick, Masi."

"I think Stone Barrington has gone up to Harlem to try and buy the van Gogh from Sam Spain. He took . . ." He looked at Joan and raised his eyebrows questioningly.

"Thirty-five thousand dollars," she replied. "It was all the cash we had."

"Thirty-five thousand dollars," Art said into the phone.

"And a gun," Joan said. "His .380."

"And he's carrying."

"How long ago?"

"Maybe three-quarters of an hour."

"Have you called his phone?"

"Just a minute, Commissioner." He turned to Joan. "Please call his cell phone."

Joan did so. "It's busy," she said.

"The line is busy, Commissioner."

*   *   *

STONE HELD UP the transparency to the overhead light and compared it to the picture, then he picked up his phone. "Arthur, the picture matches the transparency."

"Are you there with the guy with the picture?" Arthur asked.

"Yes."

"Ask him why I should pay five million dollars for a fake."

Stone sighed. "Sam," he said, "he wants to know why he should pay five million dollars for a fake van Gogh." Stone held up the phone so Arthur could hear the reply.

Sam sort of smiled. "Tell him he'll get the picture, plus you without any extra holes in your head."

36

THERE WAS SILENCE on the other end of the phone.

"Arthur?" Stone said.

"I'm here."

"What do you want to do?" Stone asked.

"I'm thinking it over."

"I don't think that's the answer he wanted," Stone said, "and it doesn't sound very good to me, either."

"I'm not sure how long it will take me to get the cash," Arthur said. "Call me back in ten minutes." He hung up.

"Well, Sam," Stone said, "nobody has five million dollars in his bottom desk drawer, but he knows how to come up with it."

"I'm feeling impatient," Sam said.

"Relax, have a drink."

"It's a little early," Sam said, "even for me."

"Let's see what's on TV," Stone said, pointing a thumb at the set on the office wall.

"Soap operas and Fox News. Neither one of 'em appeals."

"Five more minutes, and we'll have an answer."

Stone's phone rang.

"Answer it," Sam said.

"Hello?"

"It's Arthur. Hold the phone so he can hear me."

Stone held up the phone.

"Go fuck yourself!" Arthur yelled, and he ended the call.

"I tried, Sam," Stone said. "You bit off more than you could chew."

Sam put the picture back into the laundry bag and held it out to his cohort. "Deliver it," he said. The man took the laundry bag and left by the back door.

"Is the million bucks starting to sound any better, Sam?" Stone asked.

"No," Sam replied, and he reached around behind him as if to draw a weapon from the small of his back.

Stone looked at his .380; the magazine was lying beside it, and he didn't carry with one in the chamber. The cosh, however, was there, too. As Sam was halfway to his feet, Stone grabbed the cosh and swung it as hard as he could at Sam's head. It connected at the temple with a loud thud, and Sam collapsed into a heap, a short-barreled .38 revolver lying beside him.

Stone tried to get up, but his feet were still taped to the chair at the ankles. He saw a coffee mug on the desk with assorted implements in it, including a box cutter. He grabbed it and sawed his feet loose, then got up and kicked the .38 aside, grabbed his .380 from the desk, shoved the magazine into it, worked the slide, and pointed the weapon at the head of the inert Sam Spain. He prodded at the man with his toe. "Get up," he said.

Sam did a convincing job of playing the corpse.

Stone was feeling Spain's neck for a pulse when he

heard the front door of the bar crash open, followed by the splintering of the rear outside door. A uniformed officer stepped through the rear door, followed by another through the door from the bar. Each held a pistol in front of him.

"Drop it!" both of them shouted in unison.

Stone set his .380 on the desk and stepped away from it, his hands up.

"What's the matter with him?" one of the cops said to Stone, indicating Sam Spain.

"I hit him in the head with the cosh on the desk," Stone replied. "He was about to shoot me with the .38 over there." He pointed at the gun on the floor.

"Who are you?" the cop asked.

"Barrington."

"You got some ID?"

Stone reached for his wallet.

"Careful," the cop said; his gun was still pointed at Stone.

Stone held his jacket open. "The only weapon I have is on the desk." Gingerly, he fished out his wallet and handed the man his driver's license.

"It's okay," the cop said to his partner, and they put away their weapons. Sounds of others entering the bar drifted in.

Stone knelt by Sam Spain and held two fingers to the artery in his neck. "Weak and thready," he said to the cop. "You'd better call an ambulance."

"Who is he?"

"That's Sam Spain," the other cop said. "Do like the man says."

Stone didn't wait for him to move. He picked up the phone on the desk and dialed 911, then handed the cop the phone. The man called for an ambulance, then hung up.

"We're supposed to tell you that the commissioner is on his way," the cop said.

The ambulance pulled into the alley, and two EMTs took charge of Sam Spain. "What happened to him?" one of them asked nobody in particular.

"Blow to the head, left temple," Stone said.

"Blow with what?"

The cop picked up the cosh and struck the desktop with it.

"Gotcha," the EMT said. He slipped an oxygen mask onto Sam Spain, then stripped off his jacket, pushed up a sleeve, and started an IV.

"Is he going to make it?" Stone asked. He wanted Sam to make it because he wanted to know to whom the picture was being delivered, and because he didn't want to answer a lot of questions if Sam died.

DINO CAME INTO THE OFFICE from the bar as Sam was being hauled out on a stretcher; he was followed closely by Art Masi.

"Jesus, Stone, what did you do to the guy?"

"I hit him with the same cosh the other guy hit me with," Stone said. He picked up the ice bag from the floor and pressed it to his head.

"You want an ambulance?"

"No, but I want to be there when Sam Spain wakes up."

"*If* he wakes up," Dino said. "You want a lawyer?"

"I *am* a lawyer, Dino, remember?"

"Okay, consider that your rights have been read to you. Now, what the fuck happened?"

"I made Sam Spain an offer he couldn't refuse, and he refused it. He wanted five million. I got Arthur Steele on the phone, and he declined, rather rudely, to pay it. Sam put the picture in a laundry bag and gave it to his guy and told him to deliver it. The guy left, and Sam reached for that .38 over there on the floor. I grabbed the cosh from the desk and hit him."

"How hard?"

"As hard as I could—he had the .38 in his hand."

"Okay," Dino said, "I buy that. Get your money, and let's go to the hospital."

"Stone," Art Masi said, "where is the picture being delivered?"

"I have no idea," Stone replied, "and I don't know who the guy delivering it is, either. We'll have to ask Sam Spain, if he wakes up."

37

STONE RODE WITH DINO, in silence; his head wasn't too clear, and he couldn't think of anything to say.

"Can you believe they took him all the way downtown to Bellevue?" Dino complained from the front seat.

Stone still said nothing.

"Are you all right back there?" Dino asked.

"Sure," Stone muttered. Using the siren, they got downtown remarkably fast and pulled up at the ER entrance.

Stone got out of the backseat, leaned against a wall, and vomited, then he sagged to his knees.

Dino snagged a gurney from just inside the door and he and his driver got Stone aboard.

STONE STIRRED AND OPENED his eyes a little, then wider. The blinds in the room were drawn, and only thin rays of daylight penetrated. He quickly discovered that he was wearing an oxygen mask and a hospital gown, and an IV was plugged into his arm. He felt around for the buzzer and couldn't find it; he tried to reach for the phone and failed, nearly falling out of bed, then he passed out again. The only sound he heard was a faint beeping, which seemed to be in rhythm with his heart.

THE NEXT TIME he stirred, a nurse was wiping his face with a damp cloth, and Dino was sitting in a chair in the corner.

"Is he alive?" Dino asked.

"More or less," the nurse replied, "but I don't think he's enjoying it very much."

Dino got up, walked to the bedside, and peered closely into Stone's eyes.

"Kiss me, darling," Stone managed to say.

The nurse broke up.

"In your dreams," Dino said.

"Is Sam Spain talking?"

"He's barely breathing, but he looks better than you."

Stone drew a deep breath and let it out. "There, is that better?"

"Only compared to how you were before you passed out."

"Make this thing sit up," Stone said, and the nurse came and put his finger on the button. "That feels better," Stone said from a half-sitting position. "What happened?"

"You came within an ace of puking in my car," Dino said, "in which case I would have shot you."

Stone looked around the room; his was one of four beds, and one of the other three contained a lump. "Who's that?"

"The presidential suite was unavailable, so you have to share." Dino pointed. "That's Sam Spain."

"You both have the same concussion," the nurse said, "and apparently, from the same weapon. You must have hit Mr. Spain pretty hard."

"I did the best I could," Stone replied. "I'm thirsty."

"Water or orange juice?"

"Orange juice. I think my blood sugar is low."

She put a glass straw in his mouth and he sucked up most of the juice. "Better," he said.

"I've got to see some other patients," the nurse said. "Don't die on me."

"I'll try not to."

Dino pulled his chair up to the bedside. "The guy who coshed you is Sol Fineman," he said, "a well-seasoned gangster."

"Where is he?"

"God only knows."

"Where's my briefcase?"

"In my car, I think."

"There's an eight-by-ten transparency of the picture in there. Scan it and circulate it in the art world as fast as you can. Let's make it as hard as possible for him to move it."

"Hang on," Dino said. He went to the door and let Art Masi in.

"Circulate the transparency in my briefcase, Art."

"That was done when the painting first disappeared."

"Then do it again," Dino said. "Memories fade. The transparency is in Stone's briefcase in the backseat of my car. Don't steal the money."

"You got my money back?" Stone asked.

"Thirty-five thousand of it. Sam hadn't spent it all yet."

"That's all there was. Thanks."

"I'll have it brought up," Dino said. "Well, I've got to get back to solving crimes."

"One other thing," Stone said.

"What?"

"Ask the nurse to restrain Sam Spain. I don't want him coming to while I'm dozing."

"I'll get my guy to cuff him to the bed," Dino said.

"That ought to do it."

Dino left the room, and in a minute a uniform came in and anchored Spain to his bed.

Stone felt like a nap.

HE WOKE UP later to a shuffling, clanging noise. Across the room, Sam Spain was on his feet, dragging his bed around by his cuffed hand. Stone rang for the nurse, and she came in and looked at Spain in horror. "What the hell?"

"Don't touch him," Stone said. "Get two cops in here right away."

A moment later two uniforms entered the room, got Spain back into bed, and cuffed his other hand to the frame.

"That ought to hold him," Stone said. "Call the commissioner and tell him Sam Spain is conscious." They left.

"So, Sam," Stone said, "how are you feeling?"

"What did they do to me?" Sam asked weakly.

"They didn't, I did. I hit you with Sol's cosh while you were trying to shoot me."

"Sol? What Sol? I don't know any Sol."

"Sol Fineman, your guy, the one who's delivering the picture?"

"I don't know what you're talking about," Sam said. "I feel like shit."

"I'm so happy to hear that."

"Shut up."

"You know, I've always said that if people would just take my advice, their lives would be so much richer and fuller and happier. Look at you, for instance. If you had taken my advice, you'd be a million dollars richer and on a free ride out of the deep, deep trouble you're in."

"I told you to shut up."

"And you wouldn't have to be listening to me saying I told you so."

"I'm not listening," Sam said. "Shut up."

"No, I'm not going to shut up, I'm having too much fun."

"If you don't shut up, I'm going to come over there and strangle you," Sam said.

"Don't forget to bring your bed," Stone said.

38

WHEN STONE NEXT woke up it was dark outside, and Morgan Tillman was sitting next to his bed.

"There you are," she said. "How are you feeling?"

"Surprisingly well," Stone said, sitting his bed up a bit more. "In fact, I'm hungry." He rang for the nurse.

"Ah," she said, "you're still alive."

"I am," Stone said, "and I'm hungry."

"That's good news. I'll round you up something." She left again.

"Who's your roommate?" Morgan asked, nodding toward the lump across the room.

"That's Sam Spain," Stone said. "He's here because I slugged him in the head, and I'm here because he slugged me in the head."

"How'd you manage that?"

He explained it to her.

"And the picture is gone?"

"For the moment," Stone said. "Dino is on it."

"I called him when you didn't call me, just as you asked me to."

"It worked," Stone replied. "Thank you."

"When are you getting out of here?"

"I'm not sure. If I keep feeling this good, then soon."

She placed a hand in his lap. "Exactly how well do you feel?"

"Not quite that well," he replied. "Not yet, anyway. Try me tomorrow."

The nurse returned with a hot dinner and set it on his tray table. He wolfed it down. "That was surprisingly good," he said.

"I'm glad." She got up and kissed him on the forehead. "I should go and let you get some rest."

"How's Margaretta doing?"

"Not well. I spent the day with her and got some food into the house. I made funeral arrangements for Manolo, too. He was such a sweet boy a couple of years ago."

"That was good of you."

"I'll see you tomorrow. If they set you free, I'll drive you home."

"Thank you."

The nurse came back and took his tray.

"Do you know where my cell phone is?" he asked.

"Where was it?"

"I'm not sure."

She went to a closet and came back with the phone. "In your jacket pocket."

"Thanks." He switched on the phone. "I don't suppose you have an iPhone charger?"

"I'll see what I can do." She came back with one in a couple of minutes.

"I don't hear my heart beeping anymore," Stone said.

"You complained about it, so I disconnected you. Your roommate was complaining, too."

"When am I getting out of here?"

"The doctor will visit you shortly."

As if on cue, an impossibly young physician walked into the room. He did a cursory examination of Stone and said, "One more night, for insurance. You'll be discharged in the morning if you don't die overnight."

"That's encouraging," Stone said, and the young man walked over to Sam Spain and put a stethoscope to his chest.

Stone plugged in his cell phone and checked his messages; nothing that couldn't wait.

"Did you know your roommate?" the doctor asked,

"Vaguely," Stone said. "Why was your question in the past tense?"

"Because Mr. Spain is dead, probably has been for an hour or so."

"Shit," Stone said.

"My condolences," the doctor said, drawing a sheet over Sam Spain's head.

Shortly, a policeman came into the room with two orderlies and uncuffed the Spain corpse, then the orderlies transferred the body to a gurney and wheeled it out.

"Shit," Stone said again. Now how were they going to figure out whom Sol Fineman was delivering to? Then he had a thought. He got out of bed, went to the closet, and found Sam's clothes and searched them. His iPhone was in a jacket pocket. Stone got back in bed and switched it on. "Oh, God," he said.

He rang for the nurse again. "You know the corpse that just departed?"

"Yes, I'm afraid I missed that."

"Where is it?"

"In our morgue," she replied, "waiting for the autopsy."

"Listen, there's something I need from the corpse."

"I don't think it has anything left to give."

"Yes, it does. I need its right thumb."

"*What*?"

"In fact, maybe it should be a whole hand."

"I'm sorry, we don't hand out body parts here."

"I understand. How about if you wheel it back up here so I can use its thumb to get into Sam's iPhone?"

"We operate procedurally around here," she said. "We don't have a procedure for taking a corpse out of the morgue and putting it back in a room. It works the other way around."

"Okay, okay. Tell you what, don't let them take it to the city morgue until I've had a chance to get the police back here. They'll figure it out."

"I'll see what I can do," she said, then left.

Stone called Dino.

"You're still alive?"

"I'm much better, thank you. Sam Spain died a little while ago."

"Well, shit, I wanted to question him again about the destination of the picture."

"Yeah, I know, but I've got Sam's iPhone. If we can get into it, we can see a list of who he called recently."

"That's good news."

"Not yet it isn't."

"What's that supposed to mean?"

"We're going to need a fingerprint to unlock the phone."

Dino thought about that for a minute. "Was Sam right-handed or left-handed?"

"He tried to shoot me with his right hand."

"So we'll need what, his right thumb?"

"Maybe the index finger, too. The body's in the morgue, awaiting autopsy."

"Do we know who the pathologist is?"

"Whoever's on duty, I guess. I asked the nurse to see that the corpse isn't taken to the city morgue."

"I'll be right over," Dino said.

39

THE FOLLOWING MORNING Stone was sitting up in bed, waiting for the doctor to come and discharge him. Dino got there first.

"I've been down in the morgue, arguing with the pathologist who's about to do the autopsy on Sam," Dino said, sinking into a chair.

"Arguing?"

"He is unwilling to separate any fingers from the corpse."

Stone picked up Sam's iPhone, which had been charging next to his bed, and handed it to Dino. "Then take this down to the morgue and find a finger that works without amputating it. You know how it works—you've got one of these, too."

"Why didn't I think of that?" Dino asked, shoving the phone into his pocket. "I'll be back soon." He stalked out of the room and down the hallway.

The young doctor walked in. "How are you feeling?" he asked Stone.

"Just great!"

"Let me do a little checkup. He began to listen to Stone's heart and poking and prodding. "Our radiologist has pronounced your brain undamaged. You were just shaken up by the blow to the head."

"May I get out of here?" Stone asked.

The doctor picked up his chart from the foot of the bed and began writing on it, then he signed it and returned it to its hook. "You are officially discharged," he said. "You can get dressed while I get a wheelchair for you."

"I don't need a wheelchair," Stone said.

"Hospital policy—it's a liability thing. Don't move without it."

Stone got into his clothes, pocketed his phone, and sat on his bed, waiting.

Dino came back into the room. "It didn't work," he said. "I tried every finger. The pathologist said it was probably a body temperature thing, and Sam didn't have any to spare. I mentioned a microwave, but the doctor nixed that. Why are you sitting on your bed? Let's get out of here."

"I have to wait for a wheelchair."

"Hang on." Dino left the room and came back half a minute later with a wheelchair. "There was one in the hall. Hop aboard."

Stone got into the chair and was wheeled down the hall at top speed, waving at the nurses. They took the elevator to the ground floor and raced for the emergency exit. A moment later, they were cruising downtown.

"Something I should point out," Dino said.

"What's that?"

"We were going to charge Sam Spain with attempted murder for trying to shoot you, but of course he's dead now."

"So?"

"Now, since Sam is dead and you're not, we've got an assistant DA who's thinking of charging you with Sam's murder."

"That's preposterous," Stone said. "He was trying to shoot me."

"No witnesses to that," Dino said.

"I was taped to a chair, for God's sake, how could I murder him?"

"By hitting him in the head with the cosh. The DA's got the X-rays and the murder weapon."

"Stop saying that—it wasn't murder, it was self-defense."

"And when the uniforms got there, you weren't taped to the chair, and you were pointing a gun at Sam Spain."

"Of course I was!" Stone yelled. "I cut myself loose. I didn't know if he was playing possum, and his own gun was within his reach."

"The EMTs said he was unconscious when they got there," Dino said. "Look, if he charges you, I'll testify to your good character at your preliminary hearing, but you should know I'd get cross-examined pretty thoroughly, and I can't lie for you."

"Who's asking you to lie?"

"I'm just saying."

"Where's my briefcase?" Stone asked.

"On the floor beside you."

"Got it." He opened it and found the money and the transparency there.

"Anybody steal anything?"

"Nope, it's all here."

Dino handed him Sam's iPhone. "You can keep working on this. Maybe Bob Cantor can get into it."

"You remember that case recently where the FBI

wanted to get into an iPhone and Apple said even they couldn't do it?"

"Yeah."

"Well, that's what we're up against."

"Just try, okay? And get Cantor to try."

Dino dropped him at home and he entered the house through his office entrance.

"Where have you been?" Joan asked. "I've been calling everybody, including Dino. He didn't call back."

"He's been very busy," Stone said. "I took a shot to the head and spent the night in the hospital."

"Are you all right?"

"Yes, but I haven't had breakfast. Ask Helene to bring the usual to my desk, will you?" He went through his phone messages and found nothing very important, except one from Arthur Steele. He called the private line.

"Yes?"

"It's Stone, no thanks to you."

"You didn't really expect me to hand that ape five million dollars, did you?"

"You're willing to pay me twelve million to recover it. You could have taken it out of my end."

"Oh, I was going to pay the money, but you didn't call me back."

"That's because the guy was trying to shoot me," Stone said.

"Well, he didn't, did he?"

"No, because I hit him in the head. Now he's dead, and they're talking about charging me with his murder."

"They wouldn't do that," Arthur replied.

"They should be charging you," Stone said. "After all, you're the one who told him to go fuck himself and made him all mad. That's when he reached for the gun."

"It all turned out well, didn't it? You're okay."

"And Sam Spain is dead, before he could tell us who he sent the picture to."

"He sent it to somebody?"

"Yes. It was right there within my reach. If you'd agreed to the five million, we'd have it now."

"Stone, let's not drag up the past."

"It's the very recent past!"

"I can tell you're upset. We'll talk about this later." Arthur hung up.

Stone sat there fuming, until his breakfast came.

40

WHEN HE HAD FINISHED breakfast Stone called Bob Cantor.

"Now what?" Cantor asked, as if he were in a hurry.

"I've got a very important iPhone I've *got* to get into, but no fingerprint to open it."

"Where's the fingerprint?"

"In the morgue on a corpse."

"Cold?"

"Very cold."

"Then your only shot is the four-digit entry code that comes up when a print doesn't work."

"And how do I break that?"

"By entering the code."

"The code is inside the corpse's brain."

"Oh. Then you're fucked."

"There's no way?"

"If you could recall Steve Jobs from the great beyond,

maybe he could figure it out. Apple says even they can't do it."

"But somebody, some little company, got the FBI into an iPhone, remember?"

"No, I don't remember and neither does anybody else, because the FBI didn't mention their name. Maybe the director could point you in the right direction."

"Thanks, Bob, you've been a big help," Stone said, then hung up. He plugged Sam's phone into the charger on his desk; it was 66 percent charged. He tried turning it on, but only the keypad for entering the code came up. He tried to think: What numbers might be associated with Sam Spain? He had no clue, of course, having met the man only twice before he hit him with the cosh.

He tried emptying his mind, which wasn't hard, but nothing came to him. He examined Sam's iPhone, but it was the standard thing, white in color. He got up and started pacing, his hands in his pockets, then he felt a card in his trouser pocket and fished it out.

It was Sam's business card; the address on 125th Street was a four-digit number. He grabbed the phone, turned it on, and entered the number. Nothing. He threw the card into the trash can; he wouldn't be needing that anymore.

Stone slumped into his chair, but something was nagging at his mind. He picked up the trash can, found the card, and turned it over. On the back was a cell phone number. He picked up Sam's phone, turned it on, and entered the last four digits of the number.

The phone came to life.

DINO'S PRIVATE LINE RANG, and he picked it up. "Bacchetti."

"It's Stone," he said. "I'm calling from Sam Spain's phone."

"You got in?" Dino asked incredulously.

"I did. His entry code was the last four digits of his cell phone number."

"Not very secure," Dino said.

"Thank God for that."

"How the hell did you get his cell phone number?"

"It was on a card I found in Manolo Fernandez's pocket."

"Manolo, the stiff who took the dive?"

"One and the same."

"That's brilliant, Stone!"

"Now I've got a list of numbers that Sam called during the last week. There are a couple of dozen."

"Give them to me, and I'll check them out."

"I've already e-mailed them to you. Just find out who the numbers belong to. Don't start calling them, you might frighten somebody, and we don't want that."

"I'll get back to you," Dino said, then hung up.

STONE WENT THROUGH the numbers carefully. Many of them had names attached that meant nothing to him; then he saw one he had missed. The name was Nellie Fineman. "That's gotta be Sol Fineman's wife," he said aloud to himself.

Joan buzzed him. "Dino's on one."

"That was fast," Stone said.

"No, actually it was a little slow. We're still running the numbers, but I forgot to tell you that the morgue called this morning and reported a floater in the East River yesterday, up at Hell Gate."

"Anybody I know?"

"Yep, one Ralph Weede, a doorman at 740 and the chief suspect in the murder of Manolo Fernandez."

"Well, that will save everybody a lot of trouble," Stone said.

"Who do you like for Ralph's little swim?"

"Oh, Sam Spain, of course. The last time anybody reported seeing Ralph it was me, when I saw him going into Sam's bar. In fact, come to think of it, I know how he ended up in the East River."

"What do you mean, how?" Dino asked. "He took a long walk off a short pier."

"Yeah? How was he feeling at the time?"

"Like a guy with two slugs in his head, in the best tradition."

"Well, he got into the river from Sam Spain's office."

"That's a longer pier than I imagined."

"Sol Fineman told me there's a river running under Sam's bar that leads to the East River. He suggested that I might be exploring it soon."

"Ah, that all fits together, doesn't it?"

"I almost forgot, in going over the phone calls that Sam made or received, I found one listed under the name of Nellie Fineman."

"Sol has a wife?"

"In fact, he mentioned her, said she ran up his cosh on her sewing machine. Accessory after the fact in Sam's death maybe?"

"You mean, she was your accomplice?"

"Stop it!"

"Something I forgot to tell you—an assistant DA named Aaron Milestone would like to speak to you, preferably in his office. I'll give you his number so you can make an appointment."

"Okay, I've got his number, but I have no intention of calling him."

"Want a tip?" Dino asked.

"Sure."

"Call him."

"I don't have to."

"No, you don't, but it would be in your interest to talk to him before he sends somebody to look for you. It would look better."

"Look better to whom?"

"His boss."

"Oh, all right, I'll call him. I assume you've already got an APB out for Sol Fineman?"

"Since yesterday."

"Oh, good. I think Sol might be a very good chief suspect in the death of Ralph Weede, since you no longer have Sam Spain to kick around, and it's the sort of work he did for Sam. And you can always name Nellie as an accessory in the attempted murder of me, just to turn up the heat. Also, it would be a lot of fun to get a look at Nellie's cell phone."

"I'll get back to you," Dino said, and hung up.

41

IT HAD BEEN maybe ten minutes since Dino hung up, when Joan buzzed. "A Mr. Milestone on one."

Stone picked it up. "Stone Barrington."

"Mr. Barrington," a deep voice said, "this is Assistant District Attorney Aaron Milestone speaking."

"Good day, Mr. Milestone. How can I help you?"

"I'd like you to come downtown for a little chat, in the matter of the death of a Mr. Samuel Spain."

"I'd be happy to chat with you, Mr. Milestone, but I'm afraid I'm in the middle of a busy day, playing catch-up, having spent some time in the hospital with a concussion, as a result of a conversation with Mr. Spain and a colleague of his."

"How about first thing tomorrow morning?"

"Can't do that, either," Stone replied. "Tell you what, why don't you come up to my office and let's chat here? I'll make time for you."

Milestone took a deep breath and let it out. "Oh, all right," he said. "I'll be there in an hour."

"That's good for me, and, Mr. Milestone?"

"Yes."

"Don't bring a stenographer or any colleagues—that might put a damper on my freedom of speech."

Milestone hung up.

THE ASSISTANT DA made it in forty-five minutes, and Stone moved to the sofa and waved him to a chair. He was tall, thin, and in his twenties. "We sell good coffee around here," Stone said.

"Thank you, black, please."

Joan, who was lingering in the doorway, sprang into action.

Milestone clearly liked his coffee. He produced a steno pad and a silver pen. "Ready?"

"One moment," Stone said. "This will be strictly informal and off the record. You will observe that I'm not represented by legal counsel."

"You're an attorney," Milestone pointed out.

"Not when I'm being interrogated about an alleged murder."

Milestone raised his pen. "All right. When did you first meet Samuel Spain?"

Stone waggled a finger. "No, no, that's a record." He pointed at the steno pad.

Milestone capped his pen and tossed the pad onto the coffee table. "All right. I have an excellent memory."

"I thought so," Stone said. "Now, back when I was on the NYPD I caught sight of Mr. Spain a few times, but we were not formally introduced until a couple days ago."

"And by whom were you introduced?"

"The New York City commissioner of police."

"How's that?"

"We had entered Mr. Spain's bar, along with Lieutenant Arturo Masi, who leads the NYPD art squad, to discuss with him the disappearance of a painting, and Spain was known to deal in that sort of thing—or anything else, really, if there was a buck to be turned."

"You're saying Spain was a fence?"

"Well known in the industry. He also had a reputation with a knife."

"You make him sound like an unsavory character."

"Oh, all right, he was a pillar of the community—the community of thieves, junkies, and murderers. Just this morning, someone came across a corpse in the East River that Sam Spain almost certainly placed there."

"Whose corpse?"

"Fellow named Ralph Weede, a doorman at a ritzy Park Avenue apartment house. Not to worry, his death solved the murder by Mr. Weede of one Manolo Fernandez, a young junkie who had recently stolen the painting from his mother, who stole it from her employer. Manolo sold it to Sam Spain, who probably laid it off on an unscrupulous art dealer."

"You're making me dizzy."

"You've gotten lucky twice—if Spain had lived, you would have had to charge him with kidnapping and attempted murder."

"Whose kidnapping and murder?"

"That of yours truly," Stone said, pointing his thumb at himself, "and if I hadn't managed to pick up the cosh his man hit me with and hit Spain with it, Ralph Weede and I would have been holding hands in the East River when they found him."

"This is crazy," Milestone said.

"How long have you been on the job, Aaron?"

"Three weeks."

"Let me give you a tip. Nine times out of ten, the cops will do your work for you, and do it well. You should listen to them before you start investigating. The one out of ten will be the really interesting case, where the cops may have gotten it wrong, and you can knock yourself out on that one."

"One thing—was the picture an important one?"

"It's very likely a fake van Gogh, but its owner would like to have it back anyway."

"So all this is about a fake picture?"

"More than likely."

Milestone stood up. "Thank you for your time, Mr. Barrington. I'm sorry to have troubled you."

Stone stood and shook his hand. "It's Stone. Call me if you need advice."

Milestone nodded and took his leave.

Stone called Dino.

"Yeah?"

"I have disposed of Mr. Milestone, the ADA."

"You want me to pick up the body?"

"The body is on its way back to its office."

"He's not going to charge you?"

"I told him he should believe what you tell him ninety percent of the time."

"What about the other ten percent?"

"Those are the times your people screw up and finger the wrong man."

"We never do that."

"Yeah, sure."

"So you got off the hook by bad-mouthing us?"

"I told him to believe you."

"Yeah, but only ninety percent of the time?"

"I was feeling generous."

"Gee, thanks."

"I suppose I could have mentioned the number of innocent people the department has sent to their deaths who were later exonerated?"

"Prosecutors and juries send people to their deaths."

"Based on evidence provided by the NYPD."

"Well, nobody's perfect," Dino said.

"And on that confession, I will bid you good day."

"Dinner tonight?"

"Sure, Patroon at seven."

"Okay." Dino hung up.

42

THE FORMER SOL FINEMAN, born Carl Blankenship, arrived at his apartment, a second-floor walk-up on West 125th Street, and let himself in with his key. His wife, Nellie, née Cynthia Preston, could be heard in the kitchen, whistling loudly.

"Nellie!" he shouted.

The whistling stopped. "Yes, dearie?"

"Come in here, please."

She walked into the living room, untying her apron. "What's up, Sol?"

"Have a seat, honey, I've got important news."

She sat down in one of the chairs in front of the fireplace. "You look serious."

"This is serious, but it's also good for us."

"Okay, so tell me."

"Sam Spain is dead."

She sucked in a little breath. "Dead? How?"

"Not that it's important, but he took a shot to the head with that cosh you ran up for me."

"You hit Sam in the head?"

"No, no, *I* didn't do it. A guy I had already hit in the head came to, and I guess, right after I left, he got hold of the cosh and used it on Sam. That was yesterday. They took him to Bellevue, and he died this morning."

"Sol, you've made a good living out of Sam. What are you going to do now?"

"You remember I told you the day would come when we drop everything and go up the river?"

"Yes."

"This is the day. There are a lot of packing materials out in the hall. We'll take everything that's dear to us, and I'll rent a truck. You'll follow in the car."

"How much time do we have?"

"I'm not sure, but we should act like it's an emergency. The whole place has to be wiped down with Windex, too. I'll start on that while you pack your bric-a-brac and your favorite clothes. Everything else that doesn't belong to the landlord goes into black garbage bags, which we'll dump on the way."

"Do I have to keep on pretending to be Nellie Fine-man?"

"Once you're in the car, no. We'll burn our fake licenses. I got the real ones and our passports out of the safe-deposit box, along with your good jewelry."

"I can wear it again?"

"You can once we're out of here."

"Sol, you didn't tell me how you're going to make a living."

"We've got what we saved, and I've got five million that would have been Sam's."

Her jaw dropped. "Say that number again?"

"Five million," Sol repeated. "Dollars. Cash."

"How?"

"It's a long story. We'll stop at that diner on the way for dinner, and I'll tell you all about it."

They went to work.

IN THE AFTERNOON, Sol rented a truck downtown, using a fake license, and drove it to their apartment building. There were only a dozen boxes and as many garbage bags to load, then Sol took care of the super, then dropped a check to the landlord into a mailbox for the four months remaining on their lease. Nellie got the car from the garage down the street, and Sol followed her to the West Side Highway, then turned north, along the Hudson.

LESS THAN AN HOUR LATER, two detectives knocked on the door of Sol's apartment but got no answer. One of them tried the knob, and it was unlocked. "Police!" he called out. "Sol Fineman?" They walked into the apartment and found it empty of people and neat as a pin; the keys were on the coffee table. "The Finemans have legged it," the other detective said.

They went downstairs and knocked on the super's door.

A man in an undershirt holding a cigar opened the door. "Yeah?"

"I'm looking for the Finemans," the detective said.

"Apartment 2A," the man said, and made to close the door. It was stopped by the detective's foot.

"We've been there. The Finemans appear to have moved out."

"Today?"

"When was the last time you saw them?"

"This morning, when I was on the way to work. We said hello. I got back half an hour ago. They're gone?"

"They're gone."

"Well, that's between them and the landlord. Is the furniture still there?"

"Yes. You live here alone?"

"Yeah, super is a part-time thing. I get my rent and a few bucks. Rest of the time I drive a cab."

"Who's the landlord?"

The super gave him a name and address.

"Some policemen are going to come tomorrow and have a look around the apartment," the detective said. "I've already taped the door. Stay out of there until they're done."

"Okay," the man said. "Can I finish eating my supper now?"

"Knock yourself out," the detective said, and he and his partner left.

The super took another look at the two one-hundred-dollar bills Fineman had given him. Easily earned, he thought.

SOL AND NELLIE Fineman had driven north. Carl and Cindy Blankenship got out of their vehicles, went into the diner, took a booth, and ordered drinks and dinner.

"All right," Cindy said, "tell me, and don't leave anything out."

"It's like this—Sam bought a picture from a junkie for a hundred bucks. He thought it might be worth more than that, and he looked into it. First, the cops came looking for it, but I got it out of the building. Next, a guy came with a briefcase full of cash and told Sam the insurance company would give him a million for it. Sam knew better, and he said he wanted five million. The insurance company wouldn't bite, but Sam knew somebody who would, and he sent me to see the guy with the picture. He took one look and told me to come back later. I drove around in Sam's car with the picture for a couple of hours, being sure not to get a ticket for anything, then I went back to see the guy and he gave me a suitcase full of hundred-dollar bills.

"I drove back to the bar, and it's crawling with cops. I saw an ambulance drive away, but I didn't know who was in it. I got a call this morning from a nurse at the hospital telling me Sam had bought it."

"And the suitcase?"

"It's in the truck. What else was I supposed to do with it?"

Cindy smiled. "You did the right thing, sweetheart."

They finished their dinner and continued their drive up the Hudson and to the house they had bought three years before, where they unloaded the boxes and the suitcases.

"Carl," Cindy said when they had finished, "how are we going to handle the money?"

"We're going to hide it in the basement and dip into it from time to time. We'll pay cash for everything. Later, when the heat is off, we'll drive down to Florida and get a charter flight to the Cayman Islands, where we'll open a numbered bank account. They'll issue us credit cards, and we'll spend the money that way. Maybe we'll buy a condo in Florida. Nobody will ever touch us. Sol and Nellie Fineman are no more."

"I like it," she said.

"Let's unpack our stuff and break down the boxes. I'll get rid of the empty boxes and the garbage bags and our cell phones, and tomorrow morning I'll drive the truck back to the rental place, then take the train back here."

"And we'll start our new life?"

"That's the idea. The few people who know us around here know us as the Blankenships."

Cindy found a bottle of scotch, and they toasted the Blankenships.

43

STONE LET DINO into the house. "Sorry, I didn't feel up to a restaurant. Helene is making us dinner."

"I hope you didn't get out of the hospital too soon," Dino replied, following Stone upstairs.

"I called the doctor, and he says it's normal for me to feel tired for a day or two." He sat Dino down in the study and poured them both a drink. "How'd you do on the phone numbers from Sam Spain's cell?"

"Art Masi is running them down. He could have something for us tomorrow. This is not going to be easy, you know. If Sam laid it off on some buyer, nobody's going to admit buying it, and if they did, it will be with cash from a mattress—there won't be any bank records."

"Don't depress me any further."

"Why are you depressed?"

"The doctor said a blow to the head can do that. Also, I'll get a very nice finder's fee if I recover the thing."

"And you're depressed about that?"

"I'm depressed because it looks like it's not happening."

"What if Art recovers it?"

"I've made a deal with Art."

"So this search is off the books?"

"It just never happened. If it's found, I'll return it to its rightful owner, Arthur Steele can cancel payment on the theft, and you can take the picture off your computer so people will stop looking for it."

"Okay."

"If all that happens fairly quickly, there will be a nice gift in it for you, too."

"Are you trying to bribe me, you sonofabitch?"

"Certainly not, I'm trying to reward you."

"Oh, I guess that's okay."

"Where's Viv this time?"

"In Cincinnati, I think. I've stopped trying to keep track. How come you're not seeing Morgan tonight, instead of me?"

"Well, she's prettier, I'll give you that, but she demands a certain energy level that I can't meet in my reduced state."

"Oh, did I mention that Sol Fineman has disappeared? Two detectives went to his apartment and it had been cleaned out—and I mean *cleaned*. Not even a print in the place. Nobody knows nothing, of course."

"Somehow I don't think he ran from the attempted-murder charge."

"You think he's sold the painting and scampered?"

"I heard Sam tell him to deliver it. That meant he would have gotten paid for it, and Sam wanted five million for it. He may even have gotten that much. No, I think Sol has, shall we say, relocated?"

"That's a good word."

"And with Sam's money."

"Certainly."

"Ten to one, his cell phone is no longer in service," Stone said.

"I won't take that bet. He's probably on the road somewhere between here and Key West. Maybe I should put out an APB."

"Don't bother. If Sol is careful enough for Sam to trust him with a lot of cash, he's careful enough to have an identity ready to fall back on."

Stone's cell phone buzzed, and he answered.

"Hey, it's Art Masi."

"Good evening, Art. You find something?"

"I've got a couple of good possibilities, but all these gallery people know me. You want to help me out in the morning? We need somebody who looks and sounds like a credible buyer."

"Sure."

"I'll give you a call around ten AM."

"See you then." He hung up.

"What's up?" Dino asked.

"Art wants me to do a couple of walk-ins at galleries tomorrow morning. He thinks they'll think I'm a credible buyer."

"Makes sense."

Helene brought dinner, and Stone opened a bottle of wine. They dined silently for a few minutes.

"Do you have anything new about the people attacking cars with sledgehammers?"

"We've had no new reports of that activity. My guys on the case think they've crawled back into their shells and we won't hear from them again."

"That's okay with me," Stone said. "I have a thought about something else."

"Okay, spill it," Dino said. "I don't want to have to guess."

"I think it's just possible that Angelo Farina's son, Pio, and his girlfriend, Ann Kusch, are credible suspects in Mark Tillman's murder."

"You have any evidence of either, or just a wild hair up your ass?"

"Probably more of the latter than the former."

"Tell me about it."

"Couple of things. Ann told me that Pio always dresses in black, and at the time she told me that, she was dressed in black, too. They're both mountain and rock climbers and would have the skills to rappel down the side of a building."

"And that's all you've got?"

"Sort of."

"How about a motive for either crime?" Dino asked.

"Art theft—they would have the necessary contacts for unloading the picture."

"True enough, but by their own account, they took the picture to FedEx and shipped it back to Mark Tillman."

"Maybe they planned to steal it later, when a few days had passed between the murder and the picture being delivered. Or maybe it wasn't a murder, but an accident during the attempted theft."

"Stone, your theory is so full of holes as to be unworthy of consideration."

Stone sighed. "I know."

"You know," Dino said, "it's a good thing you're not a cop anymore. I'd have to fire you."

"And I couldn't give you an argument," Stone replied. "I like those kids, and I don't want them to be involved in this."

"But you felt you had to bring up the black clothes and the rock climbing?"

"I think that was just a way of clearing my head. I knew you'd shoot me down."

"I'm always happy to do that," Dino said.

44

STONE MET ART MASI at a coffee shop uptown. "Okay, Art, what have we got?"

"The calls on Sam's phone are a mishmash—a trucking company, a liquor distributor, a glassware supplier, mostly people he'd legitimately be in touch with for the running of his business, the bar."

"Anything else?"

"Two art galleries and a small auction house. One of the galleries is new, open about four months. The other is an old-line place, going back to the twenties, a third generation in charge."

"And the auction house?"

"A year and a half old, the sort of place that operates out of a gallery-like premises and rents hotel ballrooms for their auctions. They deal in everything from jewelry and wristwatches to high-end paintings and sculptures, most of them not the artist's best work."

"Sounds a little seedy. I like that."

"The galleries are closer, in the Sixties and Seventies.

The auctioneer is up in the Nineties, so let's do the galleries first. Did you bring your car?"

"It's outside."

"Okay, the Haynesfield Gallery is around the corner on Madison, on your right. I'll work the other side of the street. Whistle if you need me."

Stone got into the Bentley and gave Fred his instructions. "Slowly," he said, "we're window-shopping. The Haynesfield Gallery, on your right."

"Yes, sir," Fred replied. He drew to a slow halt outside. Stone got out of the car and checked out what was in the window. An abused Picasso print, not very large but with a matting and a heavy rococo frame, was the central exhibit. He went inside.

A tall, thin young man wearing a skinny-cut black suit with stovepipe legs and a short jacket was leaning against the rear wall, working on a puzzle in a folded newspaper. "Just a sec, be right with you," he called out.

Stone circumnavigated the small room, not finding a thing worth hanging in a powder room. Two words— cheap and nasty—characterized the place.

The young man finished his puzzle, tossed it on a counter, and came forward. "Now," he said, "what can I do you for?"

"I don't see anything good enough to buy," Stone replied.

"Well, what are you looking for?"

"Something special, something that will knock my girlfriend's eye out when she sees it."

"I gotcha. How about a Jackson Pollock?"

"She doesn't like abstracts, she likes a landscape, especially of the post-impressionist period."

"And when was that?"

"Right after the impressionist period."

"Like a Matisse?"

"More like, what's his name, who cut off his ear?"

"Ah, van Gogh. I might be able to find you something, but I warn you, it's going to be expensive."

"Money is not a problem—not that I don't want a good price. Show me what you've got."

"Let me root around in the back," the young man said.

"Go right ahead." He disappeared through a rear door.

Stone found a wobbly chair and sat down. Ten minutes passed before the young man returned.

"My colleague is looking for the van Gogh," he said. "In the meantime, I thought you might enjoy seeing this." He held up a very good Matisse.

Stone waved him closer. He was no expert, but the picture seemed authentic. He immediately thought of Angelo Farina. "How much?" he asked.

"Ninety thousand," the young man said. "I might be able to do a little better, but not much."

That wasn't much for a Matisse, Stone thought; if it wasn't Angelo's, it was hot. "Show me some provenance," he said.

"Of course." He handed Stone the picture, went to his desk, and leafed through a three-ring binder. He unsnapped the rings, removed a sheet in a plastic sleeve, and brought it over to Stone. He took back the picture and handed Stone the sheet.

"Purchased from the artist in 1899 by Eli Cornfield, a Paris gallery owner. Purchased from him in 1907 by Baron Nathan Rothschild, from Cornfield's London gallery. Bequeathed to Baron Jacob Rothschild in 1936. Removed from England in 1939 and given to Baron Edmond Rothschild, who hid it with many other works.

Auctioned from the estate of Hermann Göring, 1948, purchased by a descendant of Eli Cornfield."

"What then?" Stone asked.

"We believe the second Cornfield gave it to an American nephew, who sold it to a private owner in the 1990s. After that, we assume that his estate disposed of it, either as a bequest or in a sale to a private collector. We purchased it from that collector's estate."

"Can you document all of this?" Stone asked.

"Not so much the latter part."

"I see. I'd like to bring a friend of mine to see it. If he likes it, I'll make an offer."

"Fine, but no lowballs, please."

Stone walked to the front of the gallery and called Art Masi. "Do they know you at the Haynesfield Gallery?"

"I doubt it," Art said.

"They've got what looks like either a fantastic copy of a Matisse or a stolen one with a fantastic provenance. Come and look at it." Stone hung up and went back to his chair. "He'll be here shortly. Do you take credit cards?"

"Possibly," the young man said. "Excuse me a moment." He went into the back room and came out with a short, bearded man in a baggy suit, who introduced himself as Conrad Haynesfield.

"I understand you're interested in the Matisse," he said.

"My art advisor is on the way to give me an opinion."

"It's one of the best Matisses I've ever seen in private hands," the man said.

"How did you come by it?"

Art Masi strode through the front door and came to Stone, who introduced him to Haynesfield. Art took the painting from the young man and went to the window to see it in sunlight.

"You were telling me how you came by it," Stone said.

Art came back and stood by Stone. "I like it," he said.

"Mr. Haynesfield was just telling me how he came by it," Stone said.

"You will notice that, at ninety thousand, it is very cheap," Haynesfied said to Masi.

"Yes, I did notice that. Tell us why."

"You will notice that the provenance includes a period of ownership by Hermann Göring?"

"I noticed," Stone replied.

"Works of art with that sort of provenance cannot be successfully offered at public auction. Therefore, it behooves us to be reasonable, with regard to price. You understand?"

"Oh, yes, I understand," Stone said. He looked at Art, who nodded. "I'll take it," Stone said, producing a checkbook.

"Splendid," Haynesfield said. "I'm sure it will add substance to your collection."

"I'll make arrangements to transport it to your home, Mr. Barrington. You conclude the transaction," Art said. He took out his phone and walked away for privacy.

"Would you make it out to cash, please?" Haynesfield said.

"I'll need a receipt and the provenance on your letterhead," Stone replied.

"Of course."

Stone wrote out the check, payable to the Haynesfield Gallery, and handed it over.

Haynesfield looked at it. "I don't think I made myself clear," he said.

"Oh, you were very clear," Stone said, "but I don't think it's in my interests to handle the transaction that way."

"As you wish," Haynesfield said. "Shall we wrap the picture?"

"Thank you, just some bubble wrap."

He handed it to the young colleague, who took it to the back of the gallery.

TEN MINUTES WENT BY, then two of Art Masi's detectives walked into the gallery and flashed badges.

"I don't understand," Haynesfield said. "I was just selling this gentleman a Picasso print. Everything is entirely in order."

"Henderson!" Masi shouted, and another detective emerged from the back room carrying a painting in bubble wrap. The young gallery employee was in his other hand, in cuffs.

Masi took the painting and tore away the wrapping. "Ah, a Picasso print," he said.

"One moment," Henderson replied. He went to the back and came back with the Matisse. "There must have been some mistake," he said.

The detectives departed with Haynesfield, the young man, and the Matisse.

"Shall we get on to the next gallery?" Masi asked.

"Of course. What did you think of the Matisse?"

"A very fine one, worth at least half a million."

"Will you be able to get it back to its owner?"

"I expect so," Masi said. "We have an expert on that work."

45

STONE GOT INTO THE BENTLEY and gave Fred his instructions to the Eisl Gallery.

"Yes, sir," Fred replied. Masi got out a block short, and Fred continued to the Eisl Gallery. He drew to a slow halt outside.

To Stone's astonishment, one of his mother's paintings was displayed in the window. He walked in; a small woman sat behind a desk.

"Good morning," she said.

"Good morning. I wonder if you could tell me something about the painting in the window?"

"The Stone? Let me get Mr. Eisl for you, he's our expert on Stone." She telephoned, and a tall, elegantly dressed man came out of the rear of the gallery.

"Good morning," he said. "You are interested in the Stone painting?"

"I'd like to know something about it," Stone replied.

Eisl went to the window, removed the painting, and set it on a vacant easel. "There we are. It's a Central Park scene by Matilda Stone, who is noted for her very fine paintings of New York."

Stone inspected the painting closely. It was undoubtedly his mother's work; he remembered when she was painting it. "What are you asking for it?"

"Let me check," Eisl said. He went to the desk and the woman handed him a ledger. He turned a few pages and ran a finger down one, then returned. "Two hundred and fifty thousand," he said.

"As much as that?"

"Stone's work only rarely is found in a gallery. Most of her paintings are in private collections or museums. She has four in the American Collection at the Metropolitan."

"Will you accept two hundred thousand for it?"

"I'm afraid that's a bit too close to what I paid for it," Eisl said. "Say, two hundred twenty-five?"

"Two hundred and ten," Stone said, with a note of finality.

Eisl sighed. "Well, all right. If it's cash, I suppose so." Stone wrote the man a check and handed it to him.

"Ah, I see your first name is Stone. Any relation to the artist?"

"She was my mother," Stone replied.

Eisl looked for any trace of irony in his customer's face. "Truly?"

"Truly."

"Shall I deliver it to you? I assume you're in the city."

"I am, but my car is outside. Just some bubble wrap will do."

Eisl handed it to the woman, who took it into the rear of the gallery.

"Are you looking for anything else, Mr. Barrington?"

"I'm always in the market for something very individual, something not everyone has." Hook baited.

"I have something quite remarkable," Eisl said. "It's by a very famous artist, but its provenance, while fascinating, is not everything we would wish."

"What artist?"

"It's at my warehouse," Eisl said. "I received it quite recently. If you have a few minutes, I'll send for it."

"What artist?"

"I think you may recognize him when you see the picture."

"All right, I'll look around a bit more. Half an hour?"

"That would be fine."

Stone took the wrapped painting, walked out, and put it into his trunk. He tapped on a window and it came down. "Fred, please lock the trunk," he said. He heard it lock.

His cell phone rang. "Yes?"

"It's Art. Was that the picture in your hand?"

"No, it's something I bought. Eisl says he has something at his warehouse by a famous artist. He wouldn't say who, but he's sent for it. I'll go back in half an hour."

"Sounds like I should ask for some backup."

"Not yet." Stone walked up one side of Madison, then down the other, then he went into the gallery.

The woman was on the phone, so he waited, taking himself on a tour of Eisl's pictures. Ten minutes passed, and she hung up. "Shall I call Mr. Eisl for you?"

"Yes, thank you."

She picked up the phone, and a moment later Eisl appeared. "Ah, Mr. Barrington, the painting is on its way and should be here momentarily. May I offer you coffee or tea?" He waved Stone to a chair.

"Coffee, thanks, black."

Stone took a seat. Eisl spoke to the young woman, who went to the rear and returned with a small tray. The phone rang, and she answered it. "For you," she said to Eisl. "Rocco Maggio."

Stone had heard that name somewhere.

Eisl picked up the phone. "Yes?" He listened for a moment.

Stone saw the color drain from his face.

"Say that again?" Eisl listened. "What are we to do?" He listened again, then hung up and went to where Stone sat.

"I'm very sorry, Mr. Barrington, but the painting is not available for viewing at this time."

"Why not?" Stone asked, looking surprised.

"There has been a mix-up. Perhaps by this time tomorrow . . ."

"Where is your warehouse?" Stone asked.

"On Twelfth Avenue, but the public are not allowed on the premises for security reasons."

"Has something happened to the painting?"

"I'm not at liberty to discuss that, I'm afraid."

"Then perhaps you'll tell me who the artist is?"

"Let us say, after van Gogh."

"*After* van Gogh?"

"As I mentioned earlier, there are some difficulties about the provenance, so I am not in a position to guarantee its authenticity—not yet, anyway. I expect that to change when the painting is in my hands. I trust my own judgment above all others."

"All right," Stone said, getting up and giving the man his card.

"I'll ring you the moment I have news," Eisl said.

Stone thanked him, got into the car, and said to Fred, "Take a left, then stop." He called Art Masi. "I'm around the corner. Join me."

Masi got into the car. "Where are we going?"

"To Twelfth Avenue."

46

STONE INSTRUCTED FRED to drive to Forty-second Street and turn right on Twelfth Avenue.

"What's this little trip about?" Art Masi asked.

"Does the name Rocco Maggio ring a bell?"

Art's brow wrinkled. "Yes, but I can't place it."

"Same here."

"Sounds like a baseball player."

"That's DiMaggio."

"Oh, yeah."

"Think mob," Stone said.

Art thought. "Pietro Maggio," he said.

"Not Pietro, Rocco."

"Pietro was Rocco's father—a rather elegant New Jersey don, died five or six years ago. Had a decent art collection—paintings, sculpture."

"Any of it stolen?"

"Not that hung in his house. I got to have a close look at it once, with a warrant on a non-art case. He was rumored, though, to have moved the proceeds of a couple

of big-time art heists—one in Boston, one in Philadel-
phia."

"Were any of the pieces ever found?"

"Not a single one," Art said. "Overall value, a hundred
and fifty million, and that was ten, twelve years ago. Who
knows what it would be now, with all the billionaires bidding."

"How old is Rocco?"

"Maybe mid-forties."

"Any record?"

Art got out his cell phone and tapped away at it for a
couple of minutes. "Nothing but parking tickets."

"How many?"

Art tapped some more. "More than a hundred grand's
worth. Apparently all of New York is a parking lot to
Rocco."

They reached Twelfth Avenue and turned uptown. All
that Stone knew about the area was a big car wash and a
number of taxi garages. Yellow cabs were parked on the
side streets. A couple of more blocks, and Stone told Fred
to pull over. He did. "Back up a few feet." Fred did.
"Now hand me the binoculars in the glove compartment." Fred forked them over.

Stone trained the glasses on a spot halfway up the block
from Twelfth Avenue. "Art, see that sign, maybe six doors
up the street? The little one, near the top of the building?"

"Yes," Art said.

Stone handed him the glasses. "See if your eyes are
better than mine."

Art gazed at the sign and fiddled with the focus. "Eisl,"
he said.

"Take a right, Fred," Stone said. "Stop halfway up the
block on the right." Fred did so.

"Now, Art," Stone said, "before we cross the street

and make nuisances of ourselves or get rousted, maybe shot, tell me more about Rocco Maggio."

Art started Googling. "He's on the board of a couple of lesser museums downtown. Goes to a lot of artsy cocktail parties with fashionable women a lot younger than himself. Used to be a member of the Italian-American Anti-Defamation League—remember that one?"

"Yes, I believe it sort of faded after its chairman got himself wasted at a clam house in Little Italy."

"Right. That was twelve, fifteen years ago, when Rocco was a lot younger."

"Weren't we all?" Stone said. "I think this guy shapes up as a pretty good suspect."

"So do I," Art said. More tapping. "I thought that maybe there'd be a connection to the Eisl Gallery, that he was on the board or something, but he's not."

"And yet when Mr. Eisl calls his warehouse for the van Gogh to be brought over, he gets a call back from Rocco Maggio. Rocco doesn't strike me as a guy who works part-time as a warehouseman."

"Me, either," Art said.

"Is there a lot of art theft in New York these days, Art?"

"More than you might think. It's mostly burglaries—they take the jewelry and the silver, then maybe grab a picture or two. That's how somebody like Sam Spain gets involved. There's a museum robbery every few years, but surprisingly few big-time pieces are taken from private collections, like Tillman's. The security arrangements are pretty tight in those cases—the insurance companies insist."

"Still," Stone said, "an important piece every year or two could make it a profitable business, what with the big-time artists pulling down multimillion-dollar sales at auction. That should create a market for bargain, under-the-counter sales to unscrupulous buyers."

"You're right, it does," Masi agreed.

"Google Maggio's business connections. Let's see what his legitimate connections are."

Art tapped away. "Ah," he said, "shipping."

"What kind of shipping?"

"He's got a company that handles small-lot goods—you know, for companies that can't fill a container on their own—and . . . oh, good, an air-freight company."

"How could he compete with FedEx or DSL in that market?"

"You want to ship a grand piano, or maybe a horse or two, the big boys aren't going to deliver those to your door—or your stable. They're also not going to put multimillion-dollar artworks in their delivery trucks, or insure big-ticket items. There's a market for specialty shippers. If you want to take your Bentley along on a European vacation, for instance. Some of them even have passenger compartments, so you can travel with your goods."

"It sounds like the sort of service that could ship a stolen painting one way and bring back a suitcase or a hay bale full of cash," Stone said.

"You know," Art said, "if we could make a case for a warrant, we might find all sorts of stuff in the Eisl warehouse."

"I'm inclined to agree," Stone said, "but we come up short in the probable-cause category, so I think we're going to have to confine ourselves to a look around the place."

"Getting caught at that sort of thing is a career ender for me, Stone. I've got my pension to think about. I don't think you ought to go in there alone, either. I mean, I can come running if I hear gunshots, but when you hear gunshots you're often too late."

"You know," Stone said, "there was a time when I would just barge into a place like that, and the hell with the guards. Nowadays, I'm more likely to hire somebody to do it for me."

"Good idea," Art said.

"Is there anybody on your personal services list who might qualify for that sort of excursion?"

"I might be able to come up with a name or two," Art said. "But you'd need to handle those arrangements your-self."

"Put on your thinking cap, Art," Stone said. "And, by the way, how long would it take to scare up an arrest warrant for a hundred grand's worth of unpaid parking tickets?"

"Dino could do it pretty fast."

Stone called Dino.

47

DINO ANSWERED. "Bacchetti."

"It's Stone. You know a guy named Rocco Maggio?"

"I know a Pietro Maggio, a Jersey don."

"Pietro's son."

"I haven't had the pleasure."

"I think he's mixed up in the fencing of our van Gogh."

"You think he has possession?"

"It's a possibility. I went to the Eisl Gallery on Madison this morning and made noises about wanting something special. Eisl himself bit and said he had something by a famous artist, but with a dicey provenance. It was at his warehouse, come back in half an hour. When I came back, he got a call from Rocco Maggio, and when he heard what Maggio had to say, he went all white and said the picture was unavailable, to come back tomorrow. Art Masi and I are at Eisl's warehouse now."

"I haven't heard any probable cause for a warrant," Dino said.

"I know. What we need, in a hurry, is an arrest warrant

for Rocco Maggio for a hundred grand's worth of unpaid parking tickets."

Dino snorted. "That shouldn't be much of a problem. You're at the warehouse now?"

"Parked across the street. It might be nice if you could get his car towed, too."

"Go get some lunch. I'll call a judge and send a detective up there with your arrest warrant. Where will you be?"

"Ah, Caravaggio, on the East Side. Call me when he's on his way," Stone said, then hung up.

"I like the restaurant," Art said.

"So do I." Stone gave Fred the address, and when they arrived, he told Fred to go home and have some lunch and to be back in an hour and a half.

They ordered pasta and some wine.

"I have an idea," Stone said, "that Rocco Maggio is where Eisl got the cash to buy the painting. Not many people have a few million in cash lying around. Do you think Maggio could unload the thing overnight? I mean, Eisl thought it was at the warehouse, until Maggio broke the news to him on the phone."

"If stolen art is the business Maggio is in," Art said, "then he'll have a number of clients with a taste for rare art and no scruples about provenance. And he's got shipping at his fingertips, so the answer is yes."

"And it's possible that it could already have left the country."

"Absolutely. Maggio's shipping company website has a Boeing 737 on the title page. That could go almost anywhere with a fuel stop or two. Transatlantic would be no problem."

"That would cost a lot of fuel to transport something that weighs less than five pounds."

"Maybe he had a horse or two to ship, as well."

*   *   *

THEY WERE ON ESPRESSOS when Dino called.

"Are you still at Caravaggio?"

"Yes."

"Lucky sonofabitch," Dino replied. "I'm having a salami sandwich at my desk."

"Did you get us the warrant?"

"My guy's leaving the court now. He'll be there in half an hour." He hung up.

THE DETECTIVE dropped off the warrant. "You want some backup? I'm free."

"We don't anticipate any trouble," Stone said. "Still . . . what's your name?"

"Andy Farina."

"Any relation to Angelo Farina, the painter?"

"He's my first cousin."

"Small world. Are you in a car?"

"Yep."

"Follow us. We're in the Bentley outside."

They went out, got the cars, and headed back to the West Side. "Andy," Stone said, "give me your cell number and wait here for us."

"What if I hear shooting?"

"Assume it's at us, and get in there," Stone replied.

He and Art got out of the Bentley and walked into the warehouse. A man sat in a glass booth, reading a *Racing Form*. Stone tapped on the glass. "Rocco Maggio, please?"

The man looked them up and down. "What's your business?"

"The kind you'd rather not know about," Stone replied.

The man picked up the phone and pressed a button. "Mr. Maggio? Two gents down here to see you." He covered the phone. "What's your names?"

"Mr. Barrington and Mr. Masi."

He relayed that information and listened, then hung up. "Third floor. Elevator's over there. His office is at the rear of the building."

It was a freight elevator, but it beat climbing stairs. They got off and started walking toward the end of the building; there were stairs up half a floor, and a man stood at a window, watching them come.

Stone rapped at the door, then let Masi precede him.

"Rocco Maggio?" Masi asked.

Maggio pointed at a nameplate on his desk. "Who else?"

"Mr. Maggio," Masi said, flashing his badge and tossing the warrant onto his desk, "you're under arrest for the non-payment of a hundred and twenty-two thousand, three hundred and twenty dollars in unpaid parking tickets." He walked around the desk and produced handcuffs. "Stand up."

Maggio gaped at him. "You're kidding," he said.

"I said stand up. You want me to help you?"

Maggio stood up. "Listen, gentlemen, this is unnecessary. I'll write you a check right now." He reached for a desk drawer, but Masi clapped a cuff on that hand, spun him around, and cuffed the other hand, then he frisked the man thoroughly and came up with a small 9mm pistol.

"I've got a permit for that," Maggio said. "It's in my wallet. You can get it out for me, inside jacket pocket, left."

"Are you attempting to bribe me, Mr. Maggio?"

"No, no, listen, we don't have to go through all this."

"Let's go," Masi said. He marched the man to the elevator, then they rode down to street level, with Maggio protesting all the way.

Outside, Stone said, "Would you prefer the Ford or the Bentley?"

"Are you kidding me?" Maggio asked. He looked around. "Hey, my car is gone—it's been stolen!"

"I would imagine," Stone said, "that given your history as a scofflaw, the NYPD finally got around to towing it."

"Oh, shit!" Maggio yelled as he got into the Bentley.

Stone put him in the rear seat, then got in beside him. "I thought we'd have a little chat on the way downtown," he said.

"About what?" Maggio asked.

"Art," Stone replied.

48

FRED HEADED THEM DOWNTOWN. Nobody said anything for a few minutes. Finally, Rocco Maggio did.

"This can't be about parking tickets," he said. "I've gotta get my car back. Can we run by the towing place so I can do that now?"

"That's not the procedure," Masi said. "Your car is safe. You can get it out when you're out. It will still be there."

"C'mon, guys, how can I fix this? My kid's got a soccer game in Jersey later, and if I miss another one my wife will kill me, then divorce me."

"In that order?" Stone asked.

"Are you married?" Maggio demanded.

"No."

"Then you wouldn't have a clue what I'm up against here. Can't you empathize, just a little bit?"

"I don't remember them covering empathy at the academy, do you, Art?"

"Nope."

"Look," Maggio said, pleading in his voice, "I'm not

trying to bribe anybody, I'm just asking, sincerely, what can I do to fix this?"

"Well, paying your parking tickets is a start," Stone said.

"I've got a checkbook in my pocket," Maggio replied.

"But that alone won't do it."

"What else, then?"

Stone and Masi exchanged a glance. "You could return some stolen goods," Masi said.

Maggio's eyes narrowed. "What kind of goods?"

"I don't know," Masi said, "what kind of stolen goods have you handled lately?"

"C'mon, give me a hint. I'll help if I can."

"Oh, you can," Stone said. "Here's a hint—it's a painting by a famous artist, but with a dicey provenance."

Masi looked out the window but said nothing.

"Doesn't that sound just a little bit familiar?" Stone asked.

Still nothing.

"Okay, try this—you loaned André Eisl the money to buy it."

"Doesn't sound familiar," Maggio said.

"You're not trying hard enough, Rocco," Masi said.

"I don't know how I can help you. Anything else?"

"Well, a few days at Rikers Island while we sort out the tickets might improve your memory."

"That would make you a no-show at your son's soccer match," Stone chimed in. "Maybe several matches."

Maggio flinched, as if something had bitten him. "You want me to incriminate myself."

"Well, Rocco," Masi said, "give us what we want, and maybe you'll make the soccer match, and maybe you'll walk—if you give us *all* the information we need."

"This is screwy," Maggio said. "You walk into my place

of business wearing really expensive suits, and tell me you're cops."

"I showed you my badge," Masi said.

"How about him?" Maggio asked, jerking his head toward Stone.

Stone produced his own badge.

"And you're riding around in a Bentley?"

"The department doesn't own that," Stone said.

"I'm in the shipping business, not the art business."

"Describe your relationship to André Eisl," Stone said.

"He's an old friend. I help him out once in a while."

"Help him out at, say, ten points a week?" Masi asked.

Maggio shrugged. "I do what I can to help my friends."

"You're a prince of a guy, Rocco," Stone said.

"Yeah," Masi chimed in, "and listen to this. We're going to find that picture, one way or another, with your help or without it. If we find it without your help, we're going to nail you for fencing it and transporting it, and you're going to miss all your son's soccer matches until he's in his forties."

"On the other hand . . ." Stone said, letting Maggio finish the sentence in his head.

"I'll walk? If I tell you where the picture is, you'll guarantee it?"

"We've made our best offer, Rocco," Masi said. "You can pick it up or just let it lie there."

"It's not as simple as that—it's complicated."

"Explain it to us," Stone said. "We'll do our best to follow."

"If I give up the picture, two people are going to die."

"Which two?" Stone asked.

"Eisl and me."

"Tell us why, Rocco."

"Eisl, because he can't pay back the money I loaned him. Me, because I loaned it to him."

"So you're telling us that there are people above you who control all your actions?" Masi asked.

"Not all my actions, but I hardly ever have five million lying around the office."

"Okay," Masi said, "let's start with whose safe the money came from."

"Come on, if I wander that far astray my family dies, too."

"Okay, we'll leave out that part of the story," Masi said. "Let's start with Eisl's first phone call to you about the picture."

Maggio sighed. "Okay, he calls me and says he can lay his hands on an honest-to-God van Gogh for five mil."

"And you bought that, sight unseen?"

"Not exactly. I got a good look at it. This guy brought it to the gallery."

"Are you an art expert, with a specialty in van Goghs?" Stone asked.

"No, but I've got my ear to the ground. If something big turns up stolen, I'll hear about it. Sometimes."

"And you heard about the van Gogh?"

"Everybody in town heard about the van Gogh a year and a half ago. Lately, things went quiet, then this guy Sam Spain, up in Harlem, says he's got his hands on it."

"Yeah, we know about Sam Spain. We want to know about you and Eisl."

"Well, Eisl makes an appointment with Spain, and he sends his guy over with a picture in a laundry bag."

"This would be Sol Fineman?"

"Listen, if you know all this, why do I have to tell you?"

"Go on with your story."

"Okay, we look at it, we compare it to the notice on the Internet that went out when it was stolen from this guy Tillman. I ask Eisl if it's the real thing."

"And you have faith in his opinion?"

"André is a third- or fourth-generation art dealer," Maggio said. "His grandfather, I think, started in Vienna, then Hitler comes along and his father beats it out of Europe with a shipment of art and makes his way to New York."

"How does one get from Vienna to New York with a shipment of art in, what, 1938?"

"He chartered an airplane and flew to Lisbon, then to the Azores, then to Newfoundland, then to New York. He had Swiss francs and gold, and he spread it around on his long flight."

"So you took Eisl's word for the authenticity of the picture?" Stone asked.

"Yeah, I did. André said he could turn it in twenty-four hours for twenty mil."

"And?"

"And I made a phone call," Maggio said. "The money was there in an hour."

"Okay, Rocco," Masi said, "let's get to the point. Where's the picture now?"

Maggio heaved a large sigh. "In the trunk of my car."

49

STONE JABBED MAGGIO in the ribs. "The car that was towed?"

"That's the one," Maggio replied.

"How did it get in the trunk of your car?"

"I gave Sol Fineman a suitcase with five mil in it, then I put the picture back in the laundry bag and put it in the trunk of my car. André Eisl didn't want it in the gallery, and I didn't want it in my office. The trunk seemed a safe enough place."

"And now it's in the police garage," Masi said. "I'd say the trunk is safe enough there."

"Fred," Stone asked, "do you know where the police garage is?"

"Ah, er, yessir," Fred said hesitantly.

"And how do you happen to have that information?"

"Well, Mr. Barrington, I had occasion to visit that place—once before."

"What occasion was that?"

"The occasion when this car was towed. I'm terribly

sorry, sir, I just ran into a deli to get a sandwich, and when I came out it was gone."

"And when was this?"

"About a month ago."

"That was when I couldn't find you for a couple of hours, wasn't it?"

"It could very well have been, sir."

"All right, forget it, Fred, just take us to the garage."

"Yes, sir."

Stone leaned back in the seat. "What kind of car is it, Rocco?"

"It's a Maybach," Rocco replied. He pronounced it "My-bach."

"What is that?" Masi asked.

"It's a sort of super-Mercedes," Stone replied. "They made it for only a few years. At around three hundred and fifty thousand, they weren't selling enough, so they stopped making them. I believe they're doing very well in the used market."

"Business has been good, huh, Rocco?" Masi said.

"Good enough. I got a good deal, it was a repo."

"Let me guess," Stone said. "You gave somebody a very big car loan, and he fell behind on the payments?"

"Something like that," Rocco said.

"Art," Stone said, "call the garage and have them root out the Maybach and have it ready when we get there."

Masi got on the phone, then hung up. "It just arrived. They haven't even put it in the garage yet. They said there had been some damage."

"Damage?" Rocco spat. "Those bastards damaged my Maybach?"

"They didn't damage it, Rocco, it arrived that way. They make a note of any damage every time a car comes in."

"I'll bet the sonsofbitches did it on purpose," Rocco said. "Some people are just envious."

"Oh, stop your whining," Stone said. "You're going to get it back, aren't you?"

"And then you're going to let me go to my kid's soccer match?"

"After we see the painting, Rocco. Not until then."

THEY ARRIVED AT the police garage, and there the Maybach was, staring them in the face with its big eyes.

"Thank God," Rocco said, getting out of the car. "Will you take these cuffs off so I can pay the guy?"

Stone uncuffed him, and Rocco started toward the car.

"Hey!" the cop in charge yelled. "Don't you touch that car until you've paid the tow bill and the ticket."

Rocco reached in his coat pocket for his checkbook. "Sure, how much?"

The cop stared at the sheet on his clipboard. "Seven hundred and eighty dollars," he replied.

"Seven hundred and eighty dollars? Are you kidding me?"

"Ticket is five hundred, plus the tow."

Rocco swore under his breath. "Who do I make the check to?"

"No checks," the cop replied.

Rocco swore again and produced a black American Express card from his wallet.

"We don't take American Express," the cop said. "Visa, MasterCard, or Discover."

"This is the only credit card I use," Rocco said, shaking it in the cop's face.

"Like I give a shit," the cop said. "So you'll have to pay cash."

Rocco put away his wallet and dug into a pocket. He

counted bills. "I've only got six hundred and ten dollars," he said.

"We'll try and be patient while you go and get the cash," the cop said.

Rocco dug into his pocket and came up with an iPhone, then pressed a button. "You got any cash in the till? Bring me three hundred." He gave the address.

"Okay, now," Stone said to the cop, "we need to look in the car. It's a stolen-property thing."

"Knock yourself out," the cop said.

"Okay, Rocco," Masi said, "unlock the trunk."

Rocco got out his keys, and the three of them walked around the car and looked at the trunk. There was a hole the size of a half-dollar in the lid. Masi stuck a finger in the hole and opened the trunk. It was empty.

"I've been robbed!" Rocco yelled. "The picture was in the trunk!" He fingered the hole. "They've fucked up my Maybach!"

"Okay," Masi said, "let's get you booked." He produced the handcuffs.

"Now, wait a minute, guys," Rocco said. "I've cooperated, I've told you everything you wanted to know."

"Not yet, Rocco," Masi said. "Tell us who stole it."

"How should I know?"

Masi reached for a wrist.

"Hang on a minute, Art," Stone said. "Rocco, who knew the picture was in the trunk of your car?"

Rocco looked thoughtful. "Well, André Eisl saw me put it in there, so did Sol Fineman."

"Anyone else know about it?"

Rocco thought about it. "No one else."

"That kind of narrows it down, doesn't it?" Stone said.

"Maybe it was just some junkie, looking for stuff to steal," Masi replied.

"They didn't break into the car," Stone pointed out. "Just the trunk."

"Then the guy we want is Sol Fineman," Masi said.

"Yes," Stone agreed, "and every cop in town has been looking for him since he disappeared from his apartment, with no results, not a trace."

"Oh, shit," Art said.

"He's in the wind," Stone replied.

"Well, gee, fellows, I'm awful sorry about that. The painting getting stolen wasn't part of our deal, though. Can I go to my kid's soccer game?"

"Getting our hands on the picture *was* the deal," Stone said.

"Hey," Masi said to the cop, handing him the arrest warrant, "hold this guy until a squad car can get here to take him in for booking."

"You're going to hold a bunch of parking tickets against me?" Rocco said.

"You could have walked, Rocco," Stone said, "but you didn't come through."

Masi borrowed the cop's handcuffs and cuffed Rocco Maggio to his car door. "See you around, Rocco. Sorry about your kid's soccer match."

"Wait a minute," Rocco said, "maybe I can still help."

"Speak," Stone replied. "You know where we can find Sol Fineman?"

Rocco's face fell. "No, I just have a number."

"Which is now non-working," Masi said. "Have a nice stay at Rikers."

Rocco was weeping when they drove away.

50

A S SOON AS they were back in the car, Stone told Fred to drive them home, then he called Dino.

"Bacchetti."

"It's Stone."

"How'd you do at the garage?"

"The car had been broken into. The picture was gone."

"Oh, shit. Any idea who took it?"

"Our chief suspect is Sol Fineman."

"The invisible man? That Sol Fineman?"

"One and the same. Of course, that's per Rocco Maggio. He says only André Eisl and Fineman saw him put the picture into his trunk."

"Well, if that's all you've got."

"Have you had any reports of Fineman? Anything at all?"

"Hang on, I'll see." Dino put him on hold.

"Dino's checking," Stone said to Masi.

"I'm praying," Art replied.

Dino came back. "Not a fucking trace," he said. "It's like the guy just vaporized."

"We need him bad," Stone said.

"Sorry, pal." Dino hung up.

"Now what?" Masi asked.

"We've still got our list of possible buyers, and we've visited only two of them. What's our next one?"

Art consulted the lists. "First Lot Auctions," he said.

Stone gave Fred the address.

FIRST LOT AUCTIONS occupied a double-wide gallery space on Madison Avenue in the Nineties. Fred double-parked out front so they could see the car, and they went inside. A young blond woman in a tight black dress and chewing gum was dusting pictures and sculptures displayed for the next auction.

She stopped chewing. "Something you wanted to bid on?" she asked. "The sale is tomorrow morning at ten." She resumed chewing.

"No," Stone said, "we'd like to speak to the owner of the place."

"That would be Mr. Marx. He's in London at the moment."

"Who's in charge?"

"Mr. Michaels," she replied. "I'll see if he's available." She disappeared into a back room.

"Why do I think this is futile?" Art asked.

"If you have a better idea . . ."

"No."

The young woman reappeared and resumed her dusting. "He'll be just a moment," she said.

Ten minutes passed. "Let's go," Stone said, heading for the back door, with Masi right behind. The door opened into a hallway, with rooms on each side. In the last one they found a man packing papers into a cardboard box. He seemed startled to see them.

"What do you want?" he asked.

"Mr. Michaels?"

He looked them over. "No, he's gone for the day."

Stone walked over and looked into the cardboard box. He picked up a letter on top of a stack of papers; it was addressed to Mr. Warren Michaels.

"Okay, Warren," Stone said, "what's the rush?"

"Who are you?"

"We represent Sam Spain."

Michaels went a little pale. "Sam Spain is dead. I read it in the *Post*."

"We represent Mr. Spain's estate," Stone said, "and we have reason to believe that you are in possession of some property of Mr. Spain's."

"I'm not. I don't know anything about it."

"About what?"

"Ah . . ."

"It's a picture," Stone said. "A very rare one."

"I don't know."

"You haven't even asked what sort of picture," Stone said.

"I don't need to ask—I don't have anything belonging to Sam Spain."

"Actually, it belongs to Mrs. Mark Tillman," Stone said. "Am I getting through to you?"

Michaels opened a desk drawer, retrieved a sheet of paper, and handed it to Stone. It was the police flyer with a reproduction of the van Gogh. "This is the only thing I know about belonging to a Tillman."

"Then where is it?"

"How should I know?"

"Perhaps you'd rather talk to Sol Fineman about this?" Stone asked.

That had an effect. "Now, wait a minute, I don't want that guy in here again."

"Do you find Mr. Fineman frightening?"

"Yes, I do. The man carries a blackjack."

"Not anymore," Stone said. "We relieved him of that. Still, Mr. Fineman has other methods."

"Please, I don't know anything about this."

"Then how did you become acquainted with Mr. Fineman?"

Michaels's shoulders slumped. "He came to see me."

"And what passed between you?"

"He showed me a picture and asked if I wanted to buy it. Not auction it—he was very clear about that—buy it, for five million dollars. I don't have that kind of cash, and my boss is in a country inn somewhere in England. He wouldn't say where. I knew what it was, of course, from the flyer."

"And you reported this incident to the police?"

"Mr. Fineman made it very clear to me what would happen if I did that. He hit me with the blackjack."

"And then what?"

"When I came to, he was gone." Michaels rubbed a spot behind his ear.

Stone believed him. "Let's get out of here and leave Mr. Michaels alone with his conscience," he said to Masi.

THEY SPENT THE REMAINDER of the day visiting the rest of Masi's list. Everybody denied everything.

"I'm at my wit's end," Stone said.

"I can think of one more place Fineman might have taken the picture," Masi said.

"And where is that?"

"The insurance company."

"Arthur Steele already told Sam Spain to go fuck himself," Stone pointed out. "Why would Fineman go to him?"

"Steele has had time to reconsider. Paying Sol Fineman five million is a lot better than paying Morgan Tillman sixty million."

"No, Arthur hasn't bought it back."

"How do you know that?"

"Because he would have called me, to gloat."

"Gloat?"

"I know Arthur. He's a poor winner."

51

IT WAS NEARLY MIDNIGHT before Rocco Maggio got home, and his wife was still up and fuming.

"I know, I know," he said. "Is Mario still up?"

"He cried himself to sleep," she hissed.

"What could I do? I was in jail!"

"Jail! What have you done now?"

"Nothing, absolutely nothing!"

"Start talking or start packing," she said.

"All right, awready, it was parking tickets."

"Jail? For parking tickets?"

"For . . . a lot of parking tickets."

"How much are we talking about here?"

"Look, we're both tired, let's get some sleep and talk about this tomorrow."

"Let's talk about it *right this minute*!" she spat. "How much?"

"A little over a hundred grand."

"How much over a hundred grand?"

"Twenty-two five, give or take."

"*A hundred and twenty-two thousand five hundred dollars in parking tickets?*"

"Give or take, plus a fine."

"How big a fine?"

"Fifty percent," he murmured.

She picked up her iPhone, opened the calculator, and began punching keys. "A hundred and eighty-three thousand, seven hundred and fifty dollars?"

"Give or take."

"For parking tickets? How long were you in jail?"

"I don't know, sometime after lunch, which I didn't have, until about an hour ago. It took two lawyers and a judge to get me out, and I had to wait for two cashier's checks to be hand-delivered."

"How did you get a bank to write two cashier's checks after closing time?"

"I know people, all right?"

She was calculating again. "Do you know that you could have rented twenty garages in Manhattan for a year for that kind of money?"

"I don't need twenty garages, I just need a little space at the curb."

"At the curb, next to a fire hydrant?"

"Sometimes. Sometimes I'm in a hurry."

"Well, I'm going to bed. You find somewhere else to sleep, and don't you forget that breakfast is at six AM in this house!" She stalked up the stairs.

Maggio went into his den, took a throwaway cell phone from his desk drawer, and dialed another throwaway cell phone.

"Huh?" a sleepy voice said.

"You know who this is?"

"Sure, Rocco, I know—"

"Don't say my name, schmuck!"

"I'm sorry, Rocco—"

"Shut up and listen."

He shut up.

"You know Sol Fineman?"

"Works for the late, great Sam Spain? Sure, Rocco."

"You say my name one more time and I'm gonna come over there and shoot you in the head."

"Sorry, R—"

"I want you to find Sol Fineman and put two in his head from up close. I want him to see it coming."

"Okay. You want me to tell him anything?"

"No, but I want him to tell you something. I want him to tell you where is the five mil I paid him for a certain piece of art, and I want the five mil and the piece of art back before you shoot him. Got it?"

"Got it."

"And feel free to persuade him by any means you choose, as long as it's effective."

"Got it, Rocco."

Maggio threw the phone across the room.

"HONEY," THE FORMER Sol's wife said, "why are we leaving in such a hurry?"

"Sweetheart, it would only disturb you to talk about that."

"It will only disturb me if you *don't* talk about that."

"You know the five million we got for the picture?"

"Yes."

"Well, now we've got another five million for the picture."

"Honey, did you spend the day at the track?"

"No."

"A casino?"

"No, sweetheart, it's all from the picture."

"And where is the picture now?"

"In a safe place in Manhattan."

"What for?"

"To make the exchange easier."

"You're going to exchange the painting for something?"

"For another five million."

"Baby, you must be making a lot of people really, really angry."

He thought about that. "Only one, actually."

"And who's that?"

"Rocco Maggio."

"Well, from what I've heard, he's enough all by himself."

"Yeah, but everybody else is going to be really happy when I'm done."

"How do you figure that?"

"Like this—the owner of the painting is going to be very happy because she gets her picture back, and her insurance company is going to be really happy because they only have to pay five million instead of the tens of millions it's insured for to the victim of the theft. That leaves only Rocco Maggio, and I grant you, he's going to be very, very angry at Sol Fineman. His problem is, Sol Fineman don't exist anymore."

"Is that why we're driving west, instead of south, to Florida?"

"Yep. There are other sunny places like New Mexico and Arizona. Mexico, if things get too hot."

"You don't want to take a plane, maybe?"

"The government X-rays your luggage these days."

"Oh, yeah, it's been so long since I've flown anywhere, I forgot."

"Once the sun comes up, it will be a beautiful drive. We'll drive through Pennsylvania and Indiana—those are very beautiful states, even from the interstate."

She was quiet for a while. "Do you want me to drive for a spell?"

"No, sweetheart, I'm not sleepy, I'm excited about our new life."

She was quiet for a little longer. "Is there something else I can do for you?" she asked, unzipping his fly.

"Sweetie, you could always read my mind."

52

DINO'S SECRETARY BUZZED HIM. "Yeah?"

"Commissioner, there's a Lieutenant Levine on the line, says he's in charge of the Sol Fineman investigation."

"Put him through," Dino said, and waited for the click. "Bacchetti."

"Commissioner, it's Dave Levine, about the Sol Fineman thing?"

"Yeah, did you find him?"

"Nossir, but the thing is, somebody else is looking for him, too, and they ain't carrying badges."

"Anybody we know?"

"I recognized one guy—he works for a Jersey don named Maggio. He and his crew are tearing Fineman's apartment apart as we speak. I've had calls from two other locations we're watching, Sam Spain's Bar and a chop shop in East Harlem. People are also looking for him there."

"Have you found any trace of Fineman?"

"Nossir, it's like he never existed."

"Then follow the other guys who're looking for him. Maybe they're smarter than you."

A brief pause, then, "Yessir."

"Just kidding, Dave, but maybe they know something we don't."

"Gotcha, Commish, we're on it." Levine hung up and got conferenced with two sergeants who were working for him. "All right, guys, it's like this—we don't have to worry about where Sol Fineman is anymore, all we have to do is tail the goombahs who are scouring the city for him. We'll let them do the work, and when they grab him, we'll grab them and take the credit. Got it?"

"Got it," one sergeant said.

"Sounds good to me," the other echoed.

Everybody hung up.

STONE HUNG UP THE PHONE. He and Art Masi were sitting in Stone's office, wondering what to do next. "That was Dino," Stone said.

"Good news?"

"I don't know—maybe, maybe not."

"Tell me anyway," Art said.

"Rocco Maggio has got every soldier in the Maggio family in Manhattan looking for Sol Fineman."

"What happens if the NYPD doesn't get Fineman first?"

"Terrible things, no doubt, but Dino has them following the soldiers. The cops will let them do the work, then bag Fineman and get the credit."

"I like it, as long as the soldiers don't have Fineman for too long before the cops show up. They might get money and the picture, and then we're off to the races again."

"You're a pessimist, Art, you know that?"

"I wasn't until I started looking for this van Gogh. I

was happy as a clam, pulling down my pay and my consulting fees, and now I'm a nervous wreck because I've got a million bucks at stake."

"That's supposed to motivate you, Art, not make you nervous," Stone said.

"I think I'm going to be nervous for the rest of my life, no matter what happens."

"Art, just think about what you can do with a million dollars."

"You think that hasn't crossed my mind? First of all, I'm going to have to hand my Uncle Sam forty percent of it, and then I've got six hundred thousand. Then I'm going to pay off my mortgage, and I've got four hundred thousand. Then my wife is going to spend two hundred thousand, if I'm lucky, gutting the house and making it the way she always dreamed it would be, then she's going to spend fifty thousand on clothes and spa treatments to celebrate the dream house, and if the spa treatments don't do it for her, she'll spend another fifty thousand on cosmetic surgery, 'to make you proud,' she'll say. So now I'm down to a hundred grand, and my bookie's going to take fifteen of that, and by the time the wife and I get back from our European holiday for the month of vacation time I've got built up, I'll be back to zero, maybe even in debt again."

"Then it's a fresh start and your house is paid for, and your wife is more beautiful than ever," Stone pointed out. "That's not too bad, is it?"

"No," Art replied, "but it's depressing."

ROCCO MAGGIO SAT in the back room of an Italian restaurant in New Jersey and looked across the table at the three men who constituted the loan committee, sort of.

"So, Rocco," the taller of the three, who did most of the talking, said, "you've got your dick caught in a wringer, and we're out five mil, plus vigorish." This was how a bank's loan committee talked in Rocco's neighborhood.

"Listen, guys, this is temporary. I've got sixty men combing Manhattan for Fineman as we speak, and if that's not enough, we'll work our way up the Hudson."

"And you expect us to wait until you've found him and persuaded him to give up the five mil—call it six mil by then—to get our money back?"

"Guys, you know I'm good for it."

"That's what we believed when we loaned you the money you loaned the art guy, but even after asking politely, we're not seeing our money. Is the art guy good for it?"

"Well," Rocco said, "he's not exactly on the hook for it."

"And how did he get off the hook?"

"He never had the money. I took it to his gallery in a suitcase, Fineman showed us the picture, I gave him the money, then I put the picture in my trunk and left."

"Did the art guy ever touch the painting? That would be good enough."

"No, he didn't. He didn't say a word, he just smiled, and I gave Fineman the money for Sam Spain. Sam would be on the hook for it, but he's very dead, and we don't exactly have collateral."

"Rocco, every word you say, you're digging yourself in deeper," the chairman of the committee said.

"Look, I've got maybe two mil in ready cash spread around. I'll need a few days to collect it."

"That'll take care of the vig and some of the principal," the chairman said, "but what about the rest?"

"I've got other assets—the shipping company, the warehouse, and three liquor stores."

"It takes time to liquidate," the chairman said, "and all the while, the vig keeps going up."

"Worse comes to worst, I'll sign over a couple deeds," Rocco said.

"Worse comes to worst, you'll sign over everything, Rocco. Now get out of here and use your time well. Find Sol Fineman."

53

CHEECH, THE CAPO who ran Rocco Maggio's crew, sat in comfort on the living room sofa in Sol Fineman's apartment while his boys reduced the place to rubble. He was nearly through with the *Daily News* crossword when one of them came to him.

"Okay, boss, we've been through the place, and we haven't found anything. You want to take a look?"

Cheech wearily put his crossword aside and followed the man into the single bedroom. The pillows, mattress, and box spring had been gutted, and bits of feathers floated in the air. He walked into the kitchen, opened a couple of cabinets, and looked around. "What's that?" he said, pointing at a black plastic garbage can.

"It's a garbage can," his guy replied.

"What's that stuck to the bottom?" He pointed at a piece of paper stuck to an inside corner.

The man picked up the garbage can, peeled a portion of a sheet of paper from the inside, and handed it to Cheech.

Cheech regarded the scrap with interest.

"What is it, Cheech?"

"It looks like part of a property tax bill from Putnam County, upstate. The guy's paying twenty-four grand a year—must be a nice house."

"Is it Fineman's house?"

Cheech shook his head. "Belongs to some guy named Blankenship. The first name's missing."

"How about an address?"

"One hundred Riverview Road, Cold . . . The rest is missing."

"There's a town up that way on the Hudson called Cold Spring, or something like that."

Cheech produced an iPhone, tapped the map app, and typed in the address and *Cold Spring New York*. "Cold Spring," he said. "Across the river from West Point. Okay, let's go take a look at Mr. Blankenship's house."

MR. AND MRS. Blankenship got up early and had breakfast at an IHOP across the road from their motel.

"So what's your plan for the day?"

"I thought we might buy a new car," he said.

"The Toyota is less than a year old."

"Something nicer, something that isn't connected to New York State."

"Ah."

They drove the Toyota into the town, down a broad street filled with car dealerships. "How about this one?" he said, swinging into Callahan Mercedes.

"Why not?"

The two of them prowled the lot, and she stopped in front of a large white SUV. "I like SUVs," she said. "You can get a lot of stuff in them."

He took a good look at the plush interior, then at the window sticker; the vehicle was loaded. A man in a suit approached them, his hand out. "My name's Callahan," he said. "This is my dealership. Something I can show you?"

"I'm interested in the G550," he said. "It looks pretty loaded. Is there any option that isn't on the car?"

Callahan looked at it. "This one's got everything. We order a few loaded-up vehicles every year."

"What can you offer me as a discount?"

"We deal in list prices only. You got something to trade?"

"The Camry there, it's got only six thousand miles on it."

Callahan made a cell call, and a service technician came running out.

"The keys are in it," Blankenship said.

"Looks clean to me," Callahan said, "but I've got to run it by my service manager. Why don't we go inside and have a cup of coffee?"

THEY WERE FINISHING THEIR COFFEE in Callahan's office when the service man came in with a sheet of paper. Callahan looked at it. "Nice Camry you've got there."

"Easy to sell, too," Blankenship said.

"Tell you what," Callan said, "eighty-one thousand dollars and your car."

"You're going to make a profit on both cars," he said. "You can do better."

Callahan sucked his teeth and shook his head.

"Mr. Callahan, how do you feel about cash?"

"I'm fond of it. You mean you don't need a loan?"

"I mean I don't need a loan or a checkbook."

"Oh, you're talking about currency?"

"I am."

"You understand, there are banking laws I have to comply with. I have to fill out a federal form if I deposit more than ten thousand dollars." He scratched his head. "Besides, what would I do with eighty-one thousand in cash?"

"Seventy-five thousand," he said. "You'll think of something."

"I don't know . . ."

"Remodel the house? Buy the wife a fur coat or two? Take a really nice vacation?"

Callahan's face broadened into a smile. "Oh, what the hell? Where's the money?"

"A stone's throw," Blankenship said. "I'll go get it. You do the paperwork."

"What's your address?" Callahan asked.

"Oh, we've just moved out and haven't found a place yet. This seems like a nice town. Give us a nice address here." He could hardly register it at his Cold Spring address. "I'll be right back."

He went out to the Camry, opened the trunk, and then entered the combination of the two locks on a large aluminum suitcase. He found a shopping bag in the trunk and put seven bundles of $10,000 each into it, then counted out $5,000 from another bundle and stuck the rest in his pocket, then he walked back into the dealership and set the shopping bag on the desk. "The bundles are ten thousand each. There's seven and a half bundles."

Callahan took out a bundle at random and riffled through it. "Looks good to me," he said. "Sign right here."

Blankenship picked up the pen and signed.

"You're now a resident of one of our nicest neighborhoods," Callahan said. "Give me a few minutes and I'll send somebody down to the DMV and get you a tag, a registration, and a title. Another cup of coffee?"

They both had another cup and a doughnut. Half an hour later, the Blankenships were driving east on the interstate. At the first exit they got off, drove under the bridge, and got on again headed west.

"Our next stop is a little town called Anderson, Indiana, which has a very nice airport. We can leave the car there for a couple of days." Then he explained his plan to her.

"I like it," she said.

He ran a hand up the inside of her thigh and made contact. "I always know what you'll like," he said.

54

CHEECH ENTERED THE address into Maps on his iPhone, and he and his crew drove up the Hudson.

"Nice view," Cheech said to his driver.

"I never been up here," the man responded.

"It's what, fifty miles from home, and you've never driven up the Hudson?" Cheech asked.

"I like it fine in Jersey."

The house was very pretty—gray shingles and what looked like a slate roof. Fairly big, too. The name "Blankenship" appeared on the mailbox.

"Looks like there's nobody home," the driver said.

"I expect," Cheech replied. "If it belongs to Sol Fineman, he wouldn't be home, either." He motioned for the men in the other car to stay put.

"Where would Sol be?" the driver asked.

"Disappearing."

"Huh?"

"He wouldn't be waiting at home for us to find him."

They walked around the house peeking in windows. "Nicely furnished," Cheech said.

"Whatever."

They came to a rear door. "You any good with locks?" Cheech asked.

"Yeah," the man said; he kicked the door open.

"That wasn't exactly what I meant," Cheech said. He heard a series of beeps. "Uh-oh, alarm system. We've got less than two minutes." He ran into the house and looked for a desk or a home office, found it and went hurriedly through the drawers. Phone bill, gas bill, electrical, all in the name of Blankenship. The beeps were getting closer together. "Let's get out of here fast," he said, sprinting for the car.

The two carloads of crew drove away to the sound of a whooping alarm coming from the house.

"Slow down," Cheech said to his driver, "we don't want to get arrested for speeding."

"I just throw the tickets away," the driver said.

Cheech sighed, got out his cell phone, and called Rocco Maggio.

"Yeah?"

"We're in Cold Spring, up the Hudson," Cheech said.

"What the fuck for?"

"We found a piece of a property tax bill stuck to a garbage can at Sol's old apartment, name of Blankenship. We checked out the house. Somebody lives there, but there's no car in the garage, and no suitcases."

"So you think Blankenship is Sol?"

"I gotta think that," Cheech replied, "because there's nothing else to think. The guy knows how to cover his tracks—except for that one thing, the tax bill."

*   *   *

AS THE BLANKENSHIPS drove their new Mercedes west, Cindy got a cell phone from her purse and started to dial a number. He took it from her. "That's a no-no."

"I just want to call the maid and tell her not to come tomorrow."

"People can track cell phones," he said. He took a throwaway from his pocket and handed it to her. "Use this," he said. "On the other hand, don't use it. It's not important for the maid to know anything."

"Whatever you say, sweets."

They were coming up on a bridge. He rolled down the window and threw the phone as far as he could, into a river.

"OKAY," ROCCO SAID, "the first thing you gotta do is find out if Blankenship has a cell phone."

"He does, I saw the bill in his desk drawer."

"Did you happen to get the number?"

"Sorry, we were working fast, against a ticking alarm system."

"Hang on a second." Maggio turned to his computer and did a cell phone search for Blankenship, Cold Spring. "Here's the number," he said. "See if you can track it."

"How do I do that?"

"Hang on, I'll do it."

Maggio started tracking; this had always been a good app for finding recalcitrant borrowers. It worked this time, too. He picked up the phone. "He's at 100 River-view Road, Cold Spring."

"That's where we just came from, and we can't go back because the cops are likely to be there," Cheech said.

"Oh, never mind, this guy's smart enough not to leave

the phone there if it could do us any good." Maggio thought for a minute. "Let me check the DMV. You hang on." He pressed the speaker button and went to work on the computer again. "Got it! He drives a two-year-old Toyota Camry, silver." He gave Cheech the tag number.

"What do I do with this? Set up a roadblock?"

"I'll check it every day. He'll probably sell it, and there'll be a record of the change of title. You guys come home. Good job, at least we got a lead." Maggio hung up. He could be patient when he had to.

55

STONE CAME DOWNSTAIRS to find a large FedEx package on his desk, sent from Angelo Farina. He got a box cutter and freed the contents from their vault.

Stone was stunned. He'd forgotten his order for a van Gogh from Angelo, and here it was: a glorious view of farmlands with trees in the foreground, beautifully framed.

There was an envelope in the box, and he opened it to find a bill for $6,000 and a handwritten note. *Your van Gogh, as requested.*

Joan came in and gazed at the painting. "Gorgeous," she said.

"He really is a very talented painter, even when copying another one." He handed her the bill. "Please pay this, pronto." He took the painting up to the dining room and spent an hour shuffling things around to make a place for it.

When he came back to his desk, there was a message from Pio Farina, and he returned the call to a cell phone number.

"Pio."

"Pio, it's Stone Barrington."

"Stone, I wanted you to know that Dad has had a heart attack, and he's in the hospital."

"How bad?"

"Not good."

"Is he in East Hampton?"

"No, in the city, at the Carlsson Clinic. He has a pied-à-terre in the city, and he collapsed in the lobby of his building. The doormen got him an ambulance."

"Can I visit him?"

"They say he can see us this afternoon, and we're driving in now. I know he'd like to see you."

"I just got the painting I asked for. It's wonderful!"

"Yes, I saw him working on it in his studio."

"Call me and let me know when I can see him."

"Okay. There's something else I want to talk to you about, too." He hung up without an explanation.

LATER IN THE AFTERNOON, Stone got a call from Pio.

"They won't let anybody see him today—maybe tomorrow."

"Thanks."

"Do you mind if Ann and I come to see you? There's something we'd like to tell you about."

"Fine, now is good."

THE TWO OF THEM came in and sat on the sofa, while Stone took a chair. He waited for them to get settled with the coffee that Joan brought. "Tell me," he said.

"It's a fairly long story," Pio said.

"I've got the time," Stone replied.

"We told you about the day Mark died."

"Yes, you did."

"But not everything."

"All right, tell me everything."

"It was as we said, up to a point. Mark invited us for a drink and told us to come up in the service elevator."

"Because the main elevator was being serviced."

"That's what he said. We had our drink and started to leave. He asked us to drop off the package at FedEx."

"I remember."

"But as we were leaving through the kitchen, we heard Morgan arrive home from her shopping trip. She called out to him, 'Honey, I'm home,' something like that."

Ann spoke up. "No, she said, 'Mark, stay where you are, I want to talk to you.' Then, I assume, she walked out onto the deck where he had been sitting when we left. We closed the kitchen door behind us and took the elevator downstairs. We had parked on East Seventy-eighth, near the service entrance. As we were getting into the car we heard a sound, a loud thud, sort of. It sounded like a big balloon filled with water, hitting the ground, followed by a kind of sigh. It came from the alley behind the building."

Stone sat up. "That would have been the sound of Mark hitting the pavement."

"It had to be. We drove past the alley, but there was a car parked illegally at the entrance, and I saw it drive away in the rearview mirror. That car had blocked our view."

"Did the driver of the car see Mark fall?"

"I don't think so. There was nothing hurried about his departure."

"So you're telling me that Mark and Morgan were alone in the apartment when he fell."

"That has to be the case."

"Why didn't you tell the police about it?"

"The standard reason—we didn't want to get involved. We didn't want to spend months talking to the cops and reporters, then testifying in court. It's a privacy thing—we're funny that way."

"And why are you telling me now?"

"Because we're cowards," Pio said, "and we think you're not. You know the police commissioner, you can get the case reopened."

Stone shook his head. "That's highly unlikely."

"Why? You know now what happened."

"No, I only know what you heard. Certainly that puts her in the apartment with Mark, but she's already admitted being there. In fact, your story backs up hers, to the extent that she arrived when she said she did. And it strains credulity that she would arrive home, walk out on the terrace, and push her husband off the building."

Pio looked as though he'd just been backhanded. "What about her story about the cat burglar?"

"I think Mark's death was an accident of some sort, and she made that up on the fly because she was afraid of being accused of murder."

Ann spoke up. "Stone is right, Pio," she said.

"Jesus," Pio said, "we went through this whole conscience thing, deciding to tell you, and now what we've told you makes no difference?"

"Not in the least," Stone replied. "And I have to tell you, having gotten to know Morgan, I question whether it's in her character to do something like that."

Ann spoke again. "I think our suspicions helped form

our opinion of her character. And I think that now we have to question our conclusions."

"I know that's hard to do," Stone said, "but I think you have to try."

They were all quiet for a moment.

Then Pio said, "The doctor says we can see Dad tomorrow morning at ten. Will you come?"

"Of course," Stone said.

56

ARTHUR STEELE WAS SITTING at his desk, going over the final draft of the Steele Group's annual report, which was to go to press in an hour. The phone rang. "Yes?"

"Mr. Steele, there's a man on line two who is demanding to speak to you."

"What does he want?"

"He wants to know if you want your picture back."

Steele was about to ask what picture when he stopped himself. "I'll take the call. What's his name?"

"Sol Fineman."

The name was vaguely familiar, and he picked up the phone. "This is Arthur Steele."

"Mr. Steele, this is Sol Fineman. I used to work for a man named Sam Spain, now deceased."

"That name is familiar to me."

"First of all, I should save you some time by telling you that you can't trace this call or my location."

"What do you want?"

"I want to give you back the van Gogh you insured."

"Oh, really? How do I know you've got it?"

"I'll have it delivered to you, and you will have three minutes to inspect it, and if you find it to be genuine, then you'll give the man who delivered it five million dollars in hundred-dollar bills."

"Oh, I will?"

"Mr. Steele, you've already fucked this up once. This is your last chance to save tens of millions of dollars."

Steele didn't speak for a moment.

"I was there when you told Sam Spain to go fuck himself," Fineman said. "You can tell me that, if you like, and neither you nor your client will ever see the picture again. I'll have to destroy it—it's too hot."

"How do you want to do this?" Arthur asked.

"There's a luggage shop near your office, at Park Avenue and Fifty-sixth Street."

"I know the place."

"When you hang up, go there and buy a large black aluminum suitcase, made by Zero Halliburton. Buy the largest one available on wheels. It's about five hundred dollars."

"Then what?"

"Take it back to your office and put the five million, in bundles of ten thousand each, into the suitcase. That's how it comes from the bank. Follow the directions that come with the luggage and set the two combination locks to eight-six-nine. Got it?"

"Yes. I have the cash in my vault as we speak. When do you want to do this?"

"In two hours."

"I guess I can do that."

"A FedEx delivery man will call at your office and tell your people that he has a delivery that must be signed for by you, personally. You will allow him into your office alone. He will give you a package containing the picture and wait three minutes for you and you alone to examine it, so if you need any inspection equipment you'd better get it now."

"I see."

"While you're examining the picture, he will open the suitcase using the code eight-six-nine and count the money. When the three minutes is up, he will depart your office with the money."

"What if I need more time?"

"Mr. Steele, you have an eight-by-ten transparency of the painting. You can compare it to that, and you will know that the picture is the one you previously had authenticated. If you feel it's not the same picture, return it to the deliveryman. He will leave with it, and our business will be done, once and for all. Neither you nor your client will ever see the van Gogh again."

"I understand, and I accept your conditions."

"I haven't told you all of my conditions yet."

"Go ahead."

"Now comes the unpleasant part: The deliveryman will carry a small explosive device. If you involve the police, your corporate security people, or anyone else who attempts to disrupt this process, the picture will be destroyed by the deliveryman, who will also take a few seconds to end your life. If you stick to my conditions and allow the man to leave with the money, unhindered and not followed, he will disarm the device remotely, fifteen minutes after he leaves your office. You will get a phone call telling you that it is safe. Do you understand these terms?"

"I do."

"Do you agree to them?"

"I agree."

"Good. If you keep your word, you will be able to report to your board of directors that the picture has been recovered and returned to the policyholder. They will be very pleased with the terms under which you resolved the problem. The alternative will, I assure you, be unbearable to all concerned." Fineman hung up.

Arthur Steele immediately used his cell phone to call Stone Barrington.

"Hello, Arthur."

"Stone, there have been developments with regard to the van Gogh."

"Oh?"

"I just got a phone call from someone named Sol Fineman. Do you know that name?"

"I do. He's the man who put me in the hospital a few days ago."

"Let me tell you what he proposed." He related the phone conversation to Stone. "What is your advice?"

"Arthur, do you still intend to pay me the twelve-million-dollar recovery fee?"

"Stone, if I get it back this way, then you won't have recovered it."

"Think it through, Arthur. This recovery will not have taken place, except for my participation."

"I don't see it that way, Stone."

"In that case, I have no advice to offer you." Stone hung up.

Arthur panicked and called Stone again.

"Yes, Arthur?"

"All right, I agree to pay you the twelve-million-dollar fee if I recover the picture today."

"In that case, here is my advice. Follow Sol Fineman's instructions to the letter. Do not attempt to apprehend him or deny him the five-million-dollar payment or in-hibit him in any way. Do not report this to the police or your corporate security, and do not have him followed. Do you understand my advice?"

"Stone, you want me just to hand over millions of dollars to this guy?"

"I thought I had made myself perfectly clear. You are in a very dangerous position, Arthur. If you attempt to obstruct this exchange, the whole thing will blow up in your face, perhaps literally, and you will have to face the board and tell them exactly how you blew the opportu-nity to recover the picture for less than ten percent of its value, and how you are, as a result, going to have to pay your client sixty million for her loss. Do you understand?"

"Yes, Stone," Steele said resignedly.

"Then I compliment you on your perspicacity, and I wish you every success in recovering a precious artwork." Stone hung up.

Arthur Steele sat there sweating for a moment, then he got up and headed for the luggage shop.

57

ARTHUR STEELE POINTED at the large black Zero Halliburton case on wheels. "That one, please, no need to wrap it."

The salesman pulled down the case from the shelf. "This one?"

"That is correct." Steele handed him a credit card and waited as patiently as he could while the sale was processed. He read the instructions for setting the combination on the locks, then handed the salesman the leaflet in frustration. "I can't do this. Will you please set the combinations to eight-six-nine?"

The salesman didn't bother with the instructions. He made a few swift moves, and the combinations were set. He handed Steele the slip to sign.

Arthur pulled out the handle on the case and it followed him down Park Avenue to his office building. As he passed the reception desk, he said to the uniformed security guard, "I'm expecting a delivery soon, which will require my signature. Send him up to my floor."

"Yes, Mr. Steele."

Steele went from there to the chief accountant's office. "Please open the vault," he said.

"Of course, Mr. Steele," the man said, rising. "May I ask why?"

"Because I asked you to."

The man complied, then returned to his desk, out of sight. Steele walked into the vault and pulled the door nearly shut behind him. He took out a key and opened a steel door at the rear of the vault, exposing a tightly shrink-wrapped block of bank notes. He found some scissors and slit the pack open, then set the case on the nearby counter and began to stack the banded bundles into it, four at a time, counting aloud. When he had stacked in five hundred bundles, he rearranged the notes a little, then closed the case. He was surprised that it held all the money.

He set the case on the floor; it was very heavy, and he was grateful for the wheels. He locked the cabinet and left the vault, closing the door behind him and spinning the locking wheel. He towed the heavy case down the corridor to his office, stood it up beside his desk, and sat down. He removed a magnifying glass from a desk drawer and retrieved the 8x10 transparency of the painting from his personal safe, then set a light box on his desk and sat down to wait, dabbing at his damp face with a tissue.

SOL FINEMAN, now Blankenship, maneuvered the rented white van, on which he had pasted a plastic FedEx logo to each side. He found a space in a loading zone a few steps from the entrance to the Steele building, then he took a closed FedEx box and a clipboard, walked into the building, and approached the front desk, where a uniformed security guard awaited. Sol was wearing a khaki uniform with a matching zippered jacket bearing the FedEx logo and a name: Jenson. He was also wearing heavy-framed, tinted glasses and a thick goatee, mustache, and eyebrows.

"May I help you?" the guard asked.

"I have a delivery for Mr. Arthur Steele, requiring his personal signature."

The man picked up a phone and reported this to the receptionist on the executive floor, then hung up. "Please go up to the thirtieth floor. They're expecting you."

Sol got onto the elevator and pressed the button for 30. He felt oddly buoyant and relaxed. He got off and started toward the receptionist.

"You may go right in," she said. "You're expected. First door on your right for Mr. Steele."

Sol walked to the door and rapped lightly on it.

"Come in," a voice said.

He opened the door, took a step in, and looked around. A bald man in a black suit sat behind the desk.

"Delivery for Mr. Steele," Sol said.

"I am Arthur Steele. Come in."

Sol walked to the desk and set the box on it. "May I see a picture ID?" he asked.

Seemingly surprised, Steele produced a driver's license.

Sol tore open the paper zip of the box. "You have three minutes," he said, starting the stopwatch function on his wristwatch.

"There's the money," Steele said, pointing. He tore at the box, removed the wrapped painting.

Sol set the case on a conference table and dialed in 869. Nothing happened; the lock refused to open. "Stop!" he said to Steele.

Steele stopped. "What's wrong?"

"The combination didn't work. What did you set it to?"

"I asked the salesman at the store to set it to eight-six-nine. It *must* work."

"You're sure you said eight-six-nine?"

"I'm certain. I'm not trying to trick you."

Sol turned back to the case and tried 986: nothing. He tried 689, and the locks opened. "Got it." He reset his stopwatch. "Three minutes from now." He began counting the bundles of hundreds, flipping through them to be sure there was no plain paper hidden there. He saw a postage scale on a nearby credenza and moved it to the conference table and started weighing banded bundles at random: all the same weight. He counted the stacks and rows of bundles and multiplied in his head. Five hundred of them.

Steele had turned on the light box and set the transparency there and was peering first at the light box, then at the painting.

"You have twenty seconds," Sol said, feeling for the pistol at his belt.

With five seconds to go, Steele switched off the light box. "It's the authentic painting," he said.

Sol snapped the case shut, spun the combinations, set it on the floor, and extended the handle. He walked toward the door and stopped. "Nice doing business with you," he said, and headed for the elevator.

HE STEPPED OUT into the lobby, where his wife awaited, had a quick look around, then, satisfied, handed her the handle to the case. "Out the uptown door and turn right," Sol said. "I'll catch up to you in the next block." She started in that direction and he turned toward the front door.

The van was where he had left it. He got in, started

the engine, and pulled out into the traffic, just as a cop came around the corner toward him. He looked straight ahead, ignoring the uniform, then made a right at the corner. He made another right and started looking for his wife. There she was, near the next corner. Sol stopped the van next to her, got out and loaded the heavy case into the rear, while his wife stripped off the FedEx logo from each side of the truck. She got into the driver's seat while Sol got in beside her and started stripping off his jacket and shirt.

He ripped off the mustache, eyebrows, and goatee and wrapped them in his shirt, along with the tinted glasses, which he had wiped clean. "Take a right on Forty-second Street and head for the tunnel," he said. "Check your mirrors regularly." He reached out the window and turned the mirror so that he could see behind them.

"So far, so good," she said.

Traffic was backed up a block at the entrance to the Lincoln Tunnel, and it took another ten minutes before they were inside it. Finally, they broke out on the New Jersey side in bright sunshine and drove normally past the cops stationed there.

"Take 3 West and get off at 17 North," Sol said. He got out a cell phone and made a call. "Twenty minutes," he said to the man who answered. "Get your clearance and start an engine." Twenty minutes later they pulled up at the security booth at an entrance to Teterboro Airport. "November one, two, three, Tango Foxtrot," she said to the guard, and the bar was raised. They parked the van, and Sol got the case from the rear, while his wife gave the attendant the car rental papers and told him they would pick up the van. Two minutes later they walked out onto the ramp, where the chartered Citation was waiting.

She got onto the airplane, while Sol helped the copilot

hoist the case into the rear baggage compartment. "Got your clearance?"

"All the way to Wichita," he replied. He followed Sol onto the airplane and settled in the right cockpit seat, while Sol strapped himself in next to his wife and put on a headset so he could hear the pilots talking. He heard the other engine start.

"Teterboro ground," the pilot said, "N123TF is ready to taxi, IFR to Wichita."

"N123TF, taxi to runway one, via kilo taxiway."

The pilot repeated the instruction, and the airplane began to move.

There were two aircraft ahead of them waiting for the runway, and another ten minutes passed before they were rolling and rotating.

Sol waited until they were given a higher altitude and had contacted New York Center. "Pilot," he said.

"Yes, sir?"

"Request a new destination and routing to Anderson, Indiana, identifier AID."

"Yes, sir." The pilot did so, and ATC cleared him direct AID, where their car was waiting for them.

Sol sat back in his seat and squeezed his wife's hand. "Now we can relax," he said. "We'll sleep near Chicago tonight and get an early start in the morning. I've arranged a charter flight from New Orleans Lakefront to the Caymans the day after tomorrow, and we'll open a bank account there, then make our way back to New Orleans and drive west."

She gave him a big, wet kiss.

58

STONE WAS AT HIS DESK in the late afternoon when Arthur Steele arrived, carrying a briefcase.

"Have a seat, Arthur. How did it go?"

Steele placed the briefcase on the desk and opened it. "It went just fine," he said.

"May I?" Stone asked, reaching for the painting.

"Of course."

Stone switched on his desk lamp and held the picture up, minus its frame. "Oh, my," he said. "It's the first time I've seen it."

"I'd like you to deliver it to Mrs. Tillman," Steele said.

"I'd be happy to."

Steele took an envelope from his inside pocket and handed it to Stone. "Your fee," he said.

Stone removed the check from the envelope, looked at it, and nodded. "Thank you, Arthur."

"Don't miss the board meeting tomorrow," Steele said, rising. "Two PM. I'll need your support to convince the members that I've done the right thing."

"I don't think they'll doubt it for a moment."

Steele shook his hand and departed.

Stone locked the briefcase in his safe, then phoned Morgan Tillman.

"Well, hello there. I was about to call you and invite you to dinner tonight."

"Just the two of us?"

"Yes, indeed," she replied.

"I'll have a surprise for you."

"I hope it's what I think it is," she said.

"That, and something else."

"Seven o'clock?"

"See you then." He hung up and buzzed for Joan.

She came in. "Yes, boss?"

"Deposit this, please," he said, handing her the check, then asked her to write another.

STONE PRESENTED HIMSELF at Morgan's door, only fashionably late, and rang the bell.

She opened the door and gave him a big kiss. "Is that my surprise?" she asked, pointing at the briefcase.

"It's one of them," he replied.

"Let me fix you a drink first." She did so.

Stone opened the briefcase, removed the painting, and handed it to her. "I hope you'll give it a good home."

She took it and held it under the lamp. "Oh, my God," she whispered, and brought it toward her lips.

"Don't kiss it!" Stone said quickly.

"Why not?"

"Because if you do, you may have to someday explain to some expert how van Gogh managed to get lipstick on it."

She went to the hall closet and came back with the

frame that the thief had discarded, and a small tool kit. "Will you rehang it for me, next to the Utrillo there, while I finish cooking? I'll be done in fifteen minutes."

"Of course," Stone replied. She went into the kitchen, and he put the painting carefully back into its frame and secured it. He went to the wall and held it up to the empty space waiting for it. Then, as he started to reach for a hammer, a corner of the van Gogh struck the Utrillo and knocked it off the wall and onto the floor.

"Clumsy ass," he said aloud to himself, hoping he hadn't damaged the painting. He picked it up and found it to be heavier than he had expected, then he turned it over and discovered that the picture wire had come loose from the eye screw on one side. And as he did, he saw something that startled him.

Inside the canvas frame of the Utrillo he saw a second canvas frame that fit neatly inside the first. Another painting was concealed there. He found a screwdriver in the tool kit and gently pried the smaller picture out of the larger frame. He set down the Utrillo and turned over the second canvas.

To his astonishment, he found himself looking at another van Gogh, identical to the one he was about to hang. He picked up the framed one and held them up together, then he walked back to the table he had been sitting next to and put both paintings under the lamp. They matched, brushstroke by brushstroke. One of them had to be a fake, but which one?

He took a big sip of his drink and thought about this for a moment, then he replaced the second picture inside the Utrillo canvas's frame, re-secured the wire to the eye, and returned it to its place on the wall. It had been secreted there for a year and a half, and it was unlikely to be discovered, unless he wanted it to be.

Morgan stuck her head out of the kitchen. "Five minutes," she said.

"I'll be ready." He finished rehanging the first van Gogh and stepped back to view the wall; the painting seemed at home.

Morgan called him to dinner at a dining nook off the kitchen with a fine view of the city lights. "Will you decant the wine?" she asked.

"Sure." Stone held the bottle up to a candle and poured the claret into a decanter until the dregs started to creep up the side of the bottle.

Morgan came in with their first course of seared foie gras, and they sat down. "*Bon appetit*," she said.

"*Bon appetit*," he replied, then he cut a slice of the goose liver and chewed thoughtfully. It practically melted in his mouth.

"You seem very quiet this evening," Morgan said. "Penny for your thoughts?"

"You wouldn't get your money's worth," Stone replied. "I'm not even sure what I'm thinking."

AFTER DINNER they took a cognac upstairs and undressed.

"You're still very quiet," she said.

"I don't know how to answer you," he replied.

She fondled him. "Oh, and here's my other surprise."

"Whatever I was thinking," he said, "it just flew out of my mind."

59

STONE WOKE VERY EARLY, slipped out of bed, and dressed in the bathroom, so as not to wake Morgan. He let himself out of the apartment and, on the way down, phoned Art Masi.

"Masi," a sleepy voice said.

"It's Stone. I'm on the Upper East Side, in the Seventies. Can we meet for breakfast?"

Masi suggested a place on Lexington Avenue in the Sixties. "See you in an hour."

Stone walked slowly over to Lex and turned. He reflected that he should feel more satisfied than he actually did; he kept putting two and two together and coming up with five.

After some window-shopping, he reached the restaurant in time to see Masi getting out of a cab. They shook hands, went inside, got a table, and ordered.

"You look odd," Masi said. "What's wrong?"

"I don't know, exactly. There's an old joke—do you know the difference between a moron and a neurotic?"

"No."

"A moron thinks two and two are five. A neurotic knows two and two are four, but it makes him nervous."

Masi laughed. "Which are you?"

"I haven't been able to figure that out just yet."

"Are you hopeful?"

"Not really."

"We don't have the van Gogh, do we? No million bucks?"

"Oh, I almost forgot," Stone said, taking an envelope from his pocket and handing it to Masi.

Masi opened it and his eyebrows went up. "This is a check for *two* million dollars."

"Then you'll have more than a million after paying your taxes—and you'd better pay your taxes because there will be a record of this."

"But I didn't find the painting."

"Neither did I," Stone said, "but we solved the mystery."

"I don't understand this."

"We both worked hard for it, and we should be rewarded, and as for doubling your reward, it makes a kind of sense, because we have two paintings."

"*Two* paintings?"

"Two *identical* paintings—both the same van Gogh."

"Then one of them is a fake."

"Your logic is admirable, but which one?"

"You've seen them side by side?"

"I have."

"And you couldn't tell them apart?"

"I could not. Arthur Steele compared it to the color transparency, and he couldn't tell one from the other."

"But he paid the reward anyway?"

"He did. He hasn't seen the other van Gogh—I discovered it accidentally last night when I was hanging the first one in her apartment. It was concealed inside the frame of a Utrillo hanging next to it. A perfect fit."

"What do you make of all this?"

"I don't know what to make of it. I didn't know Mark Tillman, so I can't guess at his motivation, not with any basis in fact."

"I can," Masi said.

"Please enlighten me."

"We've talked about this—when people buy a very expensive piece of jewelry, multimillion-dollar jewelry, they often have a copy made so the wife can wear it in insecure places without fear of losing the original, which is at home in the safe."

"And you think that's why he had the picture copied?"

"Why else?"

"He was in what was, for him, reduced financial circumstances, and I think he needed the sixty million to get out of a hole, so he filed an insurance claim. I think he told Ralph, the doorman, to steal it and, when things had cooled off a bit, to fence it and keep half of whatever he could get for it. And if it was never found, Tillman still had the original."

"That makes as much sense as anything I can think of. Are you feeling better now?"

"I am, but not a whole lot," Stone said.

"Then two plus two equals four, but you're nervous about it."

"Does that make me a neurotic?"

"Very probably," Masi said, grinning.

"Now, *that* makes me feel better."

Their breakfast arrived, and they ate hungrily.

*   *   *

"TILLMAN WAS VERY SMART," Masi said over a second cup of coffee. "He would have gotten the insurance money for the fake, and the original was safe on the wall where it had always hung, and nobody was the wiser. It was so simple."

"If it was so simple, why didn't you find it when you and your people searched the apartment?" Stone asked.

"Because it was so simple. It was hidden in plain sight—well, *almost* in plain sight. It was right in front of us the whole time."

"It was very clever," Stone said, "or it would have been if Tillman had lived to enjoy both the money and the painting."

"Any new theory on why he died?"

"Well, Pio and Ann have convinced me that they didn't kill him. If they had, they would have kept the picture."

"So it was the cat burglar?"

"I'm convinced there was no cat burglar. Morgan saw the painting was gone and made up a story that explained both its disappearance and her husband's death because she was afraid she'd be accused."

"Then she didn't do it?"

Stone shook his head. "I've gotten to know her well, and I don't believe she's capable of murder."

"Everybody's capable of murder, under the right circumstances," Masi said.

"No, it was an accident. The parapet was being reconstructed and was thus low. He could have gotten too near the edge and tripped."

"Or she could have just nudged him a little."

"No. They may have had an argument—maybe she told him she wanted a divorce, maybe she was angry, thinking he'd sold the painting without consulting her, I don't know. But I think he was careless and caused his own death."

"Well, you know her better than I," Masi said.

Stone looked at his watch. "I've got to go see Angelo Farina. He's in the Carlsson Clinic, recovering from a heart attack."

"I hadn't heard. Wish him well for me."

Stone got up and reached for money.

Masi raised a hand. "No, breakfast is on me." He smiled broadly and patted his pocket. "I can afford it."

60

STONE PRESENTED HIMSELF at the front desk of the Carlsson Clinic and asked for the room of Angelo Farina; he was directed to the top floor of the building.

Pio Farina and Ann Kusch were coming out of the room as Stone arrived.

"Thank you for coming," Pio said. "The doctor says Dad is out of the woods and recovering. You can go in for a bit, but please don't overtire him."

Stone walked into the room, which was large and included a comfortable seating area for guests. The hospital bed on the other side of the room, surrounded by flickering and beeping screens, seemed almost out of place.

Angelo's bed was cranked up to a sitting position; he raised a hand and waved Stone over. He pulled up a chair and sat down beside the bed.

"You look almost as good as I do," Angelo said.

"I'm glad to hear it," Stone replied. "Are you feeling better?"

"Much better," Angelo said. "I walked into my apartment building and felt a little queasy, and I had a pain in my back on the left side. I don't remember anything else. I'm told I collapsed into the arms of a doorman, who did all the right things. I woke up here."

"I'm glad you did. I want to thank you for the glorious van Gogh you did for me. It's already in a place of pride in my house. I don't think I'll tell anybody it's a fake."

"Tell them it's an original Farina," Angelo said.

"Perhaps I will, once they get over the initial shock. I had dinner with Morgan last evening, partly to give back her van Gogh."

"They found it, then?"

Stone took him through the chain of events that had led to the picture's recovery. "The final thief sold it back to the insurance company, saving them a bundle."

"That was smart. Who was he?"

"He called himself Sol Fineman, at least for a while. Nobody has been able to find out anything else about him."

"Mark Tillman would have enjoyed that story. He was a very tricky fellow himself."

"I've come to know you're right about that."

"How so?"

"Last night, while Morgan was making dinner, she asked me to rehang the van Gogh. In so doing, I accidentally dislodged a very nice Utrillo from its place, and I got quite a surprise."

"From Utrillo? Nothing very surprising there."

"I won't argue art with you, but tucked inside the Utrillo's frame I found another, smaller frame. I pried it out and lo, another van Gogh, virtually identical to Mark Tillman's."

Angelo smiled broadly. "Did you now?"

"I did, and now I have a question for you, Angelo. Which of Mark's van Goghs is the fake?"

Angelo laughed. "Both of them."

Stone's jaw dropped. "They are both fakes?"

"Perhaps it would be more accurate to say that they are both original Farinas." He coughed a few times.

"Have some water," Stone said. He took a glass from the bedside table and held the straw so that Angelo could take a few sips.

"That's better," he said.

"Why would Mark want duplicate van Goghs?"

Angelo sighed. "Perhaps he was a belt-and-braces sort of guy," he said. "Or perhaps he had more nefarious reasons. As I say, he was a tricky fellow." He began to cough again, and Stone offered him the water, but he waved it away. Stone rang for the nurse.

She was there immediately, and shooed Stone from the room. He took a seat, and through the open door he heard a periodic beep from one of the monitors turn into a continuous tone. A doctor and another nurse, pushing a crash cart, ran down the hallway and into the room and closed the door behind them.

Stone waited for the better part of half an hour before the doctor emerged.

"Are you family?" the doctor asked Stone.

"No, just a friend."

"We did everything we could," the doctor said, "but we were unable to revive him. I'm sorry for your loss."

"Thank you," Stone said.

"I should call his son," the doctor said, and walked away down the hall.

STONE DECIDED TO WALK HOME. As he walked through the crisp morning air, he went over in his mind the chain of events that had led to this day.

He thought about Morgan Tillman. Perhaps she would discover the duplicate one day soon, or perhaps much time would pass before someone came across it. He thought he would let that happen.

He thought about Arthur Steele. Arthur and his company would never again see the five million Sol Fineman had taken from him, and Stone would hate to see Art Masi have to give back the two million he had worked so hard for.

He thought about the ten million he himself had pocketed. Still, the insurance company had saved many millions. Perhaps, Stone thought, a large charitable donation would be in order for him.

He decided not to attend the board meeting that afternoon.

ACKNOWLEDGMENTS

I must give my thanks to the artist Ken Perenyi, who knows all things about the creation, as well as the forgery, of art. His book, *Caveat Emptor*, tells (nearly) all on that subject, and I hope it kept me from sounding like an idiot on the subject. I own and treasure several of his "re-creations," and you may find his work for sale on the Internet, as well as, if rumors be true, in many museums and art collections around the world.

AUTHOR'S NOTE

I am happy to hear from readers, but you should know that if you write to me in care of my publisher, three to six months will pass before I receive your letter, and when it finally arrives it will be one among many, and I will not be able to reply.

However, if you have access to the Internet, you may visit my website at www.stuartwoods.com, where there is a button for sending me e-mail. So far, I have been able to reply to all my e-mail, and I will continue to try to do so.

If you send me an e-mail and do not receive a reply, it is probably because you are among an alarming number of people who have entered their e-mail address incorrectly in their mail software. I have many of my replies returned as undeliverable.

Remember: e-mail, reply; snail mail, no reply.

When you e-mail, please do not send attachments, as I never open these. They can take twenty minutes to download, and they often contain viruses.

Please do not place me on your mailing lists for funny stories, prayers, political causes, charitable fund-raising, petitions, or sentimental claptrap. I get enough of that from people I already know. Generally speaking, when I get e-mail addressed to a large number of people, I immediately delete it without reading it.

Please do not send me your ideas for a book, as I have a policy of writing only what I myself invent. If you send me story ideas, I will immediately delete them without reading them. If you have a good idea for a book, write it yourself, but I will not be able to advise you on how to get it published. Buy a copy of *Writer's Market* at any bookstore; that will tell you how.

Anyone with a request concerning events or appearances may e-mail it to me or send it to: Publicity Department, Penguin Random House LLC, 375 Hudson Street, New York, NY 10014.

Those ambitious folk who wish to buy film, dramatic, or television rights to my books should contact Matthew Snyder, Creative Artists Agency, 9830 Wilshire Boulevard, Beverly Hills, CA 98212-1825.

Those who wish to make offers for rights of a literary nature should contact Anne Sibbald, Janklow & Nesbit, 445 Park Avenue, New York, NY 10022. (Note: This is not an invitation for you to send her your manuscript or to solicit her to be your agent.)

If you want to know if I will be signing books in your city, please visit my website, www.stuartwoods.com, where the tour schedule will be published a month or so in advance. If you wish me to do a book signing in your locality, ask your favorite bookseller to contact his Penguin representative or the Penguin publicity department with the request.

If you find typographical or editorial errors in my book and feel an irresistible urge to tell someone, please write to Sara Minnich at Penguin's address above. Do not e-mail your discoveries to me, as I will already have learned about them from others.

A list of my published works appears in the front of this book and on my website. All the novels are still in print in paperback and can be found at or ordered from any bookstore. If you wish to obtain hardcover copies of earlier novels or of the two nonfiction books, a good used-book store or one of the online bookstores can help you find them. Otherwise, you will have to go to a great many garage sales.

TURN THE PAGE FOR AN EXCERPT

In the wake of a personal tragedy, former CIA operative Teddy Fay—now
a successful Hollywood film producer known as Billy Barnett—takes a
leave of absence to travel and grieve, landing in Santa Fe in the company
of his friends Stone Barrington and Ed Eagle. There, fate hands him an
unexpected opportunity to exact quiet revenge for his recent loss, from a man
who helped to cover up the crime. But when his enemy wises up
to Teddy's machinations, a discreet game of sabotage escalates to a
potentially lethal battle.

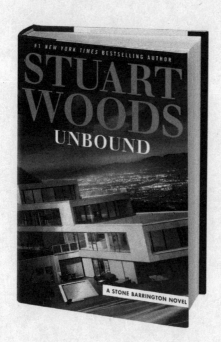

1

TEDDY FAY STARED into the smog-filtered rising sun and set his speed control to seventy-five miles per hour. The road seemed for a moment to rise into the flaming ball, then, as he crested what passed for a hill, it fell back into its proper place. He reached into the center armrest, fumbled for his Ray-Bans and put them on. No need to drill a hole into his corneas.

Teddy, who for some time had been called Billy Barnett, had done all the right things. He had identified his wife's body in the morgue, though he had winced at her injuries. The instrument of her death had been a huge SUV, driven down Rodeo Drive at an incomprehensible speed by a woman who had, reportedly, just finished a three-cosmo lunch with some friends. His wife's only participation had been to go shopping and to cross with the light in her favor. She had been the definition of innocence, and her killer had been the definition of murderer. Apparently, as he'd been told by police, the woman was the wife of one of Hollywood's most famous producers, who specialized in the kind of mayhem inflicted by his spouse on that sunny, sunny L.A. day.

Teddy Fay had done the right thing. He had engaged an undertaker, sat through a well-attended memorial service, and scattered her ashes in the surf at Malibu Beach in front of their house, a place she had loved. He had asked Peter Barrington, for whom he worked, to be relieved of his duties on a film he was scheduled to produce, and had been told to take all the time he needed. She would be missed, he had been told, having been the heart and soul of the business side of the production company and a fixture at Centurion Studios.

Billy Barnett had then packed a couple of bags, tossed them into the rear of his new Porsche Cayenne Turbo, which had, seemingly of its own accord, found its way onto I-40, pointed east, toward Oklahoma City. The car may have known the way, but Billy had no idea where he was going.

An hour after sunrise, Teddy surprised himself by feeling hungry. He had not eaten for nearly two days. He got off the interstate and found a small-town diner— he didn't know which town—and ate a big breakfast. He gassed up and got back onto I-40. He passed exits to places with familiar names, but none of them had any life for him.

He spent the night in a motel and continued at dawn the next day. He was in the western outskirts of Albuquerque when he saw a sign for Santa Fe. The name resonated for Teddy; he had visited, even lived there when he had been on the run from most of the law and intelligence services in the United States. He took I-25 north. It might be a nicer place since he had been presidentially pardoned for his many sins—more than the President knew about, but all covered.

He was at five thousand feet of elevation at Albuquerque, the same as Denver, the Mile-High City, and as he drove north the landscape rose before him, until his GPS told him he was nearing seven thousand feet. He knew the name of a hotel there: the Inn of the Anasazi. He had always liked the name, and now he phoned ahead for accommodations. He noted several calls received on his iPhone, but the ringer had been off, and he didn't feel like returning them.

HE LAY STARING at the beamed ceiling for a long time before he fell asleep.

STONE BARRINGTON WAS at his desk in his home office in New York when Joan, his secretary, buzzed him. "Your son is on line one."

They normally talked once a week, and it had only been three or four days since their last conversation, so Stone was immediately worried. He picked up the phone. "Peter?"

"Hello, Dad."

"You sound sad. Is anything wrong?"

"It's Billy Barnett," Peter said.

"Is he ill?"

"No, his wife was run down and killed by a drunk driver in Beverly Hills a few days ago, and now he's missing."

"I'm very sorry to hear that. I liked her. What do you mean, 'missing'?"

"I'm sorry, I didn't mean to sound ominous. I just mean that he asked for some time off, and I haven't been able to reach him since. I went out to his house in Malibu this morning. His car was gone, and the place was locked up."

"Somehow, that doesn't surprise me," Stone said. "Billy was a loner before he married, so maybe he just wants to be alone again for a while."

"But Billy has become more gregarious over the past few years, in his quiet way, of course. I wouldn't have expected him to just walk away from everyone he knows here."

"Peter, people don't always do what you expect them to, even when you think you know them well. Give him a while, then try calling him again, or just send him a text saying that you're thinking about him and you hope to hear from him soon."

"You're right, that's what I should do."

"When you hear from him tell him he's in my thoughts, and if he finds his way to New York he's welcome at my house."

"I'll do that, Dad." They said goodbye and hung up.

BILLY AWOKE LATE and had breakfast. As noon approached he thought he'd take a stroll around the Plaza, which was a few steps from the inn. He passed through the large group of Indian craftspeople selling their silver jewelry under the portico of the old Governor's Mansion and immediately thought of buying something for his wife but brought himself up short. He forced himself to walk on.

He was approaching some sort of commercial building when a familiar figure suddenly appeared a few yards ahead, leaving its front door. The figure was unmistakable, since he was something like six feet, eight inches tall and, further, wore a large Western hat that added another half a foot to his height. Billy walked a little faster to catch up.

Then he saw a second man, and there was something furtive in his posture and movement. He had fallen into step behind the tall man, and there was something in his right hand, bumping against his leg.

"Ed!" Billy shouted. Then louder, as he began to run. "Ed Eagle!"

Eagle turned and looked over his left shoulder but didn't stop, missing sight of the man, who was behind and to his right.

Billy lunged at the man, striking him in the lower back with his forearm and knocking him to the ground. Billy was climbing the man's back, reaching for the wrist of the hand that held the long blade, when Eagle turned around and, seeing what had happened, stomped on the wrist and kicked the knife away.

"Billy?" Eagle said. "Jesus Christ, what's going on?"

Billy had the man's left arm behind his back, his wrist shoved up between his shoulder blades.

"I think you'd better ask this guy," he said to Eagle, "but maybe you'd better call a cop first."

2

BILLY SAT AT the dining table in Ed Eagle's home, with Ed and his wife, the actress and writer Susannah Wilde, as well. The business on the sidewalk outside Eagle's offices had been handled with dispatch by the Santa Fe police, and both Ed and Billy had given statements.

"I'm sorry to hear about your wife's death," Eagle said.

"Thank you, Ed," Billy replied, "I was sorry to hear about it myself."

"Of course. What brings you to Santa Fe?"

"Four wheels and a wandering nature," Billy replied. "For some reason I suddenly craved the open road."

"I'm glad it brought you our way," Ed said. "Otherwise, I might be on a slab down at the morgue."

"I didn't get a chance to ask you," Billy said, "who was the guy, and what was his beef?"

"His name is Sanchez, and his beef was that I talked his brother into taking a plea bargain of thirty years, instead of what would almost certainly have been the death penalty. Now his brother will be out in fifteen years or so, and the other Mr. Sanchez, the one with the sword, will likely be serving life, since he opposes plea bargains."

"It was a sword?"

"A Roman sword, or a reasonable facsimile thereof. Last year Mr. Sanchez was an extra in a sword and sandal opus being shot somewhere out in the hills, and the company went back to L.A. one sword short. Except for you, they would have located it between my shoulder blades."

"I'm glad I was there," Billy said.

"I'm glad you were, too," Susannah offered. "Mind you, I've occasionally been tempted to do much the same thing to Ed with a steak knife, but I must have a bit more personal restraint than Mr. Sanchez."

Everybody laughed.

"If I'd known you were here," Ed said, "you'd be occupying our guesthouse instead of the inn. It's not too late to make the move. We'd be delighted to have you."

"Thank you, Ed, but I think I'll move on in a day or two, so I won't trouble you."

"Do you have a destination in mind?" Ed said.

"Not yet."

"Do you intend to pursue justice with Mrs. Dax Baxter?"

"She's Dax Baxter's wife? I didn't know. In any case, I'll let the law have its way with her."

"I've made a couple of calls to L.A., and I'm afraid the law appears to have lost interest in Mrs. Baxter," Ed said. "She was unconscious when the police arrived at the scene and she was taken to a hospital. Before she could be admitted or even regained consciousness, she had been moved to a private clinic, where she had previously been treated for drug and alcohol abuse, and by the time the police got access, her bloodstream was clear of any substance. Mr. Baxter has hired a very competent attorney, one Rex Winston, to represent her, and I'm afraid that by the time the district attorney has completed his investigation, Mrs. Baxter will have been found to have had a small stroke while driving and was already unconscious at the time of the accident."

"So she will just walk away from killing another human being?" Billy asked incredulously.

"That seems very likely," Ed said. "Dax Baxter is well acquainted with the wheels upon which his city rolls and knows how and which ones to lubricate."

"Then perhaps I should consider a civil suit?"

"Perhaps, but you should know that Mrs. Baxter, in her previous incarnation as Willa Mather, was a well-regarded actress, until her husband decided, given her history of substance abuse, that she should confine her career to red-carpet appearances in his company. She would probably regard taking the stand in her own defense as an opportunity for a comeback, and she would be a formidable witness."

Billy nodded. "I remember her work, and I intend to agree with your opinion of her."

"I'm sorry I can't be more encouraging, Billy."

Susannah spoke up. "Or," she said, "you could just shoot them both in the head."

Ed smiled. "I'm afraid my wife, though she is a brilliant actress, a fine screenwriter, and an ace producer and director, would make a poor attorney. She lacks the patience."

"Tell me, Ed," Susannah said sweetly, "how would patience improve Billy's situation?"

Ed shrugged. "Improvement can be hard to come by, but patience is time, and time, though it may not heal all wounds, heals some of them and usually ameliorates the rest."

"My husband is so wise," Susannah said with a smile.

"I appreciate both your points of view," Billy said, "though perhaps not equally."

THE FOLLOWING MORNING Ed Eagle made a phone call east, where it was two hours later.

"Stone Barrington."

"Hello, Stone, it's Ed Eagle."

"Ed! How are you?"

"I'm very well, thanks to a friend of yours."

"Who and why?"

"Billy Barnett, as he is now known, and he saved me from having a long piece of sharp steel driven into my back." Ed filled in the details.

"You are a very fortunate man to have *that* man come along at just the right moment."

"I am very aware of that," Ed said, "but I'm worried about Billy."

"I heard from Peter what happened to his wife."

"Perhaps you haven't heard what's happened since?"

"Please tell me."

Ed brought him up to date.

"Well," Stone said, "I tend to think that Billy would be more inclined to take Susannah's advice over yours."

"That had crossed my mind. Stone, it's been a while since you've visited me in Santa Fe. I think the news that you were coming might cause Billy to stay on for a bit, and perhaps together we might slow him down, or perhaps even keep him out of prison."

"Have I ever told you how Billy saved the lives of my son, Peter, and Dino's son, Ben?"

"No."

"Then I'll tell you over dinner tonight," Stone said. "Sit on Billy until I get there."

"Call me an hour out, and I'll meet you at the airport."

"See you then." Both men hung up.

STONE BUZZED JOAN.

"Yes, boss?"

"Please call Jet Aviation at Teterboro and ask them to have my airplane on the ramp in an hour, fueled to the gills, and cancel anything I might have on the books for the next week. And ask Fred to have the car out in fifteen minutes."

"May I ask where you're going?"

"To Santa Fe. A little vacation."

"Consider it done."

Stone hung up and went upstairs to pack.

STUART WOODS

"Addictive . . . Pick it up at your peril.
You can get hooked."
—*Lincoln Journal Star*

For a complete list of titles and to sign up for our
newsletter, please visit prh.com/StuartWoods